JADES AND AFGHANS:
THE COMPLETE ADVENTURES OF CORDIE, SOLDIER OF FORTUNE, VOLUME 3

JADES AND AFGHANS

THE COMPLETE ADVENTURES OF CORDIE, SOLDIER OF FORTUNE, VOLUME 3

W. WIRT

ILLUSTRATED BY

JOHN R. NEILL & SAMUEL CAHAN

COVER BY

PAUL STAHR

STEEGER BOOKS • 2020

TABLE OF CONTENTS

"HE'S MY MEAT!"

*The Boston Bean's yacht was a pleasure craft;
but for him and his soldier-of-fortune comrades,
Jimmie Cordie and the rest, the keenest
pleasure was in warfare, against oriental
pirates or War Lords or what have you*

CHAPTER I

AN ENGRAVED INVITATION
TO TROUBLE

"**QUIT LOOKIN' AT** them goofy Chink pictures and tell me about the time ye and another scut started ye a kingdom," Red Dolan demanded from where he lay sprawled out on a couch in George Grigsby's Hong Kong apartment. The couch sagged under Red's two hundred and thirty-odd pounds of bone and muscle as he turned to Jimmie Cordie, leader of the group of soldiers of fortune.

"Put a jaw tackle on, you red-headed ape," Jimmie answered absently as he picked up another of the rare Chinese prints.

"What did ye call the kingdom, Jimmie darlin'?" Red went on. He had nothing to do and wanted to be amused. Red, who had served with Jimmie Cordie in the Foreign Legion and later as a lieutenant in the A.E.F., had few loves. The first was the slim Jimmie Cordie, who was known over the Orient as "the black-eyed smiling one." The second was for any kind of a fight, anywhere and at any time—preferably with a sword as a weapon. The third was for any child or woman in distress. As a matter of fact, any female between one and one hundred and one could take a single look at the big red-headed Irishman and know that he was there to be bossed.

Red had a simple rule in life. He would ask "How about that, Jimmie?" or "What now, ye scut?" and the answer always satisfied Red. Another rule was "Aw, slap 'em outa the way"—no matter how many or of what breed were the ones to be slapped.

"Mexerica," answered Jimmie, smiling as he looked at the

picture of a hunting scene which seemed thoroughly comic to
him.

"Why did ye call it that, ye shrimp?" Red went on, delighted
at his success.

"Because it was an island off the Mexican coast. Quit both-
ering me or I'll come over there and take you apart."

"Oh, ye will, will ye? Twenty-nine Cordies all at once couldn't
do that, ye black-muzzled scut. What was ye in the kingdom,
Jimmie alannah?"

"Lord High Constable and Duke of Cordie. Now shut up,
you know all about it."

"What was your side-kick, Bob Gunnell?"

Jimmie Cordie put down the print and sighed. "No use," he
said sorrowfully. "Once that ape gets to chattering, who could
stop him?"

"If that is a question," George Grigsby said, putting down
a newspaper, "there is no answer known, Jeems." He was fully
as big a man as Red, but not as bulky; broad-shouldered, lean-
flanked, grave of face. Born in the Kentucky hills, he had been
a major in the A.E.F., had been in the Foreign Legion with
Jimmie and Red. He was one who fought with a little frozen
smile on his lips and in his eyes. "You might as well tell him what
he wants to know, Jimmie. You'll have no peace until you do."

"You're not telling me a thing," Jimmie answered, with a grin
at Red. "Bob was King Robert the First, Mr. Dolan."

"How many what-do-ye-call-'em did ye have?"

"You mean subjects?"

"Here's something that may interests you, Jimmie," Grigsby
interrupted. He had picked up the paper again. "It seems these
high seas piracies have worn out the British patience. On March
21st the steamer Hapsang, on the way from Swatow to Hong
Kong, was taken and looted. British men-of-war landed a party
at Bias Bay and burned a dozen buildings, which caused a lot
of smoke but failed to get the pirates. The pirates in question
seem to be very well organized, with the latest weapons. It is

*The Fighting Yid's
hand shot out and
closed on her ankle.*

rumored that the leader is a European and that his organization, which preys on white men's steamers, is a vast one with spies and agents all over the Orient. The Hapsang makes the fifth vessel this month that—"

Grigsby's house boy, aged about seventy, entered after a low bow at the threshold. "Two vely impoltant gent'men to see Mistel Gligsby and lest," he announced, gravely. There is no "r" in the Chinese language, and few Chinese can pronounce it, save some of those who have been educated abroad.

"**TWO IMPORTANT** gentlemen to see me? Did they send in cards, Chi?"

Chi advanced and handed Grigsby two cards. Grigsby looked at them and read aloud: "Mr. Abraham Cohen. Mr. John Cabot Winthrop."

"What?" yelled Red, sitting up. "The Fighting Yid and the Boston Bean? Those scuts av the world! Wid cards—and important, are they? Wait till I get the two hands av me on that Yid. I'll 'vely impoltant' him, the—"

"Show the gentlemen in, Chi," Grigsby ordered, "with all due ceremony."

The two who stalked pompously in, their hats carried at the proper angle, were in appearance as far apart as the two poles. Mr. Abraham Cohen, who was much better known all over the Orient as the Fighting Yid, was short, stocky, with shoulders as broad as the back of a deep sea going hack of the old days. He looked roly-poly and fat, but what seemed like fat was muscle. Born on Hester Street, New York, the Yid had fought all his life, in the A.E.F. and afterward for War Lords and any other potentates he could find. He owned no nerves, very few ethics, and an uncanny ability with a machine gun and in the handling of men. He was, as Jimmie Cordie tagged him once, "a soldier of fortune—neither pure nor simple."

The Yid's eyes were china blue and seemed always to be about to pop out of his head with surprise at what was happening in a naughty world. He wasn't surprised, though; nothing ever did surprise the Yid. That look had fooled several men to their cost.

Whenever he could, the Fighting Yid stuck around in the vicinity of Jimmie Cordie and Red Dolan; and if they were on the other side in a fight between War Lords, the Yid, as soon as he found it out, would promptly inform his employer where he could go, then, deserting to join his friends, would turn a machine gun against that War Lord with great aplomb and try to help that unlucky gentleman go where the Yid had suggested.

Mr. John Cabot Winthrop, as well known as the Yid in the places where fighting men gather, but known always as the Boston Bean or Beaneater or Codfish, was tall and lanky, with wide shoulders and lean flanks. His aristocratic face had a mournful, sorrowful look when in repose, but it concealed a reckless, happy-go-lucky spirit and chilled steel nerves.

He was a multimillionaire, thanks to his parents, and to two old maiden aunts who left him their fortunes, "so that poor dear John may not want." The fact that poor dear John's mother and father had already left him several millions made no difference to them.

The Bean had town and country houses at his disposal, apartments in several of the world's capitals, yachts and all that goes with unlimited money—and his one idea of a perfect time was to be with Jimmie Cordie and the rest where bullets and swords were singing the death song, his face smoke-blackened and his finger pressing the trigger of a machine gun. Failing to make contact with them, he would hunt up the Yid and go on an expedition with him after anything they decided they wanted.

"So, 'tis ye, is it?" Red demanded as they both bowed gravely. "Ye are the 'impoltant' lads, are ye? Come over here, ye Yid scut, until I see what makes ye tick."

"Keep quiet, Irisher," the Yid answered loftily. "Ve are embassadors, ain't it, Beaneater? I mean, ain't ve, Mistair Vinthrop? After, I come over und kick from you the slats, gonnif. Und if I can't, me und Jimmie can."

"Listen," the Bean reproved; "is that nice? Remember, Mr. Cohen, we are the bearers of a message; so conduct yourself accordingly. Never mind what that flannel-mouthed mick from the north of Ireland says."

"What?" yelled Red, thoroughly enjoying himself. "Ye long-legged cross between a beanpole and a—"

"Pipe down, Red," Grigsby commanded, "and let the ambassadors ambass. You have my royal permission to speak, gentlemen."

"We are bearers of an invitation for you and your questionable comrades to join Mrs. John Cabot Winthrop on the yacht Katherine Neville at once and accompany her on a cruise in the South China Sea."

"Is herself back from England?" demanded Red. "Now ye won't be jazzin' all over the lot wid this Yid omadhaun, ye scut from Bosting."

"She is, Mr. Dolan. Back and in full command. Will you

kindly give us an answer as soon as possible, Mr. Grigsby? This business of being an ambassador is getting on my nerves."

"**WAIT A** minute, Codfish," Jimmie said. "Is the Katherine Neville your new boat?"

"Yes, she was built up in the Maine yards and delivered last month."

"You said the South China Sea, George was just reading about the pirates and what-not. Is the K. Neville—er—hooked up for a proper greeting to any gentlemen that might want to look her over?"

"Well," said the Bean, sadly, "of course she isn't a man-of-war, James, but she has one or two little trinkets on board."

"And what the devil do ye care, Jimmie Cordie?" demanded Red, in genuine surprise. "Wid Winchesters and our Colts we can lick all the pirates in China."

"That's right, Red, we could, without doubt. But after we did there might be a couple coming over from the Malay peninsula to run away with Mrs. John Cabot Winthrop, otherwise known as Mrs. Beaneater."

Grigsby smiled. "Maybe Red will have a sword left. I'd like to get a couple of weeks in on the water. We haven't been out to sea since—since Putt went over the one-way trail."

Jimmie looked at Grigsby and said, hastily, "I'd like to go, too. How about it, Red?"

"Ye know damn' well I would, ye scut. It reminds me of how Putt loved to get the hands av him on a wheel. Sorry the day when he—"

"Don't start, Red," Jimmie interrupted quietly. "It may be that he will be with us in spirit,"

"He will," Grigsby said softly, "if there is any such thing. Our compliments to Mrs. Winthrop and we will be delighted to join her for a cruise."

"Putt"—Arthur Putney—had given his life in a narrow pass so that the rest of them, and a Manchu princess they were escorting, might live. He had been the fourth member of what was once called "a damn' close corporation"—Cordie, Dolan, Grigsby, and Putney. Putney had been as like Grigsby as a twin brother, although he hailed from the Vermont woods. They all missed him and his quiet, easy, practical ways. His passing had left a hole that they could not seem to fill. It was as Jimmie Cordie said, "We're like a damned three-wheeled wagon without Putt"—and Jimmie rarely used profanity.

"Und now," said the Yid hastily, for he did not like any mention of spirits—unless liquid—"that the ambassin' is over, ve vill go over und let the Irisher try und do dot takin' apart thing, ain't it, Jimmie?"

"It ain't," answered Jimmie. "Don't look for any help from me, Yid. If you're man enough, hop to it."

"Vell, maybe I vait until ve get aboard und he is seasick. My, it is a long time between drinks here at Mistair Grigsby's, ain't it?"

"I couldn't offer an ambassador a drink," Grigsby answered with a smile. "If you have come back as the Fighting Yid—that's different," and he clapped his hands together once for Chi.

CHAPTER II

PLAYTHINGS OF THE STORM

TYPHOONS COME UP swiftly in the South China Sea. One minute the sea and air are calm. The next, it is as dark as midnight and the wind comes roaring and snarling from all directions. The waters are whipped into waves that tower over the ship. The graceful, luxurious yacht, one hundred and fifty feet long, powered with twin Diesel motors, and costing over four hundred thousand dollars, was the last word in efficiency in both man and machine power. But now, as she hurtled through the darkness, caught in the teeth of a typhoon, she was as powerless as a chip tossing about in a millrace. No man power nor anything

made by man can buck a South China Sea typhoon—as many
a ship and its crew found out that night.

The Katherine Neville had been built stanch and true from
stem to stern, as a ship should be built; and now, with battened-
down hatches, she was riding it out; that was all she could do.

The young, calm-eyed English captain was at the wheel, with
a quartermaster on either side of him—not that they could do
anything except try to keep her nose pointed into as many of
the oncoming waves as possible. More than half the time her
screws and rudder were out of water.

On the bridge, clinging to the rail, stood the Boston Bean
and Katherine Neville—or rather Mrs. John Cabot Winthrop.
Two years before she had been rescued by the Boston Bean and
the Fighting Yid from the power of a Chinese War Lord. In
turn, she and the Yid and the Bean had been rescued by Jimmie
Cordie and the rest. For a year, she had been the Bean's wife.

She clung to the rail with two strong little hands and her face
showed no more fear than did her husband's; namely, none at all.
Nevilles had put out to sea in a cockle boat to fight the Spanish
Armada, and had gone down to the sea in ships for five hundred
years. This dainty blond girl ran true to her breed in hours of
stress. She was buttoned in oilskins to her little rounded chin.

Next to her stood the Fighting Yid and beyond him stood
Red Dolan, Jimmie Cordie, and Grigsby. The wind seemed to
increase while the lightning became more fork-like and jagged.

The yacht Katherine Neville spun around like a top! Suddenly
it felt as if it had been lifted by a giant hand and flung straight
at a wave that towered above the yacht's wireless antenna. As it
hit, a cross-wind came from the port side.

Katherine was snapped from her hold exactly as the end
person is snapped from the line in the old game of "crack the
whip." The wind was so strong that it literally straightened her
out and she left the rail like an arrow from a bow. It happened
swiftly, but the Fighting Yid was swifter. One arm shot out and

an iron hand closed on the ankle of a little rubber boot. But with all his grizzly bear strength, he could do no more than hold her.

Just as the wave foamed over the bow, Red Dolan let go his hold on the rail with one hand, and an arm like a python came around the Yid. He pulled in, and both Katherine and the Yid came back to the rail like rubber balls from a wall. Both of them grabbed the rail as the water surged over them.

It seemed a million years before the yacht shook itself clear, but when she did the Yid still had hold of Katherine, and Red had hold of them both.

"Thank you, Yid and Red," she gasped, as soon as she could speak. "That was a close call and—oh, my goodness!"

A vivid lightning flash had come and she had seen, looming up ahead, what looked like a dead black wall that reached higher than she could see.

"Jimmie!" yelled Red. "Are ye there, ye scut?"

"Yeah, boy," Jimmie answered. "Save your breath. You'll need— Holy cats!"

The Boston Bean reached for Katherine and got her. Now she was inside his arms, both facing and clinging to the rail. The yacht was lifted up and hurled at the black wall. But instead of hitting something solid, it seemed, as the lightning flashed, to be going through a pass or gut between black walls. On and on the yacht raced, and then all at once the black walls fell away and they were out of the typhoon's heart. It became light enough to see.

"**JOHN! LOOK!** We're—why, we're on a tidal wave!" Katherine called out. "We're in a valley and—"

"Tidal wave is quite correct," said the still calm-faced captain as he spun the wheel. This Englishman had commanded a mine sweeper in the North Sea. "If it will carry us as far as those sand dunes I may be able to put her down."

He stopped talking. The Katherine Neville was answering her wheel. The wave seemed to be slanting down as it roared across a valley, dashing up against the sides of hills on either side. The yacht sped on swiftly even as the water became mud-yellow. Then, all of a sudden, the yacht grounded. The water raced on through the far end of the valley, but now it was only a foot or so deep. The yacht settled between two sand dunes, as easily and softly as against the placed timbers in dry-dock.

As she did, Jimmie Cordie grinned. "Well, we've arrived right side up with care, anyway."

"Oi," the Yid grunted, as he let go of the rail. "Rides I have had it, many times, but never did I have it a ride like this von, ain't it, Jimmie?"

"Yid, for once I've got to agree with you. It was a cross between a shoot-the-chutes and a merry-go-round. What the heck is holding this baby up is beyond me."

"My goodness," Katherine said, "the sand is free of water already! John, what will we—"

"Heads up!" shouted Red from the starboard side, where he had gone to look over to see what kept the yacht almost on an even keel. "Look at 'em come!"

From the hills on the right and left side of the no longer flooded valley came columns of men. It could be seen from the yacht that these were disciplined troops. They came down at a double, in ranks of fours, led by their officers. In all, counting both parties, they numbered some one hundred men. Their bayoneted rifles glittered in the sun, which was now shining as if there had never been any such thing as a typhoon.

"Chinese," Jimmie announced. "Get your men to their battle stations, Bean. Don't show anything, though. If it comes to repelling boarders, we'll use the machine guns. No use of showing our hand unless we have to."

A moment later a bugle blew General Quarters, softly. The forty-odd men of the yacht crew and their officers started for battle stations from where they stood or sat.

The Bean's yacht was not a man-of-war, as he had told Jimmie Cordie; but there is no question but what he was telling the truth when he added that there were one or two little "trinkets" aboard. He might have said that the Katherine Neville carried the complement of a cruiser, and still would have been within the truth. And there was not a soul on board with the exception of Katherine and Ming Li, her Chinese "topside boy," who had not served in either the American or British forces, on land or sea.

"Only show two machine guns, one forward and one aft," Jimmie called from the bridge to the Bean, who stood on the quarterdeck forward. "Line the rails with Winchesters."

The lean brown muzzle of a Browning came up from behind the breakwater before he had finished speaking. Red and the Yid had shed their oilskins and gone below as the bugle blew. There were some guns on the berth deck that they wanted to handle.

Grigsby stood with Jimmie on the bridge. The Bean, followed by the bugler, came up on the bridge just as the Chinese halted. They had seen the two machine guns and had also seen ten or twelve men line the rail on both starboard and port sides.

The promptness with which the yacht had shown teeth had evidently come as a surprise. A pleasure yacht, such as the Katherine Neville seemed, might reasonably be supposed to carry a brass saluting cannon, and the officers might have rifles; but to see two machine guns instantly manned and the rails lined with grim-faced men who handled Winchesters as if fully accustomed to them, was something else.

THE YACHT lay between the sand dunes, her keel about ten feet above the sand. Forward and aft there was about fifty feet in the clear. The sand dunes that held her firm blocked some forty-five or fifty feet amidships, the sand coming about up to her portholes, some five feet below the spar deck level.

The Chinese stopped when within a hundred yards and the officers of both columns ran together. They looked at the yacht and at the silent men on the bridge and along the rails. There was a consultation, then an officer strode forward. He climbed up to the top of the sand dune on the port side. When he halted, he was within ten feet of the men at the rail. Jimmie Cordie,

Grigsby, and the Bean, all now wearing cartridge belts and Colt forty-fives in their holsters, walked over to the port end of the bridge. The Chinese officer saw them and called in English, "Who is in command of this ship?"

"I am," the Bean answered.

"Then flom you I demand the sullendel."

"Oh, you do?" asked the Bean, gravely. "Are you speaking as an officer of the Chinese National army?"

"I am speaking fo' myself. Sullendel this ship at once. If you do not I will take it and all who sulvive will suffel Ling-Chi, the death of a thousand cuts. You cannot fight one hundled men."

"That's quite a lot of men," the Bean answered. "You say you speak for yourself. Just who are you?"

"Let me take the deck, Bean," Jimmie Cordie said softly. As he spoke, his .45 Colt seemed to leap into his hand. Before the Chinese officer could move, he was staring straight into the round black muzzle.

"Come on board," Jimmie commanded. There was death in the voice although it was not raised above a conversational level. And there was death in the cold black eyes behind the Colt. The Chinese officer knew it and without making the slightest attempt to draw the gun in his own holster, he stepped as close to the rail as he could.

"Help him over," Jimmie commanded, leaning over the bridge rail so he could see. "That's right: bring him up here."

The Chinese columns had joined on the port side, a little forward and to the right of the sand dune. They saw the action, but were too far away to hear what had been said. As the officer disappeared in the arms of two husky sailors, another officer snarled an order and drew his gun. Down came the bayonets and the Chinese charged straight at the sand dune and up the sides.

As the officer drew, the Bean said to the bugler, "Commence firing," and the bugler blew the call. The two men guarding the Chinese officer were at the foot of the bridge ladder with him when the machine gun, forward, went into action. The aft gun had no target, to the deep disappointment of its crew. The rifle-men on the starboard side ran through the superstructure to port so as to get in the fight.

"Disarm him and take him below," Jimmie ordered, as he saw the men and the officer. Then he ran back to the end of the bridge, his Colt already going *pow-pow-pow!* There were few men in the Orient that could equal Jimmie Cordie with a Colt.

RED DOLAN and the Yid, seeing there was no chance to fight one of the heavier guns, came up on deck like two jacks-in-the-box and ran to the bow. The Yid had a Winchester, which was the weapon he liked next best, and Red had a .45 Colt.

" 'Tis fooled we are, Yid," Red mourned. "They didn't wait for us, the spridhogues."

Red had a right to be sad, loving a fight as he did. There were few of the Chinese left by the time he and the Yid arrived. It was a foolhardy charge, this charge of one hundred men against a machine gun and twenty-odd Winchesters. The rest of the Bean's crew were at their battle stations.

It would have been foolhardy even, if the men behind the guns were amateurs. But with men serving the weapons who could qualify for the Distinguished Marksman's badge, it was suicide.

The Chinese fell away like leaves from a tree in the fall winds. The charge had not won halfway up the dune when all who could, turned and ran down and across the valley. None of them would have reached the shelter of the hills if Grigsby had not suggested, softly, yet regretfully, "Cease firing, Bean."

The Bean gave the bugler the order and a moment later the yacht was still.

"Get a first aid party over the side, Codfish," Jimmie said. "If any of the wounded can walk, start them back to where they came from."

Red and the Yid arrived on the bridge. "Oi, Jimmie, such a business! Vy didn't it you tell Red und me dot you was goin' to cut loose mit only de poppers?"

"Why didn't you and that big ape stick around? You high-tailed down to get the chance of playing with those three-inch babies, didn't you?"

"Well, ye cross between a small-sized chimpanzee and a flat-faced gibbon," began Red, "ye start off widout—"

"Tell him about it later," Grigsby interrupted. "We'd better get at the how-come of this as fast as we can. This boat lies in an exposed position if the welcome committee here have any heavy guns. Let's get below and see if we can get some dope from the gent who asked us to surrender."

The Bean had been talking to Captain Paulet. "We'll darned soon know about where we are," he announced, as he rejoined the group at the end of the bridge. "Paulet will shoot the sun and—"

"Me, I am going to shoot a tall cold von," the Yid interrupted, firmly. "Wot with de ride und den gettin' fooled mit de fightin', I need von, ain't it, Jimmie?"

"It certainly is, Mr. Cohen. Let's go get it."

CHAPTER III

WAR LORD OF PIRATES

UP IN THE hills at the end of the valley, an Englishman was lying flat on the ground close beside a big bowlder. As he looked through field glasses at the yacht, he talked to the Russian beside him. Both were dressed in white linen, cut like a naval officer's whites. Both wore the pith helmet of the tropics.

"She's tight between two sand dunes. My word! That yacht's a beauty. There go Tzu-kung and his men. I say, did you hear that, Boris?"

"No. What?" the Russian asked in a thick voice.

"I couldn't tell, but it sounded like a bugle note. Hullo, she's going to show fight. There's a machine gun coming up forward—

and one aft. By Jove, the rails are lined with men. Well, Tzu-kung has enough men to eat her up. He'd jolly well better obey orders. He's stopped and gone forward alone. Probably to demand her surrender.

"I say! He shouldn't leave his men bunched that way, the bloomin' ass. It's hard to teach these bounders any sense.... He's going on board. May the foul fiend fly away with these glasses! He's—there they go! At least I've taught them to charge; they'll—my God! Look at them go down! Hear that fire? That's from men who know how to shoot. It's—no—yes, by gad, it's over! They run, the blighters, those who can."

He lowered his glasses and turned so that he could see the other man. Even in this reverse there was a smile on his handsome English face. The eyes, though, were a little too close together and the lips a trifle full.

"Your remark, my dear Radischev, about the gods having brought us a plum on the crest of the tidal wave may have been a little erroneous. The plum has turned out to be a lemon, what, what?"

Boris Radischev, a Russian Communist sent to China to further the Red cause, smiled also as he answered in good English, "From your description of the attack, it is very probable you are right about the kind of fruit, Henry. I would like to have seen it. If this inflammation of my eyes does not get better, I do not know what I will do. You say few came back?"

"Not more than ten," answered Henry Warrenne, young son of a noble English family. Waster and remittance man, he had been cashiered from the army, expelled from clubs and all social life, and now was the leader of Chinese pirates. He had been born a gentleman, lived like a rotter, and there was nothing he would not do or had not done to gratify his lusts. There was only one good thing he had and that was the courage that went with his name. "Let's be getting back, old thing."

Radischev had come to the headquarters of the pirates to see if he could not get Warrenne to throw his men and ships in with the Communists who at the moment were sweeping through China toward Hankow like a plague of rats, devouring and destroying all that stood in their way.

Radischev had offered Warrenne a free hand in slaying and looting. But Warrenne had laughed and answered, "I have that now, wherever I am strong enough to make it stick, old top. Can the Soviet show me some gold? Say a million pounds. If it can, I will put two thousand men and twelve ships at their disposal."

Radischev had said that the Soviet could, but that he did not have the authority to send for it. He would send a messenger for a commissionaire to meet Warrenne in Peking or Hong Kong.

While waiting for an answer, Radischev stayed with Warrenne, liking very much the "wine, women and song" that Warrenne could and did offer in unlimited quantity.

THE PAIR reached Warrenne's headquarters before the last of the fleeing party of Chinese. It was more like an orderly village than the lair of pirates. The houses were laid out in streets; the docks at which several vessels were tied were clean and orderly. Uniformed soldiers patrolled the streets and docks, much like British bobbies on the streets of London. They were Chinese, young men, with the alert look that is common now in "young China."

Back of the village proper there were long lines of tents and over at one side, an artillery park. Most of the guns in it were old muzzle-loaders of the vintage of the first part of the Eighteenth Century, but here and there were batteries of modern guns, among them some French seventy-fives taken from a French supply ship that Warrenne had captured.

The tidal wave had carried the Katherine Neville to the east side of the island, which was fringed by a range of mountains. By the grace of whatever gods have the lives of ships in their hands, the yacht had been hurled through a pass and into the valley. The floor of the pass, in ordinary water was some twelve feet above high tide. The wave had covered it many feet and the yacht had gone through with plenty of water under her keel. The range spread out from the pass and almost surrounded the valley, then went back to the sea on an angle. The west side of the island was free from mountains and faced the coast of Anam, below Hue.

Warrenne was sitting at a plain table in front of the stone house he used as headquarters when the fugitives came up. There were twelve of them, all young men. None of them carried their rifles, having thrown them away in the frantic effort to get beyond reach of the yacht's deadly guns.

They lined up in front of him, came to attention and saluted. Their young faces were gray and their lips livid; they knew that Warrenne was merciless. Behind Warrenne there was lined a company of infantry. Radischev was not in sight, having gone to bathe his inflamed eyes.

"You have left your rifles somewhere?" Warrenne asked, silkily, in perfect Chinese.

A man answered, "We charged, Lord of the World. We charged and met the fire from machine guns. When there was no chance for us to take the ship, we—we—"

"Why hesitate, Meng? You what?"

"We—we ran, Mighty One. If you can find it in your resplendent heart to have mercy on—"

"I can find no mercy for dogs who run," Warrenne interrupted. "Why did Tzu-kung go on board?"

"One of the foreign devils who stood on the bridge pointed a revolver at Captain Tzu-kung and ordered him to come aboard."

"Ordered him! I see. Now, you who ran: run now—out on that pier." He pointed to a long pier that went out into the shark-infested water. "And when you get to the end, see if you can run over the water to Anam. Start—unless you prefer the boiling oil death."

The dozen Chinese turned and ran out on the pier. There was nothing else they could do. Out, and into the water. The fins of sharks came in sight almost as soon as the bodies struck the water, and in less than a minute, there was a flurry and splashing. Then the water became red in spots.

Warrenne sat with impassive face until the onlookers who had been near the pier turned away. Then he beckoned to the captain of the infantry company. He came forward and saluted. "Bring Wang-sun to me," Warrenne ordered curtly.

The captain returned in a few minutes with an elderly Chinaman who was not in uniform. "You may dismiss your company," Warrenne said. The captain saluted and retired.

"**SIT DOWN,** honorable elder brother," Warrenne said.

The old Chinese obeyed, his wrinkled face placid. He began fanning himself with an ivory-handled fan as he said, "Yes, it is wise that you go to the ship that now lies on dry land and see for yourself what she is."

"Where you get the power of reading my mind like that is beyond me, honorable one. You are a mighty soothsayer. I will go, then. Do I not always follow your counsel?"

Wang-sun did not answer, his eyes now looking out over the waters.

"I will go under a flag of truce," Warrenne finally went on. "That is all, elder brother." The Chinese left.

Radischev had come up in time to hear the last of it, and he smiled as he sat down.

"Do you believe in that sort of thing, Henry?" he asked.

"I don't know whether I do or not. That old heathen Wang-sun has foretold lots of things. He can look at a man and read what is in that man's mind. I've seen him do it a hundred times."

"We have them in Russia," Radischev answered indifferently. "What are you going to do about the yacht—shell it?"

"No, not yet. I'm going in with a flag of truce and take a look. It may be that I can decoy them away from her. If I can, I'd try and float her."

"You would—how?"

"By bringing her over here. Bigger boats than she have been hauled inland, old thing."

"I know, but—"

"Take her to the cañon and through it. From there it is easy—a straight down-hill pull to the water. But there are some hurdles to jump, first," Warrenne added with a smile.

"Will you try to get the crew to join you?"

Warrenne shook his head. "No, they are either Yank or British. Yank for choice, as the boat has Yank lines. They wouldn't join, Radischev. I will do to them what I have always done to all others but the Chinese: turn them over to the executioners."

"That is wise," Radischev answered. "It is a true saying that dead men tell no tales."

CHAPTER IV

THE BOARD OP STRATEGY

JIMMIE CORDIE, THE Bean, Red Dolan, Grigsby and the Yid sat on one side of a long mahogany table in the library of the Katherine Neville. Captain Paulet had shot the sun and got the position of the island.

"Longitude 110 and latitude 10. We are on an island. We must have blown directly south through the Formosa Strait," he had reported.

Now, as they waited for two sailors to bring up the Chinese officer, Jimmie said, "We can't be such a heck of a ways from the coast of lower Indo-China. I have a hunch that we've landed right—"

The sailors brought the Chinese officer up to the table, saluted and went out.

The officer's face was impassive as he stood at attention, his eyes at gaze.

Grigsby spoke first. "What is your name?" he asked, courteously.

"Tzu-kung."

"Your rank?"

"Captain."

"What service?"

"I will not answel."

"I will answer for you. You are in the service of the pirates who make this island their headquarters. Do you know the fate that captured pirates meet?"

"Yes."

"Then, if you do not tell us on what island we are, and what force is on it, you will swing from the yardarm in five minutes."

"I will not tell you foleign devils anything."

"And yet you are led by a foreign devil," Grigsby said, quietly. It was a shot in the dark, but it landed. The officer's eyes widened:

"You know that? Then why ask me?"

Red leaned across the Bean and whispered to Jimmie, "How did George know that, Jimmie?"

"Guessed it from the uniform and equipment. Keep still, Red."

"What is his name?" Grigsby continued his grilling.

"I see no leason why you should not know. My leadel's name is Wallenne."

"Warrenne, eh? What force has he and what guns?"

"I will not tell you."

"You hang, then."

"I am not aflaid to die. I would die happy if I could take with me some of you foleign devils. Wallenne will avenge my death on youl bodies."

"It may be," answered Grigsby calmly. "You want to question this man, Jimmie?"

"No. Call your men in, Codfish, and have him put in irons. We may be able to use him in some way."

As the Chinese captain was being taken out, Katherine came in. She heard Jimmie saying, "And if this gent has any artillery, he can place it up on the top of any of those hills and blow us halfway up the golden stairs."

"If who has, Jimmie?" Katherine asked as she sat down next to the Bean.

"Warrenne," Jimmie answered. "We got the name of the chief pirate out of the gent that is visiting us. We've lit right smack in the middle of a pirate island, Mrs. Winthrop. Chances are that he will come over to take a look-see as soon as word gets to him about the way we greeted his assistant pirates. He may come close, or he may not; depends on his nerve."

"He has plenty of that, Jimmie," Katherine said quietly, "if it is Henry Warrenne. All the Warrennes have. It must be he, because I've heard that he—"

"For Pete's sake! You know him, Katherine?"

"Yes, all my life. Their place in Essex joined ours. The Nevilles and the Warrennes have known each other for five hundred years, Jimmie."

"Vich is some knowin'," put in the Yid.

"He wasn't like this when we were little," Katherine went on. "He seemed to change when he was about sixteen. I haven't seen him since I was fourteen. He went away to school. Once he came home and—and made love to me. He said that he always had loved me," she went on hurriedly. It is hard for the English to talk about such things, but Katherine felt that the big, tanned, tight-lipped soldiers of fortune, who were to her as brothers, ought to know all they could about this pirate.

"What kind of a bird was he?" Jimmie asked. "Easy to frame?"

"To frame? I don't—oh, you mean was he easy to spoof?"

"That's it—spoof," Jimmie answered with a grin. "Was he?"

"No, Jimmie. Just the opposite. We never could fool him in the games we used to play. He is very clever."

"Well, that's something to go on. Here's what old Gineral Cordie says. To wait and let him bring up heavy guns and post them on the hills would be a darned bad error in strategy. At the minute he doesn't know where he's at. I say to unload some of the Beaneater's heavy trinkets over the side pronto and in great haste, and get them on top of those three hills. Once there we can make it darned unpleasant for him to try to place any guns on the others. We can take up Brownings, also. Leave gun crews up there with the guns. That will take, say, thirty men. It stops any shelling of the yacht until after he has mopped up—and that will be one hard thing to do. If he attacks, the men on the yacht can go to their help."

"RIGHT YE are, ye scut," Red announced. " 'Tis what I had in me mind. Come on, let's get 'em out and—"

"I knew you figured it, Red," Jimmie said with a smile at his big Irish comrade. "I beat you to it in the telling, that's all. Now, question: can we get set up there before he comes over to take the said look-see? It takes time to drag four-inch rifles up hills, gents, and our mule power is represented in Red, the Bean, and the Yid. George and I, being ginerals, couldn't be expected—"

"Me?" Red demanded. "A mule, is it? If ye was bigger than a half-baked shrimp, ye omadhaun, I'd show ye about mules."

"Und dot goes double for me," the Yid said with a smirk. "Maybe-so de Codfisher vill—"

The Bean looked at Jimmie gravely. He started at Jimmie's feet and slowly looked all the way up to his hair, then shook his head. "Perhaps if the three of us would jump him all at once we could make him—"

"Listen," interrupted Grigsby, "do your kidding later. Get on with it, Jimmie."

"Hearing and obeying," Jimmie said with a grin as Katherine wrinkled her pretty nose at him. "I say to get the guns up there, right now. Many a battle has been lost, gents, by saying 'Let's wait until.' The lads that run may not have got all the way home yet—and Warrenne's got to come all the way back. If we step on it, we may get set before he shows. Then we are in a position to take the play away from him. My thought is to decoy him and his merry army into the valley and then give them all we've got from both hill and yacht. Afterward we will go through to his headquarters, take a ship and yorricks and away."

"Oh!" Katherine stood up, her eyes shining. "Let's do it right away."

They all laughed and as they rose the Yid said, "Vait. If ve got it two ginerals ve might as vell have it a admiral. Katherine is Admiral Vinthrop, or I von't play."

"No playee, no eatee, Mr. Cohen," Jimmie announced. "You and Red get below on those guns you wanted to shoot so badly this morning. Admiral Winthrop, will you see that they stay on the job, please, sir?"

CHAPTER V

BRIEF TRUCE

WARRENNE HAD NOT hurried. He knew that the yacht or the people on her could not get away from the island. The people might, on a raft, but to do it they would have to face the surf on the west side. He strode slowly along with only two officers. It was roughly some five miles as the crow flies, seven or eight on foot across the mountains. There were no horses on the island, so Warrenne walked.

"When we get to the cañon," he said, "I will go forward, alone. I am going in under a flag of truce. You remain here until I return. It may be that these men who hold the ship will not recognize a white flag. If they do not, you may return and bring up your regiments. We will take her, this time."

When they got to the opening in the hills, he walked forward alone. It did not occur to him to look up at the tops of the three highest hills that commanded all the others. There was nothing in his mind to make him do so. As he came out into the valley, he stopped, took from his pocket a white cloth about the size of a pillow case, and waved it.

In a minute or so, there was a white flag waved from the yacht.

Warrenne smiled scornfully as he walked toward the yacht.

The smile was erased from his face and a frown took its place as he saw a figure dressed in the uniform of a captain, with a black cloth over the head, dangling and swaying from the wireless mast. As a matter of fact it was a dummy, dressed in Tzu-kung's clothes; but to Warrenne it was the body of Tzu-kung.

"Curse the beggars!" he said, through tight lips.

As he climbed up the sand dune and walked as close as he could to the yacht rail, his keen eyes looked her over from bow to stern. She looked like any millionaire's hundred-and-fifty-footer. There were one or two sailors in evidence, both forward and aft. No one on the bridge and no guns in sight at all.

A plank had been run from the deck to the sand dune and a section of rail removed. On the yacht, standing by the rail, was a tall, lanky man, dressed in yachting clothes. The man called, "Come right on board. It is far too hot for you to stand out there, Mr.—"

"Warrenne," answered the renegade, politely, as he stepped on the plank. "Henry Warrenne. And you?"

"I am John C. Winthrop, Mr. Warrenne. Come on board."

Warrenne, as he reached the yacht's deck, stopped and looked at the Boston Bean, then laughed. "I say—that's a bally good one, what? You are the Boston Bean, aren't you?"

The Bean grinned. "That's right, I am. I didn't think I was so well known."

"It is my business to know things, Mr. Winthrop. And this is your new yacht, the Katherine Neville, that was sent you from Maine not long ago. I—no wonder my one hundred men got 'eaten up,' as the jolly old Zulus used to say. May I ask if Mr. Cordie, Mr. Dolan and Mr. Grigsby are on board? It is rather a foolish question after seeing or rather hearing the machine guns start to work, isn't it?"

"Yes, they are on board, Mr. Warrenne. Also Mr. Abraham Cohen."

"No, you are not by any chance spoofing me, are you? The Fighting Yid! My sainted aunt, what a haul!"

"You haven't pulled the net in yet," the Bean answered gravely. "Come below and meet the gentlemen, Mr. Warrenne."

"I will be very glad to, Winthrop, and while *en route,* let me tell you that I do not need to pull in the net. The tidal wave did that for me."

The Bean said soberly, "Be careful how you reach in to take the fish out, Mr. Warrenne. I have heard that there are very poisonous fish in these waters."

"I will be," answered Warrenne, with a smile. Whatever else he lacked, he had two things: courage, and a sardonic sense of humor.

JIMMIE, RED, Grigsby and the Yid rose as the Bean ushered Warrenne into the library.

"This gentleman came from the hills under a flag of truce," the Bean said, "which I acknowledged from the bridge. He is under it until he returns to the hills. His name is Henry Warrenne. Mr. Warrenne, from left to right, these gentlemen are Mr. Cordie, Mr. Dolan, Mr. Grigsby and Mr. Cohen. May I ask you to be seated?"

As they all sat down, Warrenne looked curiously at the men whose exploits and fighting ability were known all over the Orient.

They looked at him with impassive faces—faces like those of officers sitting on a court-martial.

"Why do you come to this yacht under a flag of truce, Mr. Warrenne?" Grigsby curtly demanded.

"Because I want to see who it was that destroyed one hundred of my men; also to find out what the yacht had, besides machine guns and rifles," Warrenne answered calmly.

Whatever plans Warrenne had made before had vanished when he found out who was on the yacht. Jimmie Cordie laughed. "A direct answer to a direct question, Mr. Warrenne. You have seen who the men are. We regret that we cannot show you more guns than you say you have heard or seen. I don't remember seeing you in the charge."

"I was on top of one of the hills, Mr. Cordie, with glasses. Near enough to hear a little and see quite a lot. That reminds me, you hung Captain Tzu-kung?"

"Did you see him at the wireless?" Jimmie answered. "Sorry we didn't have the regulation yardarm, that all pirates eventually swing from."

Warrenne laughed. "Not at all, Mr. Cordie. I am sorry you thought it necessary to execute Tzu-kung. I am afraid that the Chinese will insist on reprisal."

"Vell," said the Yid, with one of his smirks, "never mind, Mistair Varrenne, ve save it a place for you on de vireless."

"And if that don't satisfy the likes av ye," Red, who had been staring at Warrenne out of frosty, hostile eyes, stated, "I'll take ye apart wid me two hands and scatter the pieces around, ye black-hearted scut av a—"

"Steady, Red," Grigsby said quietly; "and you also, Yid. This man is under a flag of truce."

"And well for him he is," growled Red.

Warrenne laughed. "The bull and the bear, what, what? Led by the nose. Well, listen, Mr. Bull and Mr. Bear, I stopped being frightened by animals some time ago. If either one of you or both of you would like—"

"Steady for you, also," Grigsby interrupted, sternly now. "Unless you wish to start for the hills. You are under a flag of truce for safe-conduct. If you violate it—"

Katherine Winthrop entered the room. "Oh, John, I beg your pardon. I have been asleep and didn't know that any one—why, it's Henry Warrenne!"

Warrenne rose, his eyes wide with astonishment. "You, Katherine! Here with these men! What does it mean? I thought you were in England. My word, I'm glad to see you," and he advanced with outstretched hand, ignoring the men in the room.

Katherine held up a slender little hand. "No, Henry. You have forfeited the right to do that—ever."

Warrenne stopped as if hit by a bullet. His hand dropped

and his face grew white. "So you are like all the rest, are you?" he asked. "I am not fit to touch you, now? Well, by the red bull of Warrenne, I will make you—"

The Boston Bean stepped in front of Katherine, facing Warrenne. He had to stoop a little to get his eyes on a level with those of the renegade, who was plainly almost beside himself with anger.

"I find nothing," the Bean said, very softly, "in a flag of truce that prevents a man from saving his wife annoyance. Address yourself to me, Mr. Warrenne. Better yet, waive your rights and let me get you a Colt .45. We can argue the matter further, out on the sand."

WARRENNE DID not give back an inch, at first. It was evident that he was getting hold of himself. Finally he stepped back and smiled, then bowed to Katherinc, who had stepped to the Bean's side.

"I am more than sorry if in any way I have offended you, Mrs. Winthrop. Please accept my most humble apologies." Then he looked at the Bean. "That Colt thing will have to wait, old dear. I cannot waive my rights just at the moment. There is business toward."

He looked at the men sitting at the table, at Katherine again and then at the Boston Bean.

"All right," he said, in the rasping voice of an officer on the parade ground. "Here it is. Surrender this yacht to me, now, and I will let you live. Don't, and I will take it, and you will die under torture if you are alive after the assault. You know who I am, I see. What you don't know is that I have some two thousand trained men and three thousand more at call on the China Sea. I do not—"

"Vell," interrupted the Yid, "if de two t'ousand and the t'ree t'ousand ain't no better than the vons you sent to say it mit bayonets, maybe-so ve mop up on dem and come and get you for de vireless, Mistair Tough Guy."

"Cut it out, Yid," Jimmie said, with a grin that he couldn't suppress. "Let him get it out of his system. Go ahead, Mr. Warrenne. You were just past the place where we all die by torture when Mr. Cohen interrupted."

Warrenne looked at Jimmie and then laughed, with real amusement. "I have heard much about you, Mr. Cordie," he said. The rasp was gone from his voice. "It will give me great pleasure to see you, as you Yanks put it, 'strut your stuff.' I was going to say that I do not care how many guns or men you have hidden on this yacht. For every one you have, I have twenty. You cannot fight against such odds. Surrender now and you may live."

"I will speak for all," Katherine said, her head held proudly. "We will not surrender. We are not afraid of you or of your thousands of men and your guns. If we can, we will—we will do what the Fighting Yid says. We will hang you to the wireless for a pirate."

"Und dot," said the Yid, "is Admiral Vinthrop speaking, Mistair Varrenne."

"Is that your decision, gentlemen?" Warrenne asked.

"Yes," answered the Boston Bean.

"Yes," from Jimmie and George at the same time.

"It is," Red said, grimly. "Watch the steps av ye carefully, ye scut av the world. I'm comin' to get ye for the wireless."

"Und me vid him," added the Yid.

Warrenne bowed, a courtly bow he had learned in a stately old English castle before he had gone bad. "That being the case," he said calmly, "I will go back to the hills."

Neither the men nor Katherine returned his bow, and as they stood there with immobile faces Warrenne turned on his heel and left the room. The Bean followed him and escorted him to the plank without a word. Warrenne was silent until he stepped on the sand dune. Then he smiled and said, "Touching that Colt .45 thing—you need not get one for me. I prefer a Webley, old topper. See that you have your Colt in your hand when we meet next."

"I will," answered the Bean gravely, his thin face mournful.

"Come and see us again—without the flag." His face may have looked sorrowful, but the Bean's heart was singing with the joy of a fight to come.

CHAPTER VI
BRINGING UP THE BIG GUNS

FRENCH SEVENTY-FIVES AND four- and five-inch rifles are heavy pieces of ordnance; but the pyramids were built by man power, and the Chinese, under the stimulus of Warrenne's stern presence, moved them forward little by little to the hills.

The formation of the island leading up to the hills, especially the three high ones that commanded the valley, made it possible to get the guns almost up to them through a fairly wide, gently sloping pass—the one of which Warrenne had said, "a straight down-hill pull to the water."

"I do not like it, Yang-lu," an officer said to his second in command as they stood on a little knoll watching the toiling lines of men dragging the guns along the skids. "It is too quiet. Many tales I have heard of these foreign devils. It does not seem possible that they would lie supine and let us mount guns that will destroy the ship in which they came."

"I do not like it either, O Shun. I was at Ta-hsiang when those men fought for General Peng Teh-hue. There they led us into an ambush and few escaped. It was told me that the English-man spoke to the Russian about them when he returned. He mentioned their names. The ones called the—the—*aie*, what names!—called the 'Fighting Yid' and the 'Boston Bean' are the most to be feared for what he called the 'flame'—I cannot say it. For tricks, that is it. All of them fight like wounded leopards. If we take the ship, elder brother, what profit to us?"

"I know not. Yet there is less profit if we do not, Yang-lu. See, here comes the Englishman. Hurry your men."

Warrenne came up, Radischev with him and a few officers.

"Too slow, Shun," he said curtly. "Your men are not working up to the limit. Put men with whips among them. Start those five-inch guns up the hill to your right."

After he gave the order he walked away, followed by his staff.

After he had gone, Shun looked at his second. "Whips," he said softly, "Whips… It may be that some day the—"

"He looks back, elder brother," warned Yang-lu as he started for the men.

Warrenne went along the lines of men, giving orders for more speed to the officers. He intended to place the guns, shell all around the yacht to show the men on it that they had no chance, and afterward send his men in to take it. He wanted the yacht as little damaged as possible; but most of all he wanted Katherine Winthrop.

To him, it was a simple matter. He would break the morale of the crew and the men who had defied him, he would take the yacht, slay all the men, take the girl he had always wanted and bring the yacht overland to his headquarters. That the Boston Bean or any of the others would kill Katherine rather than let her fall into his hands he knew, but that chance he had to take.

He would advance his men under cover of a barrage and trust to the quick taking of the yacht to prevent that misplay. The expression in the eyes of the men who had sat behind the table, and the tone of voice with which the Bean had spoken to him, had dug deep under his skin. He wanted to see and hear them scream under torture if they were still alive when he took the yacht.

"Very good," he said to the colonel in command, as the last seventy-five reached the foot of the hills. "Take two up on this side."

A BUGLE blew "Commence firing," and the crowded pass became an inferno of bursting high explosive shells and machine gun bullets. From each of the three commanding hills came the fire. It was fast and absolutely merciless: one- and two-pound

*"If you cannot take a small yacht that carries
fifty men—" the Russian sneered.*

rapid fire guns, three-inch rifles, and, worst of all, the deadly
sleet of steel-jacketed machine gun bullets.

The men around Warrenne's guns had absolutely no chance.
They went down in heaps as they milled around. Shells landed
squarely on the guns and burst to send steel fragments in all
directions. It was a massacre—nothing else.

There was no chance to fight back.

The men pulling on the ropes had laid aside their rifles and
the officers had only their side arms. Warrenne had failed in one
of the most essential points of strategy: he had not sent advance
parties up the hills to occupy them while he was bringing up
his guns.

He knew the men on the yacht, at least by reputation, and he
should have realized that they would not let him plant heavy
guns to command the situation if they could prevent it. That
they too could have heavy guns had never dawned upon him.
He knew they probably had machine guns other than those they
had shown, but he had not dreamed that they would leave the
yacht to do the fighting rather than remain on the defensive.

As the firing started he was a little over to one side. The first shell came from the hill on which the bugle had blown. He looked up and shouted an order. "Peng! Take your men—"

The other hills joined in, and Warrenne knew that he had been caught. There was no need to order a retreat. His pirates were fighting men, highly organized and disciplined; they were under his eyes; and yet, in that hell of flame and steel, they reverted, as all men do, to the animal instinct to save themselves. The noise, the flame, the flying steel that were deafening, burning and tearing them, wiped all else from their brains but the desire for a place to hide from it.

They ran in all directions and Warrenne and the officers ran with them. As they scattered out, the heavy gunfire ceased. But the machine guns went on with the *rat-tat-rat-tat-tat!*

There had been some five hundred men with the big guns. Now, as they ran, there were less than four hundred. Warrenne and Radischev were fairly close to a little foothill, and they made it safely around a curve—though not before Radischev had taken a bullet in his left arm and Warrenne's pith helmet had jumped from his head.

The Yid, who was firing the machine gun that tried for them, grunted in disgust. "Oi, vot shootin'. Maybe-so I go to de old man's home, ain't it?"

As a matter of fact the Yid did more than well when he got that close to them. He was six hundred yards away and up on top of a hill. They were running fast and he had to swing his gun around and shoot from an almost impossible angle to try for them at all. But to the Yid, the fact that he missed them as much as he did was very displeasing. As it was, he blasted away the lives of the officers a little to one side of Warrenne and Radischev.

Warrenne climbed up to the top of the foothill and flung himself full length on the ground where he could look over the crest.

His face was white and like that of a devil. He, Warrenne, leader of pirates, a man who had trapped many a ship and many a land force sent against him, had been ambushed like a coolie in a dark alley. He saw his guns, some dismounted now. He saw the bodies of his men, saw the survivors fleeing. He saw the relentless machine guns pick up group after group and destroy them; and the foam literally seeped through his lips. He knew that it was his fault, and that made it worse.

Then he saw, from each hill, a line of uniformed men, dressed in natty navy whites, armed with bayoneted rifles and cutlasses, and led by three officers, start down the hill at the double. One of the officers he recognized as the Boston Bean.

Disregarding the chance of getting a machine gun bullet, Warrenne jumped up, drawing his Webley.

Then he came back to his senses. He knew that he could not stop the charge by himself. If he stayed, he would surely die. He was not afraid, but he wanted to live to capture the men who had shown their contempt for him. He turned and ran down the foothill.

Radischev was already on his way to headquarters. Warrenne shouted as he passed some of the officers who had not run as fast as the men, waiting to see what he would do.

"Get back! Get back! Order Tsing's regiment forward to the mouth of the cañon! Order Ling to land all men on the ships and support him!"

As he ran, his one thought was to retake his guns if he could before they were put entirely out of commission. The inevitable loss of men meant absolutely nothing to him. There were plenty of men. What made him physically sick was the thought of the smiles that would be on the lips of the men who had tricked him.

"I—I will cut them off," he panted, as he ran. "I will make them eat the—" He stopped talking and ran.

"**AND THAT'S** that," the Boston Bean said, as the charge stopped at the guns. "No use in chasing them around the corner. He may have some support back there."

"Oi, vot a sucker he is," the Yid announced. He had left his

gun and joined in the charge down the hill when he saw Red
Dolan start. "If he is a fighter, I am a—"

"Hester Street A.P.A.," Jimmie Cordie interrupted. "Who
told you to leave that gun, you ape?"

"Oi, Jimmie! It vos all over, ain't it? I see the Irisher start and
I come to protect him," and the Fighting Yid smirked.

"Oh, you did? All right, Yid; some one had to go along to
protect Mrs. Dolan's little boy. He—"

Captain Paulet and his men were destroying the mechanism
of the French seventy-fives and the other guns, and Jimmie
stopped as he watched them.

"Man, howdy," he said. "I hate to see guns like those get
ruined. They're darned near human."

"If you had spoken about it a minute before, James," the Bean
said, mournfully, "we could have saved them for Mr. Warrenne.
Had you rather face what comes out of them?"

Jimmie laughed. "That will be about all, Codfish. Wait a
minute: he's got to come up this way to get to the—no, he hasn't
at that, unless he got some more modern— We could hold 'em
right here. No, not so good. There may be twenty other ways of
getting to the valley."

"All of which is plain as mud," the Bean said. "Let's get back
and hold a council of war."

Red Dolan walked with the Fighting Yid. " 'Tis wan devil av
a thing," he said bitterly, "that it is only wance in so often that
ye will find any av them damn' Chinks that will stand up to ye.
Wouldn't ye think now that some av them scuts would have
waited for us?"

"Vell," said the Yid seriously, "maybe-so they didn't like vot
ve started to play vid dem vid."

That night a message was sent, carried by a wounded
Chinaman: "Speaking of surrender—come and get hanged." It
was signed, "Admiral Winthrop."

When Warrenne read it his eyes narrowed. He was back
in headquarters and had regained control of himself. He had

already lost more than two hundred men, his French seventy-fives, his four- and five-inch rifles, and, what was more important, he had lost some of the confidence of his men.

"It's only the first round," he said aloud. "You win it. I know now that you have more than two machine guns. So—I'll see if I can't arrange something to turn your flank, old dears."

CHAPTER VII

CHEMICAL WARFARE

"**IT'S A LEAD-PIPE** cinch," Jimmie Cordie said, "that Warrenne won't pass over what we've handed to him. Here he was, all set on his island, everything his own way—and we come riding in on a tidal wave and bust up his playhouse. He'll use more care the next time he attacks."

"What the devil now?" interrupted Red. "Let's go and smack him into the sea. There are fifty av us. Can't we take—"

"No, Red, we can't," Grigsby interrupted. "He is not to be caught twice. There is one big difference between bushwhacking an outfit and shooting our way through it, old kid. We caught him by taking advantage of his conceit this time. Don't think for a moment that fifty men can shoot their way through a thousand, if the thousand are fighting men."

They were sitting on the quarterdeck aft, all of them, including "Admiral Winthrop," as they styled Katherine.

"What he will do is this," Jimmie said. "He'll try to frame something that will pull us away from the yacht, or make a direct charge with all he's got from some other direction. At the same time, he'll throw his men against the hill positions. We can't shoot guns two ways at the same time, and he will figure that if he can keep the hill guns busy, he's got a chance at the yacht from another direction."

"Are we to be holed up here like a fox in the den av him, while that scut figures what he will do to us?" demanded Red. "We sit here like a lot of ould ladies. Are we to let a scut av the world like him take what time he needs to frame the likes av us?"

"What would you suggest, Mr. Dolan?" asked Jimmie. "Your plan of going over and slapping them into the blue sea hasn't seemed to meet with general approval."

" 'Tis the only way I know, Jimmie, darlin'."

"And a darned good way, if we can't dope out any other. We've smacked him where he lives, and it's a cinch that he'll let go all holds and get us if he can. Bean, have you got any high explosives on board?"

"You mean outside of shells?"

"Yeah, dynamite or what-not."

"No. That time up on the Red River, I just happened to be packing that stuff up to a bird who was mining in Sangshu. Why?"

"I've been looking over the cut where we came in. If we could blow that fifteen or twenty feet of rock that is holding back the sea, it would fill this low valley and maybe-so we could buck her and go out the way we came in, after the valley filled."

Grigsby sat up straight in his chair. "Say that again, Jimmie."

"I said that there is a wall of rock about fifty feet thick and twelve or fifteen feet high that is holding the sea out of this sunken valley. We came over it on the tidal wave, which evidently spread over the rest of the island and got soaked up. If we can blow that wall, the yacht might be floated. We're below sea level—this sandy valley was once sea bottom."

"Maybe-so, Jimmie. Depends on how badly the yacht is damaged."

"Why, she is hardly damaged at all, George," Katherine said. "The engineer told me that she could float. He said that some of her seams were opened when she settled and he was fixing them. I—oh, I wish we could!"

Jimmie smiled at the pretty little Mrs. Winthrop. "So do I,

Katherine. But if the Bean hasn't any explosives, I don't see how we are going to blow up that much rock."

"Vait," interrupted the Yid. "Ve got it plenty of shells, ain't it? Ve take the guncotton and the T.N.T. out of dem und—"

"There isn't enough in all of them to make a ripple in that much rock. And what we've got we'll sure need once Warrenne gets started again. Your suggestion, Mr. Cohen, is all wet."

"**TOO MUCH** wah-wah," Grigsby said bluntly. "Here it is, down to cases. Warrenne will get his men together, find another place to plant what guns he has left, and throw everything he's got against us. This time we won't catch him off guard. He may come in from the west."

"That's right, George," Jimmie agreed absently. "He may."

He looked at the hills, at the narrow eastern pass the yacht came through, at the cañon through which Warrenne had started to bring his guns. He whistled softly as he looked. Grigsby watched him, a smile on his lips. Red started to speak but Grigsby caught his eye.

Finally Jimmie said, "How long do you think it will be before he makes a play, George?"

"I don't know, Jimmie. Depends upon what men he has left at his base and what he figures on doing. That's like 'how long is a piece of string?'"

Jimmie grinned. "My idea was to—it's a cinch that he won't come back for a couple of days, anyway."

"Vy is it?" asked the Yid. "Vy can't he go right back and get it his men und come?"

"He could—but he won't, Yid. You sabe Chinese as well as I do. He's got to work them up to a point before they will do business again. I don't give a darn whether they are pirates or not; right now, they wouldn't charge against a jackrabbit. For all his training them, he can't change the nature of the beast. Here, if you birds will take over the job of holding him off for say five days, I may be able to make enough high explosive to—"

"*Make* it?" echoed Red, who had worked in high explosives. "What with, ye shrimp? Sure it takes nitric and sulphuric acid and glycerin and wood pulp and—"

"I know what it takes, Red. I wasn't figuring on dynamite. I was figuring on guncotton."

"Guncotton?" the Boston Bean asked, surprised. "That's harder to—"

"Go ahead, Jimmie," Grigsby interrupted. "We haven't got all the time in the world to sit here. If you get a certain length of time, you can make guncotton enough to let the sea in, eh? Well, old kid, we'll see that you get the time."

"Fair enough," Jimmie answered with a grin. "I don't know whether I can do it or not. I know that I saw some cotton growing in a little valley from the top of the hill I was on and I also saw some blamed funny-looking fumes coming from another. If it is what I think it is and the Bean has some pots and pans his chef isn't using, maybe-so can do. I'm going to see."

"I'll go wid ye," Red announced, promptly. "If any wan can make the damned—'tis beggin' your pardon I am, alannah, for the cuss-word."

"It's quite all right, Red," answered Katherine, smiling at the big Irishman. "I said it too when John wouldn't take me to the top of the hill this morning. When are you going, Jimmie? I'd like to take a walk."

"Right now. Come on if you want to go. It's on this side, George. We can get back easy enough even if Warrenne starts anything. The gun crews will pick him up quick enough for us to get back."

Grigsby smiled. "If he comes that way, Jeems. Better take some men and a couple of the Brownings. He probably won't want any more of our game until he figures out a better plan than mounting guns on the hills, but better safe than sorry, young feller me lad. Especially if Katherine is going along."

"I'll do 'er, George. Throw out some two-men patrols on this side and stretch them out to cover those two spurs. If you scatter them—"

"You are teaching your granny how to fry eggs. Get going, Mr. Powder-maker," the Bean said.

"Come on, Codfish," Jimmie answered. "I need your chemical knowledge."

"I go mit, too, Jimmie," the Fighting Yid said. "Red und I will be the army vile you do it the expertin', ain't it?"

"It ain't," Grigsby answered for Jimmie. "You and Red both stay here. Red, you get up on the hill, the one in the middle. Yid, you take out the patrols. Any one would think you birds were out on a picnic instead of being in the middle of a war."

Red glared at Grigsby. "Supposin' that they hop Jimmie and the Beaneater?" he demanded. "Wid herself along. What then, ye omadhaun?"

"Why, then," Grigbsy said, "they will have to take hold of hands and run, Mr. Dolan. You and the Yid can go to the rescue if that comes off. Make it snappy, Jimmie, if you are going. This bird Warrenne isn't going to wait any longer than he can help."

CHAPTER VIII

A NEW THREAT

WARRENNE SAT IN his headquarters with some of his higher officers. He could not punish those who ran, this time; he had run himself. The loss of the guns affected him very little. He could not use them on board ship—at least on the vessels at his command. The loss of men affected him still less. What did affect him was his loss of "face."

His Chinese officers were as respectful as ever and moved to obey his orders with the unquestioning speed they always did. There was no contempt shown in their eyes or on their impassive faces; and yet—Warrenne knew that his power over them had weakened badly. He had led his men into an ambush that ordinary precaution would have avoided, and in China a leader does not make many mistakes like that, and retain his command. He is lucky to retain his life.

Warrenne knew that he had to do something to regain his "face," and do it quickly. He had some fifteen hundred men in all, counting the crews of the vessels at anchor.

"What was the trouble over in your lines last night, K'ang?" he asked an old officer who had captained a pirate ship before joining Warrenne.

"The dogs heard the wailing of the spirit of Tzu-kung in the hills, Lord," K'ang answered seriously. "It told of death for us all."

"His spirit? Then it is known that he died?"

"Yes, mighty one. The wailing told of his body swinging from the wireless of the ship held by the sand dunes, and called upon his friends to go and give it honorable burial. Two of the bravest crept up in the hills and then down close. The moon was out and they could see the body swaying in the wind, O Leader of Thousands."

"Tell them that I, with Wang-sun, whose mystic power they know, will quiet the spirit of Tzu-kung, and that soon—very soon—the body will receive honorable burial. That is all for to-day, gentlemen."

The officers rose, saluted and went out. Warrenne sat there, staring at the floor. He was in a bad jam and knew it. He must destroy or capture the yacht and the men who held it. He could not do any less and retain his prestige and power. That they only had a certain amount of food and water on board he knew. He could throw a cordon around the yacht, far back in the hills, and wait until starvation and thirst drove the defenders away from it. But how long it would take, he had no way of figuring.

Counting the men there must be at the guns, the men in the charge, and those without question held in reserve at the yacht, he had figured that the Katherine Neville was a good deal more of a fighting ship than a pleasure craft. He knew that fifty or sixty men led by the soldiers of fortune whose fighting ability was known wherever fighting men gathered, and as well armed as they were, could and would put up a terrific resistance.

A direct assault against machine guns and rapid fire guns, coming across the open valley, would be suicide for the attackers, even if they started out fifteen hundred strong. His Chinese pirates were fighting men but he could not lay down a barrage for them now that the hills were occupied; and to send them in without it—he shook his head. No fifteen hundred men of any race could go through the sleet of steel that would greet them the moment they started.

"If I had enough men," he thought grimly, "I would throw them at the yacht until she ran out of ammunition." But he hadn't. He might try for the guns on the hills—take them and turn them against the yacht. But the Chinese fought for loot and his men might turn on him if he tried to send them up against the guns that had already destroyed so many of them. It was up to him, though. If he tried to starve them out, the Chinese would think that he was afraid and had lost his planning ability. There must be some way....

Warrenne looked up impatiently as Radischev came in. The Russian's arm had been given first aid and he carried it in a sling. His eyes still looked inflamed, and from the flush on his face he was running a fever.

"SIT DOWN, Boris," Warrenne said. "I am trying to think of some way to draw the fox."

"Draw the fox? I do not understand—oh, you mean some way to take the yacht?"

"Yes. Here it is, old thing. My men are fighters, I'll give the rotters credit for that. But they fight for what there is in it for them. The chance to loot the city or what-not. This yacht comes in and to them it is only a small craft with probably little of value on it. One hundred of them go to take it and are promptly mopped up. Then, in trying to place guns on the hills, some two hundred more are wiped out. I will admit the last was my fault if it will help any, which it won't. I should have sent advance parties up."

"That is," said Radischev smoothly, "what an American I know calls 'water under the bridge,' Warrenne. It is what you are going to do now that counts. I am afraid that if you cannot take a small yacht that carries some fifty men, with all your forces, my people will think you cannot be of much service to them in larger matters."

"What your people think does not worry me, Radischev. I have fought on my own for some years and can continue to do so. It is what my people will begin to think if I do not take that yacht and wipe out the men who killed so many of them."

"You have over a thousand men. Would not a direct assault—"

"No. It would cost me too many men, even if it went over."

"This woman you were telling me about: if you could take her you could make them do anything you say. I know the Americans and the English. They are fools about their women. In Russia we do things better."

"I know you do. Let me think for a minute. What you have said has opened up a line of thought. If I could get hold of Katherine—by gad, I'll try for it."

"And while you are," Radischev said, "I will go to the mainland and get my arm and eyes fixed up. And I have thought of another thing. First, this matter of the million in gold: if I help you destroy the yacht will you divide with me?"

"Yes," answered Warrenne without a moment's hesitation. "I will divide with you, Boris. But help does not mean the suggesting of things for me to do. It means actual help."

"That is satisfactory. While I was speaking I remembered that in Hanoi there are two bombing planes and their pilots. The Soviet sent them there to be ready, when needed. They were shipped there to the War Lord Fokien, who is with us. I can send them to you, Warrenne."

"My word! If you can and will do that, Boris, I wall not only split the gold with you, but you may take a double fistful out of the jewel chest. What a pay-off! By all the gods of war, I'll teach the bloomin' bounders to play with Henry Warrenne. When will you go?"

"Now. I will stop at Hanoi and send them to you. They can land on the parade grounds. Do you think that the yacht people can see or hear them come down?"

"No. Not five miles away. If they did it wouldn't make any difference, although I would much rather have it come as a surprise to them. They couldn't put up any defense against a bomber."

RADISCHEV LOOKED at Warrenne through his swollen eyelids. "If the yacht is bombed the woman will no doubt be killed," he said softly, "and I know you want her, Henry. I could tell that as you spoke of her."

"That is quite right, old top," Warrenne answered with a smile. Since Radischev had told of the planes he had regained his usual suave manner. "I do want her. But if I cannot figure out some way to get her before the bombers come, why she will jolly well have to take her medicine with the rest. My word, what a feather in my cap if I could outplay the famous Boston Bean and the Fighting Yid and the rest, what, what? I can get all the men I want after that. If those bombers will do the work for me, Boris, I will guarantee to join you with ten thousand men."

"They will do it," Radischev answered as he rose. "I will go and pack."

"I can land you at Hanoi in a day. How soon will the planes be here? They can fly it in three hours if they have any speed at all."

"I do not know, Warrenne. It may be that the planes are not yet assembled. They must have been taken down when shipped by steamer. If they are assembled and the War Lord Fokien is there and still friendly it would mean another day. It is quite a distance to his palace, and you know as well as I the delays that might arise. Say three days from now. Then begin to look for them."

"Right. I will pass the word through Wang-sun that soon all

will be shown the yacht and men destroyed without the loss of another man. That will keep them quiet and start the regaining of my face. In the meantime I will see if I cannot put to use some of my old-time ability to make the fly walk into the spider's parlor."

Radischev smiled, "My English is not good enough for me to follow into the spider parlors. I go to pack now. Will you have the ship ready in half an hour?"

"Yes. In less time than that if you wish. Will you have a little drink?"

"No, thank you. When I come back, yes. I do not wish to make my eyes more inflamed." Radischev bowed and went out. Warrenne still sat at the table, but now there was a real smile on bis lips.

After he had seen Radischev off on the fastest vessel of the pirate fleet he went back to headquarters and sent for Wang-sun. That old Chinaman listened, nodding his head, and finally said: "It is good, little brother. I will pass the word. Let the ships that fly come as a surprise."

He shut his eyes and in a moment went on: "I see them landing—now they rise in the air—now they hover over the ship between the sand dunes—something falls—it hits the ship—there is a loud noise—flames rise—and—and—" He opened his eyes. "That is all I could see, O War Lord. It is true that I am getting old. *Aie, aie,* I wish for the time when I could close my eyes and see plainly to the end. Now I can see but a little."

"What you see, O most honorable elder brother, is sufficient. Will you order Hui to have my launch ready in an hour? I am going to the other side of the island and see if any guns have been mounted."

CHAPTER IX

JUGGLING GUNCOTTON

JIMMIE CORDIE AND the Boston Bean sat on a ledge of rock overlooking a little valley. Katharine was with them, and a little farther back six men of the yacht's crew lay beside two Brownings. On a hill quite a bit to the left of them stood a sentry and to the right was another.

The Boston Bean and Jimmie Cordie were gazing intently at the smoldering relict of an ancient volcano. Just below its base ran a wide fissure or gulch, which was filled with hot white vapors.

"What does that look like to you, Brownbread?" Jimmie asked.

"Sulphuric acid fumes," the Bean answered promptly.

"It does to me, too. I'm going down and get a cupful. I mean I would if I had a cup."

"You better go slow, James. See those bones lying around. You'd need a gas mask, old kid."

"No, I won't. I can tie my shirt around my head. What the heck can we use as a cup?"

"We can send back to the yacht for one, Jimmie," Katherine said, very much interested. "Supposing it is sulphuric acid?"

"Well, if it is, we've got the cotton and the—what I don't savvy at the minute is the red tinge that comes up in the fumes. Send one of your men back for a quart Mason jar or any small glass pitcher or what-not that is handy."

The Bean dispatched one of the men, then said, "Where has your chemistry gone, Jeems? That red shows nitrates are being introduced into the fissure—but how and from where?"

"Darned if I know. Wait till we test some of it in that dinky laboratory of yours."

"It is not a dinky laboratory," Katherine protested. "It is a very fine laboratory, and John is a dandy chemist, Mr. Jimmie Cordie. Why, he spends most of his time there when he is on the yacht."

The Bean patted her hand. "That's the girl. You straighten out this darned ignoramus about me."

Jimmie grinned: "I meant that the laboratory was a very fine one and John a dandy chemist, Mrs. Winthrop. 'Dinky' means all of that. Sit here and hold hands while your Uncle Jimmie takes a look-see."

The man got back with the Mason jar just as Jimmie returned. Cordie, with his soft flannel shirt wrapped around his head, leaving only a slit for him to see through, went cautiously to the edge of the fissure. He came back with the jar half full of heavy, hot liquid which gave off clouds of vapor.

"It's sulphuric, all right," he announced, "and of darned high concentration, if you ask me. Let's get back to that fine laboratory and test it."

It was of high concentration, as the Bean announced a little later, "and practically anhydrous, containing no water."

Red was standing next to the Yid, both of them having come to the yacht as they saw the party returning. "What the heck does that 'anhydrous' mean, Yid?".

"My, such ignorance," smirked the Yid. "It means dot dere is no vater in it."

"In what?" demanded Red.

"Vy, in de—in de anhydrous, you dumb Irisher."

"Yeah? 'Tis ye that say I'm—"

"Get the heck and high water out of here, you two chattering apes," Jimmie ordered. "My gosh, how can we figure if you are going to start a fight in here?"

"We're shut, Jimmie darlin'," answered Red, who wanted to stick around.

"Well," the Boston Bean went on, "nitrates are being introduced into the fissure, as I said, young feller. But where they come from is the question."

The shell burst about a hundred yards from the yacht.

"Must be from above," Jimmie said. "Let's go back and do some prospecting."

"Come on," the Bean agreed. "Katrinka, you stay here with George. It may be a long pull."

"I will, John."

"That's a good girl. We'll be back pretty soon."

"**RED, YOU** and the Yid get back to your posts," Grigsby said.

"What the divil is the need av that?" Red demanded. "I will go with Jimmie. Let the Beaneater go up on the hill."

"Are you a chemist?" asked Jimmie. "I'll answer for you—you are not. It takes a chemist for this job, old settler. Go up on the hill, you red-headed gibboon, and guard us."

" 'Tis wan hell av a lot—there now, ye have made me curse before herself, Jimmie Cordie. The sin be on the head av ye. Ye need no—"

"Oh, for Pete's sake! Listen, Red, will you do me a favor? Go up on the hill and let us get at this thing. Once we get it, you can be my chief assistant guncotton maker, no foolin'."

"Sure I will, Jimmie alannah. I was only jokin'."

As Red and the Yid started back with the patrols, Jimmie and the Bean went back to the ledge.

"See that hill on the other side?" Jimmie asked. "Let's climb it and see if we can spot anything. It's a cinch that the nitrates must seep down."

An hour later, on an upper plateau, some distance away from the old volcano and above it, Jimmie and the Bean stood and looked at each other, pleased grins on their faces. They had found a large natural deposit of crude crystals of sodium nitrate, known as Chile saltpeter. It was constantly being leached out by the tropical rains and finding its way through cracks or channels in the underlying rock to drip into the mouth of the crater.

"Holy cats," Jimmie said. "Here is where she comes from; but what happens, Beaneater?"

"Easy, Jeems. Listen to old Professor Winthrop. The nitrate gets down into the subterranean caverns inside the volcano where it oxidizes the sulphuric vapor to sulphurtrioxide. Is that plain to you, Mr. Cordie?"

"Yes, if you go slow. My chemistry at Boston Tech has slipped me for many a year, professor."

"I see. Well, the said sulphurtrioxide escapes through cracks in the side of the volcano where it combines with the moisture in the soil and air to form sulphuric acid which in turn dribbles down into the fissure or whatever you want to call it. Hence, Jeems, the sulphuric acid you dipped up in the jar."

"Fair enough," Jimmie answered with a grin. "We can make the nitric by cooking the Chile saltpeter crystals with the sulphuric acid, can we not, teacher?"

"We can—if we can find a big stoneware pot, Jeems. If we can't—an iron one will do."

"Well, by the Nine Red Gods, we've got the sulphuric, the nitric, and the cotton. Stick around and watch your old Uncle James make guncotton."

"Not close," the Bean answered as they started back. "Have you ever seen a guncotton wringer fume off, James?"

"Yeah. At an English war plant. Not once, Duke of Boston, but many times. Let the nitrators wear their slickers and goggles. It won't hurt them unless some lands on their skin. I'll do the dirty work with Red—he was so darned anxious to get in."

"Where are you going to get the goggles? Do you think the yacht is a department store?"

"What kind of a question is that to ask the superintendent of the Cordie guncotton works? You're only a chemist, feller. All chemists are silent unless asked for information."

"Most of them that I know aren't very silent," answered the Bean, solemnly. "None of us wear glasses and—"

"Listen—take a rubber sheet and cut slits in it to look through. If she fumes—turn your back—what could be sweeter?"

"Lots of things," answered the Bean firmly. "You and Red can do the nitrating."

Jimmie laughed. He knew that the Boston Bean would try anything at any time, no matter what he might say or pretend.

"All right, Codfish. We'll do 'er. Are you afraid to analyze the product?"

"I'll try to screw up my nerve that far," answered the Bean mournfully.

THE MAKING of that guncotton by Jimmie Cordie, with Red as assistant superintendent, the Boston Bean as chemist, the Yid as general foreman, the crew as laborers, and Grigsby and Katherine as observers, directors, stockholders and what-not, is a story in itself. They used everything on the yacht that could be used, except, as Jimmie said, "our spotless reputations." Nothing was sacred. The chef produced a huge earthen carboy—which, he claimed, had held his private stock of rice wine. The Yid grinningly insinuated that judging by the color of the chef's nose, it had held brandy.

They cooked the Chile saltpeter crystals with the sulphuric acid in it. The neck of the carboy was sealed with mud in which was stuck a large bent glass tube that had been used to siphon wine. The tube was wrapped with cloths that were kept constantly wet with cold water from the yacht's ice plant. That condensed the vapors from the carboy and the nitric acid dripped from the end of the tube into a big glass punch bowl.

"Well," Jimmie said, with a grin, as the bowl slowly filled. "We have now, ladies and gents, nitric and sulphuric acid. *Allons, mes enfants.* What now, chemist?"

"Mix two thirds sulphuric and one third nitric and you have your mixed acid for nitrating, super."

"I know that. What temperature do we nitrate at?"

"As low as you can get it, Jeems, or rather, keep it."

"I know that also. What the heck was the old proportion? Twenty pounds of cotton to four hundred and eighty pounds of mixed acid? But we can't go that strong; about five to ninety-five is our limit. Something like that anyway. Yid, round me up some more crocks—big ones; also get me a tank to set 'em in. Then run in an ice water line. This stuff has got to be kept cool, you hear me?"

"Oi, Jimmie! Sure I hear you. Vare am I to get dem?"

Jimmie stared at the Yid. "Listen," he said firmly. "Are you general foreman of this plant? If you are, don't come running up to me and asking fool questions. If I have to tell you where to find things, I don't need you as foreman. Go and find them yourself, and make it snappy."

"I'll go with you, Yid," Katherine said. "Let's go up to that old temple on the hill. Maybe we can find some crocks up there."

They found several, made of native stoneware; and brought them down to the yacht with the help of some of the crew.

Jimmie and Red stuck the first batch of cotton down in the acid after it was cooled by the ice water around the crock and the rest moved hastily back. The charge promptly burned up in the acid.

"**NOW WHAT** the heck and high water is the matter?" demanded Jimmie, as he and Red ran from the red and black and yellow fumes.

The Bean examined the wild raw cotton. "Too many seeds," he announced. "The oil from them is what did it, Jimmie. This cotton must be picked clean."

"Oi," said the Yid, "vot a job. As foreman I don't have to did it."

"Every one has to 'did' it, old kid," Jimmie said firmly, "Come on, let's get at it. Wait—did it ever occur to any of you that our boy friend is keeping darn quiet?"

"He's framing something, probably," Grigsby answered. "Let him take all the time he wants. We're hooked up for him."

"Maybe-so," Jimmie answered. "But I'll feel a darned sight better when we get to sailing over the deep blue sea. Latch on to some of that cotton, Red. What do you think you are, a passenger?"

They cleaned the cotton and after two or three more fume-offs, they nitrated it for thirty minutes, then drowned cotton, acid and all in a barrel of water. They washed the cotton with cold water, they boiled it all day in several changes of water to stabilize it, then they spread it out to dry in the not too hot sun.

"Watch it now, Jimmie," warned the Bean. "It's dangerous and sensitive now."

"I will. How are we going to compress the darn stuff?"

"Can't—except what you can do by ramming it hard with a wooden rammer when you are loading the holes. I hope she'll go."

Jimmie looked at his acid-scarred hands and grinned cheerfully. "So do I, Codfish. Next thing to do is to drill the holes. I've got the engineer making some drills, and the rock isn't very hard, praise be. How will we detonate her, Bean?"

"Take the fulminate of mercury caps out of some cartridges."

"Holy cats! Here's where Mr. Cordie's son Jimmie resigns as superintendent. Can do, Bean?"

"Darned if I know. We can try."

"Maybe-so the electrician can dope out some way to detonate

her by putting wires into the cartridges so as they touch the cap. That 'taking-out' thing don't sound so pleasant to me."

"Perhaps he can, Jimmie. There is plenty of wire, anyway, he tells me. We'll put the detonating division under him."

"That's a brilliant suggestion, Codfish. We'll make another batch and then shoot the works."

CHAPTER X

WARRENNE STRIKES

KATHERINE CAME UP to where the Yid was sitting under the awning on the quarter-deck aft. "Yid, I want to go up to the temple again. There are some carved stones that I want to examine in the light. I didn't have a chance when we were looking for—"

"Oi, vat a business in de hot sun," the Yid protested. He had really been working very hard and was, for the first time since the guncotton-making began, actually taking it easy. "Look at how far it is up dare. Vait till it gets cooler."

"Why, Yid! It's cool right now. Come with me."

"I vould in a minute," the Yid lied, "but ven I hooked it up de last tank I sprained my ankle. Vait till after dinner, maybe-so it gets better, ain't it?"

Katherine laughed. "It'll be much hotter then, Yid—and probably your ankle will be much worse. Well, I'm going."

The Yid straightened up in his deck chair and looked around. He could see Jimmie Cordie and the Bean with some of the crew over by the rocks, drilling holes. Red was up on the highest hill with the gun crew, the Yid knew. Grigsby was below with the engineer. There were three or four sentries in sight on the various high points. The temple, what was left of it, was in plain sight.

So the Yid grinned and said, "You have my royal permission,

Mrs. Admiral. Take mit you some of de crew," and he settled down to take a nap.

Katherine did not see any reason why she should take any of the crew away from their work, and she sauntered down the sand dune alone.

She walked to the foot of the temple hill and sat down a moment to rest. As she did she waved her hand to Jimmie and the Bean, who she thought were facing her; but they didn't see it. She smiled as she realized how engrossed they were with the guncotton; and after a few minutes she went on up the hill and entered the ruins.

The Yid was sound asleep when Jimmie Cordie shook him awake.

"What kind of a general foreman are you?" Jimmie was demanding when the Yid opened his eyes. "Corked up in the middle of the shift. Didn't you hear that mess call?"

"Vot mess call? Oi, I just closed it my eyes for a minute und—"

"And kept them closed all the morning. You're fired, Yid. This afternoon you can swing a nine-pound hammer."

Red, down from the hills, came up in time to hear the Yid's demotion.

"What has that scut been doing?" he demanded. "Sleepin' here in the shade whilst I am meanderin' up and down hills?"

"My vork vas done," the Yid defended; "I got it a right to—"

"Sure you have, Abie," Jimmie agreed with a smile. "Red is jealous, that's all. Let's eat."

Jimmie, Grigsby, Red and the Yid were sitting at the table when the Bean came in. He had gone to his stateroom when he came on board.

JIMMIE LOOKED up. "Where's Katherine?" he asked.

"Why—I don't know. I thought she was here," the Bean answered. "She and Scotty are side-kicks; maybe-so she is down in the engine room with him. I'll send a steward down."

"No, she isn't," Grigsby said, putting down his fork. "I just came up from Scotty."

"She vent to the temple," the Yid said, "just before I vent to sleep."

"Who went with her?" Jimmie demanded, rising.

"Vy—nobody, I guess. I told her to take it some of de crew, but I don't think she did."

"You let her go by herself! General quarters, Bean! Red, get up on the hill! If you see a party going toward the cañon, get 'em with the gun crew. Yid, get out and circle with the patrols. Swing in toward the yacht. It may be that she is still there!"

The Bean had run out of the dining saloon and at once the bugle blew.

"Take the deck, George. The Bean will want to go with me."

"Hold it a minute, Jimmie. If Warrenne has got her, as he probably has, look out for an ambush up near the temple. Take all the men except a couple of machine gun crews. We'll hold the yacht until you get back if he attacks."

"Right. It may be a mare's nest, but—" The Bean came in. He had his cartridge belt on and was carrying a rifle.

"All set, Jimmie," he said, quietly—too quietly.

"Steady, John," Jimmie said gently. "We'll get her. He will not harm her until—"

"Let's go—if you are coming," the Bean interrupted. "I can't stand any talking."

"How many men at their battle stations?"

"Twenty-five."

"Order fifteen forward with us. George will stay here. Come on and—Winthrop! Snap out of it!" Jimmie's voice held the snarl of command. "You are an officer about to lead men."

The Bean's eyes became sane once more. "I'm all right, Jimmie, thanks. Let's go—*please!*"

Red and the Yid had, without a word, started for the hill and the patrols.

There was no ambush at the temple or anywhere else. Jimmie sent an advance guard far ahead, but it was unnecessary. There was not even any sign of a struggle anywhere around the temple.

"He's got her, Jimmie," the Bean said. "Let's get back and go through to where she is with all we've got."

"We will, Bean. Relax, old kid. Listen to reason. He won't touch her. First he'll use the fact that he has her to try to make us surrender. That's a-b-c stuff, John."

"Jimmie, my brain won't open to hear anything. He's got the woman I love better than anything in the world and I'm going to—"

The Yid came up with all but two of the men who had been on the patrol.

"On de next hill, facin' de vater," he said, "are two of our men—dead—mit daggers in de backs."

The Yid's face was not very handsome under any circumstances and now it looked like some stone-carved demon. "It is my fault," he went on, "und I vill go und get—"

"Steady, Yid," Jimmie interrupted. "No time to talk about whose fault it was. We all had her to protect, and now she is gone, that is all. Let's get back. Did you see any trace of a party?"

"No. Ve circled around from de hill vare Red is to de sea and den in to here."

"He took her through some hidden passage, then. Let's go."

BACK ON the yacht, Jimmie Cordie, the Yid, and the Bean went up on the bridge where Grigsby stood with Red Dolan and Captain Paulet.

"Here it is," Jimmie said curtly. "There's no question but that Warrenne has captured her. How he got by the patrols, I don't know; and it does not make any difference. I have told the Bean that I do not think that Warrenne will in any way hurt Katherine, but will use her in some way to force us to surrender. He may figure that we will start out to rescue her, which is just what he wants us to do."

"What else is there for us to do?" demanded Red. "Are we to stay here talkin' whilst that scut has herself? We'll take the Brownings and shoot our way in and if he has touched wan hair of her pretty head, I'll—"

"Pipe down, Red," Grigsby ordered quietly. "That's the last thing to do—go rushing in. He will be hooked up for us, as Jimmie says."

"What else is there for us to do, George?" asked the Bean with insulting smoothness. "Wait here until he condescends to send my wife back to me? Well—rush in or not, I am going to take every man on board this yacht and the gun-crews on the hills and go and get her. Captain Paulet, order every man over the side, full equipment. One machine gun to every four men. Rifles, Colts and all ammunition that can be carried. Jimmie, are you going with me?"

"No," curtly answered Jimmie Cordie. "After you damned fools get killed, which you will, George and I will take her from Warrenne—if he does not kill her when you come blundering in."

"That's right," Grigsby said. "I won't go with you, Winthrop." Not "Bean" or "Codfish" now; it was Major Grigsby talking to Lieutenant Winthrop. "You are leading your men to certain death."

The Boston Bean stared at Jimmie Cordie and then at Grigsby, as if not believing his ears.

"What the divil do ye mean by that, Jimmie Cordie?" demanded Red, in equal surprise. "Have I lived to hear ye backin' away from a fight? Sorry the day!"

"No, you haven't, you red-headed ape—and you won't, either. If it were just us I'd be right alongside—and well he knows it. But I've Katherine to think of. I love her myself, and by the Nine Red Gods I'm not going to jeopardize her safety while I've still got the sense I was born with. Right now, Winthrop is as goofy as the devil."

"Is he, Jimmie? Be quiet now, Beany darlin'. 'Tis us that will take care of ye as we did up in that desert av—"

The Boston Bean looked at Red, then back at Jimmie Cordie. Slowly he said, "You win, Jimmie. I'm sane. That 'jeopardize her safety' thing knocked some sense into me. I withdraw that order, Paulet. Go ahead, Jimmie."

"I hoped I could jar you loose, Bean," and Jimmie breathed his relief. "The first thing to do is to find out where Katherine has been taken. For all we know, she may be halfway to the mainland by now. Personally, I think she is at his headquarters and he is figuring a play to make us holler 'uncle.' If you birds will give me until morning I can find out. Then during the 'Oh, will you, won't you, will you?' stuff, we can start a little backfire and snatch her out from under, smacking Mr. Warrenne down while doing so, to teach him to lay off our admirals. Use sense, Bean. He won't touch her until after whatever bluff he puts up has failed—and don't forget that Katherine is no weak sister, herself, as far as that goes."

"All right, Jimmie," the Bean answered quietly. "Take the deck. But whatever you do, I'm going to be right along."

"We won't do anything until after dark. Then the men that are chosen can ease off, one by one and—"

"And wan av the wans will be me," interrupted Red, firmly.

"And anodder of de vons vill be me," stated the Fighting Yid, just as firmly.

Grigsby laughed. "Don't start any picking, old kid. We'll all go if there is to be a party."

"I say," the young English captain said, "I want to be included, you know. Mrs. Winthrop was on board and I was in command. It was up to me to see that she was guarded. You chaps all—especially Mr. Winthrop—you all rank me, but—"

"You will be included, Paulet," the Bean said. "I know how you feel."

"Well, for Pete's sake," Jimmie said, "the whole blame crew will want to go. This is to be just a scouting party."

LITTLE MING Li, who had been with Katherine's uncle when he met his death on a mountain trail, and who had stayed with her ever since, came up and bowed.

"All right, Ming Li," Jimmie said. "What's on your mind?" All of the hard-bitted soldiers of fortune liked Ming Li, Red especially.

"This, honolable captain," Ming Li answered firmly. "Pilates take my Missee Katheline. I go to find missee, light now."

"Oh, you do? Who is going to do the wailing in the hills after we get eaten up by the pirates? You're supposed to wail 'em into an attack with your ghost-wailing for Tzu-kung, young feller me lad."

"No get eatee up," answered Ming Li positively. "Plenty dead men alound. Me catchee unifolm. Pilates no know evelybody on pilate ships. I go in as wounded man, vely weak—all coveled with bloody lags and evelything. Find whele Missee Katheline is; come back; tellee you, honolable eldel blothels; you go and get."

"Well, I'll be darned," Jimmie said. "I'll bet you could, at that."

"If ye can, ye scut," Red announced, "I'll give ye that chance to play wid a machine gun that ye have been pesterin' me for."

"Can do! I go now."

"You will not," Jimmie answered. "Wait until dark. Then you can, Ming Li. Right now you listen to me. Don't try any rescue stuff yourself or I'll skin you alive. You go in, find out all you can, and come back to where we'll be waiting for you in the hills. Is that plain to you?"

"Plentee plain, eldel blothel. No do any tly lescue stuff all alone."

"That's her, Ming Li. You remember that and I'll make you a present of a gun and a belt."

IT WAS about two o'clock in the morning when Ming Li came to where the party from the yacht lay hidden in the hills.

"Missee Katheline is in house of Wallenne. No hult yet.

Vely easy fol me to find out. Plentee new pilates on ships. All vely angly at Wallenne fol losing so many men and not cutting down 'body' of Tzu-kung. Plentee aflaid of Tzu-kung's spilit wailing in hills."

"How many men are there on shore, Ming Li?" Grigsby asked.

"Vely many. Maybe-so one thousand, maybe-so fifty thousand. Plentee on ships in halbol."

"Where is Warrenne's house?"

"By the piels and the ships. Two legiments alound it."

"Come on," Red said impatiently. "What are ye waitin' for, Jimmie? What the heck is two regiments av them damn scuts? Herself must be worryin' bad. We'll slap 'em outa the way."

"I know Red, but wait a minute. We know that Katherine is not hurt in any way. What else did you find out, Ming Li?"

"Plentee, Captain Coldie. Thele is a mighty magician named Wang-sun that the pilates go to see so he may tellee them what his eyes see when he sends them abload. They go to him about the wailing of Tzu-kung's spilit. One, a man flom the nolth, say that Wang-sun vely top-side man; Wallenne say, 'will I do this, O vely honolable Wang-sun? Will I do that?' Me, I do not believe that Wang-sun can send his eyes—"

"Nor do I. Now, wait a minute, Ming Li," Jimmie interrupted. "Did you find out where this mighty magician lived?"

"Yes. In a stone house close to the hills, captain."

"Is there a regiment around his house, also?"

"No. One in flont. I went to see if I could get—"

"All right, Ming Li. The gun and belt are yours. Pull out for a minute. Wait—go over to that hill and do a little high-class wailing. Make it strong about how mad Tzu-kung's spirit is at them all, and at Wang-sun in particular."

"What's the idea, Jimmie?" the Boston Bean asked. "We are standing here and—"

"Stay put, Codfish. Something is commencing to buzz around in the place where I ought to carry a brain. If we can get this—

no, not so good; a message would be rotten. What the heck is the matter with me? Here I want to decoy Warrenne out in the open and—by gosh, I've got it. Listen to this...."

CHAPTER XI

IN THE SOOTHSAYER'S HOUSE

OLD WANG-SUN, THE seer, sat in his stone house, which consisted of one large room and a couple of smaller ones back of it. He was not feeling very well and so could not sleep. A knock came on the door and he called testily, "Enter."

A young wounded Chinese came in, bowing very low.

"Who are you and what do you want?" Wang-sun demanded.

"I am Ming Li, of Yi-yin's regiment, O all-powerful one who speaks with the gods. My spirit is troubled and I would that you, resplendent one, ease it."

"Come to me in the morning. I am tired and must rest."

Ming Li took a gold chain from his blouse and laid it at the feet of Wang-sun.

"Put it in my hand," the old Chinaman commanded, his eyes showing his lust for gold.

Ming Li obeyed and, as he did, said, "It is this that troubles my spirit, O mighty one. Tzu-kung's spirit wails to us, his brothers. To-night two of us went as far into the hills as we dared and it talked to us. It is wrathy and threatened even you, who were its friend when it inhabited the body."

Wang-sun didn't like that at all. For all his half-unconscious faking, he believed in spirits and what an angry one could do.

"Me?" he quavered. "It threatens me? But I always was a friend of Tzu-kung's. Why is it angry with me?"

"Because you have not prevailed on Warrenne to go out and cut down its body and give it honorable burial."

"But he—I—Warrenne is waiting for— Tell the spirit of Tzu-kung that it will be done soon."

"We attempted to tell it, O mighty one, but it is very angry. It said that it would come and tear your spirit out of the body and whip it through the cold outer darkness forever unless you proved that you were doing all you could."

"Proved? But how?" demanded the very much scared old Wang-sun. He didn't doubt in the slightest but what the spirit of Tzu-kung could do just what it threatened to do.

"We, his brothers, asked that—knowing you would demand what proof was desired. We knew, great one, that you could send your spirit out to talk to the spirit of Tzu-kung if you wished, but we thought that we—"

"You did right, Ming Li," interrupted Wang-sun hastily. "I could, but at the moment I am ill. What did the spirit of Tzu-kung want?"

"It told of the capture of a woman from the ship who is now with Warrenne. It cares nothing for the woman, but it wishes to be reassured of your power over Warrenne. You are to send for the Englishman, telling him to bring the woman for you to see. When he comes you will go over whatever plans he has with him. The spirit of Tzu-kung said it would be here to listen. It cannot read Warrenne's mind. This will tell the spirit of Tzu-kung that you are still a friend."

If Wang-sun had taken time and coolly thought over the request, he might have got suspicious. But he was not feeling well, he was afraid of spirits, he did believe that Tzu-kung's could do as it had threatened. He swallowed the bait, hook, line and sinker.

"I will send at once," he said, rising. "Remain here with me, Ming Li. I—I do not care to be alone."

He went to the door, opened it and called to one of the sentries.

The man saluted and came up to the door. "Send Captain Ch'e to me at once."

When the captain came, Wang-sun said, "Go to Lord Warrenne and tell him that I feel my sight returning. Ask him to come here to me as I am not well. Ask him also to bring with him the woman he captured. I have seen her when I sent my eyes abroad. Tell him to bring her as it will help me see."

The captain saluted, turned on his heel and started toward Warrenne's headquarters.

AS WANG-SUN shut the door and started back to his chair, he said: "Truly, I hope that the spirit of Tzu-kung will soon be pleased with me. It—"

The Fighting Yid's brawny arm came around Wang-sun's neck and the rest of the speech was lost in a gurgle as the sooth-sayer's wind was shut off.

In a moment or two the Yid laid him down on the floor. "If you've choked him to death," Jimmie Cordie whispered fiercely, from the door of one of the little rooms, "I'll take you apart, you Yid baboon."

"Vot? I just pressed a little. He is down, but not out, poppa."

"Yeah? Drag him in here and make it snappy. Ming Li, you beat it out the back way and back up the hill. You can come down with the rest if they charge. No; no argument. Obey me."

Ming Li shut the mouth he had opened in protest, and started.

"Take off your coat, Yid. Come on, Bean, help me get the robe off this gent."

"Why didn't you let Wang-sun wait for Warrenne? We could have—"

"I know we could. But it would have meant one more to get in the way if Warrenne brings others with him besides Kather-ine. Now the Yid will be right up in front. Hurry up, Yid. Some one may come to see you before Warrenne gets here. If they do, go to the door and—"

"Oi, Jimmie! Vot kind of a Chink vill I make it? Von look at my nose and avay goes de ball game." The Yid was taking off his coat.

"A damn rotten one; but it's the best we can do. You needn't take off your pants and shoes, Yid. Roll your pants up. This, robe is like a nightgown. Put that belt and holster down, you nitwit. Who ever heard of a Chink with a—"

"Vait, I slip it the Colt up de sleeve, ain't it? See, now it don't show. De cap is too big."

"All the better for you. Get out and sit in that chair till we see how you look. Oh, my gosh! Double rotten. Yid, if any one comes, for Pete's sake talk from the chair, and hold the fan up."

"Talk in vot?" demanded the Yid, very peevishly. "I don't know Chink, Jimmie."

"You don't? I thought you were a Chinese scholar. Well, talk in Yid, then. They'll think you have the gift of tongues and are under the influence."

"I vish to heck und—"

"Steady," whispered the Bean, who was standing as close to the little slit of a paneless window as he dared. "Here comes—Katherine! She is walking beside Warrenne. How about that light, Jimmie?"

There was a kerosene lamp over on a table in the corner. The chimney was dirty, and the wick needed trimming, so there was not much light.

"Let it alone. There's enough. Remember, Yid. Let them get all the way in. As soon as they do, motion Katherine to stand over by the light. As if you wanted to get a good look at her. If you shoot Warrenne, the Bean and I will climb your frame. He's our meat."

"He's *my* meat!" corrected the Bean softly, as he and Jimmie slipped back into the darkness of the little room.

A knock came at the door and the Yid called something that he hoped would be taken for "Come in."

The door opened, and Warrenne, with his hand on the knob,

stepped to one side and bowed ironically as Katherine Winthrop entered.

"Enter, my dear," he said. "You are now in the presence of the mighty magician, Wang-sun. He is known—"

One of the Yid's shoes was sticking out less than an inch from beneath the robe, and Warrenne saw it. He had not gained the leadership of thousands of Chinese pirates by being slow, either physically or mentally. As quick as the stroke of a leopard's paw, his Webley came out of the holster. He shot—not at the Yid, but at the lamp. He hit it, and as the darkness came he jumped back through the door, slamming it behind him.

IT WAS fast, very fast. Too fast for Jimmie Cordie, the Bean, and the Yid, who were all fast men. As it was, the bullets from their Colts thudded into the door. One second less speed from Warrenne and he instead of the door would have received the bullets.

The Bean had Katherine in his arms before the door-slam had died away. The Yid shed the robe as Jimmie said, "Fair enough. Out the back and up the hill, children!"

As he spoke they could hear Warrenne shouting orders which were being repeated by company commanders.

"Hop to it," Jimmie said, as they ran out the back. He, the Yid, and the Bean, had slipped down the hill under cover of darkness and into the rear of the stone house. The Chinese regiment and the sentries never even dreamed of an attack, and the sentries, as Chinese sentries often do, had almost all gone to sleep.

"I hope that the reserve heard the shots," the Bean said, as he tenderly lifted Katherine over a rough place. At that second he had audible notice that they had. Two machine guns opened up from the hill and down charged Red, Grigsby, Captain Paulet and six of the crew.

The Chinese regiment was flowing around the house on both sides, and when the machine guns opened up, there must have been two or three hundred of them. Two machine guns manned by men who had operated them in France, opened up on the Chinese at almost point-blank range, shooting into the "brown." They blew wide swaths through the Chinese on both sides. But those behind came on, like fighting men.

The charge down the hill stopped as it reached the four, Red letting out a wild Irish yell of joy.

"We can't hold 'em here!" Jimmie shouted. "Back up the hill. Red, quit that! Start back!"

Back they went past the machine guns. "Get ahead with Katherine, Bean," ordered Jimmie.

Two machine guns and ten rifles responded and the regiment of Chung melted away. But another took its place.

"Fall back a hundred yards," Grigsby commanded. "Back, Red! Get to the top. We'll hold 'em there."

They made it, but before they did three of the crew went down. Pirates were firing now from the roofs. The Yid grunted as a bullet tore into the muscles of his shoulder at the back. Jimmie staggered as one caught him in the calf of the leg, but did not fall.

Red saw Jimmie stagger and ran to his side. "Are ye hit, Jimmie darlin'? Will I carry ye?"

"No. I can make it. Get those guns back, Red. Yid! Cover the guns!"

Back they went, then halted and drove the Chinese back down the hill. Back once more and another halt.

Warrenne was like a crazy man. But he was not so crazy as to lead a charge. He knew that five of the best shots in the Orient would crack down on him the moment he showed. He threw his men at the hill, as many as could get on it at a time.

The moon came out a little, which made the shooting light better—for him as well as for the yacht party. But the refugees had reached the top.

The Bean and Katherine were close now. Jimmie shouted, "Get back to the yacht, Bean. George, go with them! We'll hold 'em off until you—"

Scotty, the yacht's engineer, arrived with every man who had been left on the yacht plus those who had been at the guns on the hills. With them arrived rapid fire guns, more Brownings.

"I couldna stay longer," Scotty panted. "The goons dr-r-rew me." Scotty, whose name was Douglas, had fought with the Scots Greys.

"Glad they did!" Jimmie answered tersely. "Get in action with 'em."

Warrenne tried twice more, and both times got driven back with frightful slaughter.

He finally saw that what he was doing only resulted in the loss of men, and ordered that the charges cease. "We will circle," he said to a high officer with him, "and get between them and the yacht."

CHAPTER XII

THE RED THREAT

AT A TABLE in a fairly crowded Hanoi restaurant much frequented by the Europeans in that Indo-China capital, sat a young Chinese flyer with an Englishman, John Cecil Carewe.

Carewe was young, reckless, and—though they perhaps had not recognized the fact on the one momentous occasion they had met—as like Red Dolan, inside, as twin peas. Outside, there was no resemblance, Carewe being slim and quite English.

"You look as if you had lost some one you love," the Chinese flyer said, with a smile. He had first met Carewe in England, years before. "It is not a natural look for your face to wear, John. Generally you are smiling as if all the world were a joke."

He spoke in Chinese and Carewe answered in the same language, but more slowly and with many mistakes in his voice inflections. One Chinese word may mean several things, according to the way the tone is raised or lowered.

"It is true that I am sad, O observant one," Carewe answered lightly.

"If it is a question of money, brother of the air, or of the recent loss of your plane, I can—"

"No, it is not, Liu-hsia. Thanks for the offer though, old dear. It is true that I have lost, not a loved one, but several that I—" The clean-cut, good-looking young Englishman leaned a little across the table. "It may be that you can help me, Liu-hsia,"

"As you helped me in England, John. Anything I can do, I will."

"You know of the Americans called Jimmie Cordie, the Boston Bean, Grigsby, Red Dolan and the Fighting Yid?"

"Who does not?" answered Liu-hsia, with a smile. "Are they the cause of your sadness? It is true that they have made many men sad; and some glad—those they fought for."

"Liu-hsia, one time in the north, not very long ago, I got into a bad place. A very tight place, to be frank. Those men pulled me out of it and I fought at their side. I have fought in many places since I left England, Liu-hsia, and with many men, but none with whom I would rather be."

Liu-hsia nodded. "It is considered an honor to fight at their side, brother. That I know. Why do they make you sad?"

"They don't know that they are doing it," answered Carewe, with an effort at casualness. "I went to Hong Kong ten days ago to find them. I wanted to—be with them again if they would let me. They had left Hong Kong on the yacht belonging to the Boston Bean. You remember the typhoon that swept the China Sea about then?"

"Yes, very well. Many ships were lost. Also many planes."

"Among them mine," answered Carewe grimly. "I thought the old crate was secured, but the wind lifted her up and smashed her against a wall. Well, since the typhoon, the yacht on which they sailed has not been heard from. That is why I am sad, Liu-hsia. You said loved ones. I answered, not a loved one. I lied; I love them all, as deeply as one man can love another."

"You have searched for the yacht, John?"

"No. I cannot raise the money for another plane at the moment. And where should I search? The South China Sea is broad and long, brother of the air. I came here hoping to get a job flying."

THREE MEN passed the table. Two of them were young men, both more than a little drunk. They smiled and waved their hands at Liu-hsia. That is, the two young men did, the older one nodded curtly.

"Two Soviet flyers—the drunken ones," Liu-hsia explained after they had passed. "The other is Radischev, a Soviet agent."

"What are they doing here?" Carewe asked indifferently.

Liu-hsia smiled, "That I do not know definitely, brother. I am here to find out. There is a War Lord here who, it is thought in Peking, has been bought by Soviet gold. It may be that when he decides to do what you call 'show his hand,' they will fly for him. I know that planes are being assembled. I have spies in the War Lord's palace and— Truly my brain must have been wandering! What other yacht and men could do as they have done?"

"All of which, old dear," Carewe said softly, "is as clear as mud. Start at the beginning."

"It may be nothing, John. My spies report everything that happens in the palace. Last night I was told a tale of the arrival of Radischev and of a conversation Radischev had with the War Lord."

"It was overheard? My word, your spies must be highly placed."

"In a Chinese palace there are many ways to overhear a conversation, brother. Do you wish me to take the time to explain?"

"My sainted Aunt Maria, no."

Liu-hsia smiled. "I did not think you did. Radischev spoke of an island and a pirate leader named Warrenne."

"I've heard of that rotter."

"Radischev asked the War Lord for the loan of the two flyers who had come with the bombing planes. The War Lord asked why he wanted them and Radischev told him of a yacht that had been carried by a tidal wave onto the island. Warrenne had attacked this yacht and had been driven back with heavy slaughter. He tried again to post guns on the hills to destroy the yacht and went into an ambush that cost him more men."

"Oh, I say! It is the Katherine Neville and— Your pardon, Liu-hsia. I'll not interrupt again."

"The War Lord asked why he should send flyers to help a pirate take a yacht and Radischev explained that this pirate Warrenne had agreed to join the Soviet cause with all his men and ships. Radischev wanted him with as many men as possible and if help was not given him he would be very likely not to have many men left by the time he took the yacht. The War Lord was ready to refuse, then Radischev mentioned a gold payment and offered to divide with him. That changed the situation for the War Lord and he agreed to send the flyers."

"What have they got?" Carewe asked, his eyes shining.

"Bombers—latest type."

"Where is this island?"

"Off the coast of Anam below Hué. A three-hour flight to the south."

"When do they leave?"

"That I do not know, brother. You think it is the yacht of the Boston Bean?"

"Think, my eye!" Carewe said in English. "I know jolly well it is. What other could— Don't turn around, Liu-hsia. Radischev is leaving. After he goes, look around and catch their eyes. Beckon them to join us. I've got to find out when they are taking off."

A FEW minutes later the two young Soviet flyers were sitting at the table with Carewe and Liu-hsia. With the freemasonry that exists among all birdmen, they were at ease from the introduction. Drinks were served and, egged on by Carewe and Liu-hsia,

the Russians began to boast of their exploits with women and
with planes.

Carewe was well known as a reckless soldier of fortune, who
flew for any honorable potentate who could command his
services and pay enough for them. Liu-hsia was an ace in the
army of the South. The two young Russians had heard of them
both after coming to China—and wished to impress them with
their ruthlessness and their skill.

Finally Carewe said, "My hat! That type bus must be a swanky
thing, what, what? I'd dearly love to take her up once." It was
in English. Neither of the Russians spoke Chinese, but they
did know English, as well as French and German—like most
Russian officers.

One of them answered, "But why not, Carewe? As soon as
they are assembled, you can take—"

"You forget that we are ordered to leave at once, Dmitri," the
other interrupted. "When we come back it can be arranged."

Carewe drew back, very much disappointed. "But I leave for
Peking as soon as I get orders which I expect any minute. How
long will you be gone?"

"See," laughed one of the Russians, "how disappointed the
Englishman looks, brother. Do not cry, little one. The planes will
be ready in two days. We go only a short distance and will be
back in less than a day. Cannot you delay that long?"

Carewe brightened up. "Why, yes. I know I can, I say, you
chaps, if I can ever do anything for you in return, don't hesitate
to send out the flamin' call and all that sort of rot, what, what?"
As he said it, his handsome young face and blue eyes smiling,
he was saying to himself, "I'll do something to, not for you, you
blighters, if I have to steal a crate and a rifle."

"Glad to do it," grunted the one called Dmitri, lurching to
his feet. "We must be getting back, Ostrov."

The other rose promptly. "That is so. We are already over our
leave." He steadied himself by holding on to the table, grinning
foolishly. "Cheerio!" he said, gutturally but triumphantly.

They all laughed at the English farewell and the way he pronounced it. Then the two Russians tried to walk out, very dignifiedly.

Before the pair had reached the exit, Carewe leaned forward. "Liu-hsia, get me anything that can fly. Steal it if you have to. I've got to make Hong Kong by morning."

"Hong Kong? But the—"

"Listen, brother who flies. There is no time to explain. Can you get me a plane? I will see that it is brought right back."

"Yes. Not mine because it is an army plane. There is one owned by the warden of Yin that I can—"

"Come on, then. Pardon me for interrupting, old thing. But time is of the jolly old essence."

Liu-hsia smiled as he rose, tossing a bill on the table to pay the reckoning. "Come, then."

YEN YUAN was lord of life and death over four million members of the dread secret society of the T'aip'ing. Fat, bland, with fingernails enclosed in sheaths of gold, he sat placidly in the flower-scented garden of his palace in Hong Kong. Like all Chinese he loved his garden and spent as much time there as possible. A palace official came to within ten feet of him and bowed.

"You have my permission to speak, Shao."

"One begs to see the Lord of Life."

"Who is the distinguished person that honors me by requesting an audience?"

"An Englishman, whose name is Carewe."

"I know no Englishman named Carewe—yet the name has come to my ears before. What does he want?"

"He would not tell me, illustrious one. He said to tell you that it is for the Black-eyed Smiling One that he—"

Yen Yuan came near losing the impassiveness for which all Chinese strive. His hands spread wide open as he dropped his fan and his eyes opened wide also.

"Fool!" he snarled. "Worthless one, lower than the belly of a snake! You knew that, and stand here? Bring him to me. By my honorable ancestors who sit on high, I will have you boiled in—"

The palace official was on the ground, his face to the dirt, and Yen Yuan regained his control. "Rise," he ordered. "I will forget your fault. Go quickly, Shao."

Jimmie Cordie, while at Boston Tech, had saved the life of a young Chinese student who lay sick with a contagious fever, alone, in a strange, and to him, hostile land. Jimmie had nursed him and "kidded" him back to health.

The boy was the only son of Yen Yuan, absolute head of the T'aip'ing. Jimmie had not known that when he nursed the boy and it would not have made any difference if he had. He himself had once been sick and alone in a strange land, and he cared for the boy as he would have liked to have been nursed.

Later, in China, he had encountered his former classmate, now a member of the powerful T'aip'ing "Board of Foreign Affairs," and had been taken by him to Yen Yuan. That plump, bland old Chinaman had risen from his inlaid gold and mother-of-pearl chair and bowed low to the slim, smiling American.

"You are my honorable elder brother," he said in Mandarin Chinese which his son translated. "Deign to mention anything you may wish, elder brother, and it is yours, as is this miserable hovel where I abide and all I possess."

Jimmie had laughed and answered, "I would ask for nothing but something cool to drink, O mighty Yen Yuan, father of my friend."

From that moment, old Yen Yuan had accepted Jimmie as another son sent him by the gods—and word had gone to that effect through all the countless ramifications of the T'aip'ing.

TWO MINUTES after Shao had done so, Carewe bowed to Yen Yuan, who bowed in return.

"Honor me by being seated, Mr. Carewe," Yen Yuan said in Chinese, ready to change into English if Carewe did not understand.

"Thank you," Carewe answered, sitting down on a stone bench near Yen Yuan's chair. "The matter is this, O mighty Head of the T'aip'ing. In—"

"You are sure of that, Mr. Carewe?" asked Yen Yuan blandly.

"Of what? Oh, of your being Head of the T'aip'ing? I was with Jimmie Cordie in the north where also was your war captain, Shih-kai."

"You know where is the Black-eyed Smiling One, my honorable elder brother, Mr. Carewe?"

"I have a flamin' good idea. In Hanoi last night," Carewe began, telling Yen Yuan what had happened. Yen Yuan sat like a stone image as he listened. Carewe ended with, "I remembered that Jimmie Cordie was your honorable elder brother, O Yen Yuan—and I have come to you. I want a fighting airplane. One with machine guns mounted on the scarf yoke and—"

Yen Yuan held up his hand. "I know nothing of the details about fighting ships of the air. Whatever you wish, you may have, Mr. Carewe. The ships of the society have searched the waters and all the brothers have been hunting for the Black-eyed Smiling One. You have gladdened the heart of an old man. The flying ship will be ready for you in two hours. It may be sooner. What else?"

"My word!" Carewe lapsed into English. "That's rippin', old dear." It is very probable that never before had any one called the Head of the T'aip'ing "old dear," but Yen Yuan smiled.

"You are," he said, "very like the Black-eyed Smiling One—and more like the Lord of the Flaming Hair, who is called Red. I shall make certain arrangements of my own; but is there anything else you can use?"

"Why, I'd like to have a man as gunner. It would take time to pick up an English or American flyer and it would need a lot of explaining, also. Can you furnish me one?"

Yen Yuan clapped his hands together once. An officer stepped out of a little pagoda close by and bowed.

"Send Captain Wen Chih to me."

Three minutes later a young Chinese officer saluted and stood at attention. "You will secure a fighting ship of the air for this gentleman, who is Mr. Carewe. Do not be longer than two hours, Captain Wen Chih. You fought the little guns that go with the ship of the air, under General Ch'ang K'ung Ch'iu?"

"Yes, all-powerful one."

"You will go with Mr. Carewe, under his orders. This I will tell you, O little brother: he goes to rescue the Black-eyed Smiling One, my honorable elder brother. Conduct yourself accordingly. You have my permission to go. Mr. Carewe will join you in a moment."

The young officer saluted and retired.

"Will one ship of the air be enough, Mr. Carewe?" asked Yen Yuan. "You may have as many of them as you wish."

Carewe knew the power of the T'aip'ing and he did not doubt that Yen Yuan could produce fifty planes if necessary; but he shook his head.

"One will be enough," he promised grimly.

CHAPTER XIII

UNWILLING TARGETS

THE WAY BACK to the yacht was a running fight from the mouth of the cañon. Warrenne had hurried some of his pirates between the rescue party and the yacht, but not enough to hold them trapped until he could bring up reinforcements.

The Chinese met a reckless, happy fighting outfit now. Katherine was in the middle and it would have taken many more men to stop them than the pirate band who made the valley. Charges were met by a withering fire and, long before the valley was half crossed, by counter charges. The Americans and Englishmen, led by Red Dolan and Captain Paulet, would cease firing, lower their bayonets and charge, as often as the Chinese got near enough. To give the pirates credit, almost to a man, they waited to receive it, in the open.

"Once more, Red," Jimmie Cordie shouted. "We can make it this time. Over to the right! Paulet, take ten men to the left!" They made it quite easily.

As they reached the yacht the Bean said, "Well, here we are home from the wars."

"We are going to get some more war brought right here to us, Codfish. Look over to the hills," Grigsby announced.

"Holy mackinaw," Jimmie said. "He's ganging up on us. Darned if he isn't going to try to take us by direct charge. We'll need everything we've got this time."

Grigsby, as he reached the quarterdeck, said, "Red, the guns on the hills? How did you leave them?"

"How did I leave them? I left them right where they was, where else? When herself was captured, could I think about guns on hills?"

"I forgot them myself," Jimmie said. "I know the gun crews came up with Scotty. By gosh, I'll bet that we'll be on the receiving end of our own guns in a minute. Warrenne has got 'em by now."

Captain Paulet came up. "You are speaking about the guns, Major Grigsby?"

"Yes."

"The men who made up the crews told me that they hid all the gun ammunition down a deep cut before they left to join Scotty."

"Well," Jimmie said, "here's hopin' that Warrenne doesn't find that cache, and hasn't any ammunition of his own to fit. If he has, they can blow us out of here in ten minutes. I'll leave you gents to entertain Mr. Warrenne's children for a few minutes. My leg is commencing to tell me things."

"I'll fix it for ye, Jimmie," Red said. For all his size he was a gentle and competent first-aid man.

"I go mit, also," the Yid announced. "I got it von in de back some place."

"I'll cut it out av ye, Abie," Red assured. " 'Tis likely I'll cut the heart av ye in doing it, ye scut. Ye won't mind that, will ye?"

The shriek of a shell came and every man on the yacht's deck froze as he listened. "Too high," Jimmie Cordie said, "and too far to the—" The shell burst about a hundred yards from the yacht, sending up a geyser of sand.

"I have a feeling," the Bean said, gravely, "that he has found the shells."

"Your feeling"—another shell came from the higher hill, this time much closer—"is correct."

"**GETTING THE** range," Grigsby announced. "We can't stay here, Jimmie."

"Not if he's going to send that kind of calling cards. Only one thing to do, George, unless we abandon ship; and that is to go up and take back our own guns. Bean, bring everything you've got to bear on the hill. I'll take a party to go spike 'em. You lay down a barrage for us."

"I'll go wid ye, Jimmie," Red announced. "Come on."

"Me, too," the Yid said. "As a gun-spiker I am de best in de—"

"And as wounded men both you and Jimmie are damn' fools," interrupted Grigsby. "I'll take the party. Red, you can come along. Jimmie, you work one of those two-pounders if your leg will let you. Yid, you and the Bean can play with a couple of machine guns. Detail me ten men, Captain Paulet."

The spiking party could have walked slowly across the valley to the hill and all the way up it, for that matter. Jimmie Cordie, the Fighting Yid, the Boston Bean, Captain Paulet and the crew of the Katherine Neville not only laid down a barrage of steel in front of them but also on both sides.

It was sent from every gun mouth on the yacht except those in fixed positions fore and aft, and those raked the hills on both sides as far as they could swing the muzzles. The Katherine Neville ceased to even look like a pleasure craft. From her superstructure and from every porthole, from the quarterdecks forward and aft, she became a battle wagon.

But the spiking party ran instead of walked. They knew that Warrenne would, without question, send men to reënforce the gun crews and they wanted to beat him to it. The Yid and the Bean, both past grand masters of a machine gun, laid a railing of steel-jacketed bullets on each side of the party, not more than half a dozen feet away from them on either side.

As the raiders swung out to the right or left, the "rail" moved out with them, never getting closer or farther away. Scotty and the rest of the crew with anti-aircraft guns, three- and four-inch rifles, put down a barrage that advanced ahead of the party just as fast as they were running.

It was an exhibition of accurate shooting that made Warrenne, from where he lay on one of the hills near the old temple with glasses jammed against his eyes, say to an officer who lay beside him: "My word, what shooting! But Tsai Wo's regiment will beat them to the guns and they will be fifteen or twenty men the less in a few minutes. They can't have all the ammunition in the world either."

But the regiment of Tsai Wo did not beat the party to the guns. As a matter of fact they would have done so, but a make-shift bridge across a deep, swift stream fell and before they could swing around and get across much lower down, fateful minutes were lost.

The Chinese at the guns, as shells and bullets began to whistle overhead and the big foreign devils came over the crest, rose from the guns to give battle as best they could. They fired one scattered volley that did no harm and then death was among them.

Over the guns and past went Grigsby, Red and the crew, and back again. A quick destruction of the mechanism and back to the slope of the hill from which the yacht could be seen.

Jimmie Cordie stood up as he saw the raiding party halt. "What the—oh, wigwag stuff. Looks like Red's shirt."

"Vait, I get it," the Yid said. " 'Ve c-o-m-e,' vot de deuce kind of vigvag is—oi, sure: 'down und—go—to—de—odder—hills—von—by—von. C-o'—vot de deuce kind of a letter is dot? Oi, he means it a 'v.' 'Cover us.' Dot's it, Jimmie: 'Ve come down—'"

"I heard you the first time. Get on that gun again. Hold 'em back, Bean! Look at the top!"

Tsai Wo's regiment had arrived to find the guns put out of commission and the gun crew dead. They started after the foreign devils, who were, it appeared, fleeing. It was worse than going over the side of a vessel to slay its crew and passengers. They were literally blown back from the top of the hill by the steel from the ship that met them. Tsai Wo tried to rally his men, but fell before he had shown more than his head and shoulders.

Warrenne had said that he would like to see Jimmie Cordie "strut his stuff," and now his wish was being gratified. Not only Jimmie Cordie, but the Bean and the Yid and the crew were obliging, and they had plenty to "strut" also.

THE OTHER two hills on which guns were mounted were not as high, nor were the guns as heavy. The men on the yacht saw that Warrenne was not going to send more men across the valley, and the guns were stilled.

Not one was fired until the party reached almost to the top, then the yacht's guns poured steel over it for a minute. There were few men on either hill. Warrenne had sent men to see if the hills were still occupied. If they were, his men had orders to surround the gun crews and hold them. He knew that most of the yacht's crew must have been in the force that met him above the stone house of the soothsayer Wang-sun.

There was even less resistance on the lower hills than on the highest one, and the spiking party reached the yacht without the loss of a man, though three of the crew were wounded. Red and Grigsby were untouched. With them they triumphantly dragged two of the lighter guns from the third hill.

"You done noble, gents," Jimmie greeted them, "and Admiral Winthrop and Gineral Cordie will recommend that you all get a D.D."

"Mit palms," smirked the Yid. "Dey go vid it. Vy didn't you get killed, you Irish gonniff?"

"I came back to do that bullet-cutting thing on ye, Yid darlin'," Red answered, "and now 'tis double deep I will probe, ye Hester Street chimpanzee."

"While Red and the Yid are telling each other about it," Jimmie said, "I'll start once more to get this darned leg tied up."

Katherine came into the yacht's sickbay, as Red was bandaging Jimmie's leg. The Yid was sitting against the wall, waiting his turn.

"Ye better get outa here, alannah," Red said. "I start on the Yid in a minute and maybe-so it is that his yells will not sound good to the pretty ears of ye."

"Why, Red! You wouldn't hurt the Yid, would you?"

"I would—and plenty. 'Tis many the time he has poured the iodine into the wounds of me and said, 'Keep still, you Irish loafer.' It will be music to the ears av me, the yellin' that he'll be doin'.... That's all, Jimmie. Climb up on the table, ye Yid beneath notice, until I cut ye open."

Katherine and Jimmie laughed. They knew that Red, unless fighting, was as gentle as a woman and would never give unnecessary pain to any living thing. The Yid pretended to be terrified as he lay face down on the table and Red cut away his shirt.

"Oi, Oi, vait! Cut lighter mit de knife, doctair, I esk you!" he yelled.

"Well, ye big booby," Red said, bitterly, "I have not touched ye at all."

"I felt it," moaned the Yid. "Vay down to de bottom of my feet. Oi, admiral, come und hold it my hand."

"Yid," Katherine said, sternly, "you are making that all up. Red hasn't even touched you."

Once Katherine had screamed when a Chinese War Lord, by whom she had been captured, twisted her arm. The Yid had broken out of a punishment cage hung below a window, when he heard the scream, and had come through the window like a great gorilla to kill that War Lord with the Chinaman's own sword. From that moment he and the lovely English girl had been, as the Yid expressed it, "pardners, ain't it?"

"But vot he is going to did!" yelled the Yid, who really had chilled steel nerves and had fought on many a field with much worse wounds and smiled as he got rough first-aid later.

"Jimmie," Red said, "take herself outta here. This gibboon will not quit as long as ye are here."

"That's right, Red. Come on, Katherine."

As they left, the Yid's yells miraculously stopped.

"JIMMIE," KATHERINE asked, as they walked along the corridor, "what do you really think? Will we be able to get away from here alive?"

"Well," he answered gravely, "darned if I know, Mrs. Admiral. To tell the truth, it doesn't look that way, unless the guncotton we've been manufacturing will blow a big enough hole for the sea to come through. We might fight our way through to where Warrenne has his ships and capture one, but I doubt it. A surprise is one thing and a direct attack through hills is something else again, Katherine. He won't be surprised again, that's a cinch. In the hills his men can pop it to us from all sides and angles. You saw the time we had getting back to the yacht; and then we had the advantage of surprise, with his men being scattered. Now, not so good."

"But Jimmie, if we cannot fight our way through, and the yacht doesn't float when the guncotton goes off—what will we do?"

"Make it for the pass we were washed through, and start to swim to the Philippines," Jimmie answered with a grin, "One thing is certain, old lady Winthrop, and that is that he can't take the yacht until our ammunition runs out; and your husband has more ammunition than I ever saw on a cruiser, no foolin'. He must have ballasted her with shells."

"Jimmie, Warrenne has more guns. He bragged about them to me. He can bring them up and shell us, can't he?"

"Yeah, boy. But the ones he has aren't the right kind to do much accurate shooting with. If he does, we'll go out and get 'em. How did he treat you?"

They had reached the quarterdeck aft and as they sat down, the Bean joined them.

"That's what I want to know," he said. "How did he act, Mrs. Winthrop?"

"Why—he acted all right. That is, he didn't touch me, if that is what you mean. I was circling a fallen stone in the temple, and a blanket or something came over my head. I couldn't yell or anything. I was picked up and carried. When they took the blanket off, I was on his launch. He just sat there and smiled at me, the way he used to do when he won a game when we were children. A satisfied, conceited smile. He called you a—a long-legged gargoyle, John."

"He did?" asked the Bean gravely. "That sounds pretty bad, Katrinka. What brought out that—"

"Very realistic description," finished Jimmie Cordie for him.

"It is not!" Katherine defended promptly. "John is a very handsome, distinguished-looking man, Jimmie Cordie—and you know it."

"That's right," agreed Jimmie with a grin. "I know it and I'm as jealous as the dickens."

"When you get through discussing my peerless beauty, I'd like to hear what came off," and the Bean patted Katherine's hand. "Never mind this half-pint of nothing, admiral. Go ahead."

"I won't, John. I mean I won't mind him at all. There isn't much to tell. Warrenne maintained that supercilious attitude as if I were a little girl and he was a—what was it you said the other day, Jimmie?"

"What did he say the other day?" The Bean shook his head. "How can he pick out any one thing he said? He's always saying something. Be more specific, Mrs. Admiral."

"Oh, I remember. Warrenne acted as if he were a little tin god on wheels. I say, that's a very fine description."

GRIGSBY CAME up. "Where do you birds think you are, in Hyde Park? Take a look around, Jeems—especially at the hill-tops."

"Lend me your glasses," Jimmie answered, rising. In a minute he lowered them. "Not so good. It looks as if he were bringing up all the artillery he has. We'd better try to make it as hard for him as we can, pronto and in haste. I can see gun muzzles sticking up hither and yon. We can't let him place any on the crests where he can point directly down. If we hold him to shooting up and over, he'll have one sweet time hitting us. Katherine, your sad story will have to wait."

Katherine and the Bean rose, and as they did, she said, "Why, there isn't any story. He took me to his house and said as soon as he made a widow out of me, he was going to make me his wife, whether I wanted to be or not. I laughed, and he said that he'd show you some tricks. He was very cynical and—and blasé, as he always pretended to be."

"All right, Katherine," the Bean said. "I'm glad he confined himself to being that. You better get below."

Katherine drew a long breath to tell her "handsome and distinguished-looking" husband just what a Neville thought about being ordered below in time of battle. But the Bean was already on his way to the bridge with Jimmie and Grigsby.

The yacht began firing at the hilltops. Steady, well placed shots they were, and more than one gun muzzle disappeared in a cloud of dirt and flame. But Warrenne placed many guns, old-type cannon and mortars he had collected from ships he had captured, just behind the hilltops and in lower cuts and little valleys.

That he had a clever artillerist among his forces became apparent very shortly. The gunfire from the yacht prevented him from placing guns that would have a direct range. He tried it twice with some of his modern guns but gave it up as the men dragging the guns into position fell the moment they came into sight. But he opened with everything he had, firing on angles figured by his gunners.

As Jimmie said, to hit a yacht one hundred and fifty feet long and some thirty feet of beam, lying in the middle of a valley, would take some shooting—like making a direct hit on a trench. Most of Warrenne's remaining guns, all of the old ones, shot solid iron balls. If a hit was made it would be more a fluke than anything else.

The balls landed and buried themselves in the sand all over the valley. Some went on over the hills and out into the water. If the yacht had plenty of ammunition, so did Warrenne, for the guns he was putting in action. One ball hit within twenty feet of the yacht's bow and another buried itself in the sand dune on the port side.

Grigsby looked at Jimmie. "We can't stay here, Jimmie. Sooner or later, by the law of averages, he'll knock us down. Pass the word for the Bean to cease firing. No use of wasting ammunition. He won't try for the hilltops again."

The yacht's guns became quiet and Red, the Yid and the Bean came up on the bridge. And so did Katherine. She had been at Red's gun with him and had been firing it. The Bean looked at her and grinned. "I see you went below."

"I did—as far as Red's gun," answered the daughter of the Nevilles.

HERE IT is," Grigsby said. "If we stay here, sooner or later he'll make contact. When he does it may damage the yacht so that there will be no chance of floating her. Personally, I don't care at all about sitting down and letting any gent rain iron on me until he beans me."

"Vell," said the Yid, "vot to do? Me, I'm for doin' somethink, but vat?"

"Yid, if you could only answer your own question, you'd get promoted to be a corporal," Jimmie answered. "George is right about that sitting-down thing. There's only one thing to do—"

"Shoot your horse, crouch behind his carcass, and if the cattle, in the mad stampede, don't—" the Bean began, gravely, then stopped and said, "Pardon me, gents. That 'There's only one thing to do' reminded me of—"

A cannon ball made a direct hit on the quarterdeck aft and crashed through.

"What does that remind you of?" Jimmie asked, as he started to see what damage had been inflicted.

The ball had gone through two decks and into the hold, just missing the propeller shaft; caroming off a steel plate, it had hit a bulkhead door, denting it.

"Thirty feet forward and it would have smacked us where we live," Jimmie said. "One of those babies caressing the motors and we're sunk."

"Sunk is good," the Bean said, as they went up on deck. "If he can hit the coon's head once, he can again. Proceed with the 'one thing to do,' Mr. Cordie."

"I will. I think we've got enough holes drilled. I'll go over and load 'em and touch her off. If the water comes in we may be able to give our playmate an imitation of a naval battle on the way out. If she doesn't—we can lower the boats and try for the opening. That's all I can see to do."

"All right, Jimmie," Grigsby answered quietly. "There's no use in trying to shoot our way through to his ships. They'd get us before we had gone a mile."

"Yeah, boy. Bean, send that electrician to me, with plenty of wire."

"He 's made a blasting machine, Jimmie, and some caps from—"

"I don't care what from, Codfish, as long as they'll go. Hot damn! That one was close, no foolin'. Time we moved out. Ten men will be enough. You birds cover us. Whoever stays to touch off the blast will have to swim or climb a tree."

"The electrician says that he will, Jimmie. He tried for the Channel swim two or three times."

"Yeah? Well, he'll think this is another try. Red, you want to be chief assistant?"

"Try and stop me, ye scut."

"Vait," protested the Yid. "I am de general foreman, don't forget dot, Mistair Superintendent."

"You were also fired, don't forget that. Nothing doing, Yid. Your back won't let you do any running or swimming either."

"Und I suppose dot your leg vill let you do both, ain't it?"

"Red's going to lend me an arm. Let's go, Codfish. You gents hold 'em off us and watch the guncotton experts bring in the China Sea."

CHAPTER XIV

CATASTROPHE

BEFORE THEY GOT a hundred yards from the yacht, the firing from the hills ceased. Warrenne had gone back to his headquarters when word has been brought that his Russian flyers had landed and were waiting for him.

The Chinese had been ordered to keep up the fire on the yacht and to hold their men in the hills ready for a final charge after the bombs dropped by the planes had done their work. Now they saw a party leave the yacht and start for the pass through which the yacht had come on the tidal wave, and they did not know what to do.

If they sent their men in to wipe out this party, they would have to stop the bombardment of the yacht. It would be hard enough to force a charge against the deadly guns they all knew the yacht carried, without adding the possibility of getting killed by their own barrage. Yet the party that had left the yacht was going after something in a businesslike way, the Chinese officers could see through their glasses.

The ranking Chinese officer lowered his glasses. "We must stop the foreign devils," he announced. "I will take the responsibility. Order that the firing cease, Ch'en. Yi-yin, lead your regiment and destroy them. Yang Huo, take your regiment around and occupy the pass. We will wipe them out."

Just before the guns in the hills became quiet, Jimmie Cordie began to laugh.

"What are ye laughing at?" demanded Red. He and several of the crew were carrying gunnysacks full of the cotton. "Will I carry ye. Jimmie?"

"No. I'm all right if I take it easy. I was thinking that if a cannon ball hit any of you birds that are packing the stuff, we'd all get a first-hand demonstration of whether the guncotton would work or not."

"And that is wan hell av a nice thing to be laughin' at, ye scut av the world. 'Tis close to ye I'll walk, ye omadhaun!"

"Keep away—holy cats! He's coming to get us! The Bean better start—there! And it's about time."

From the hills on that side charged Chinese—not in close formation, but in waves, the men scattered out. The guns on the yacht began picking them up, and again the steel rail was set up. This time a barrage boxed the party in. Some of the Chinese in the charge knelt down and began firing with their rifles. A bullet could go where a man couldn't—through that murderous steel barrage.

One of the yacht's crew pitched on his face, the gunnysack falling with him. Another spun around and went down as the party reached the rock. Now they were more sheltered, at least from rifle fire. The barrage dropped, lifted from in front of them and redoubled in intensity on either side.

Jimmie grinned as Red, who had got on top of the rock, reached down an arm as big around as a boa constrictor's body, and pulled him up.

"Thank you, Mr. Dolan. All right, let's go. Load the holes and tamp with those wooden poles. Ram it hard."

"Wait a minute, Mr. Cordie," the electrician said. "Better let me take it over. The detonating caps ought to go in with the second or third foot."

"Hop to it, old kid. My gosh, I hope the Bean's shells hold out. Look at 'em come now."

"All set," the electrician announced twenty long minutes later, as he stepped beside his blasting machine. "Get back, everybody."

"Go on, Red. You men also. I'll stay here." As Jimmie spoke, the first company of Yang Huo's men came over the rock from the sea side.

The wires ran about two hundred feet back from the rock to the blasting machine and when the electrician announced that it was all set, the whole group were standing near it.

"Cut 'er loose, feller," Jimmie said quietly. "We'll swim for it."

THE ELECTRICIAN grinned cheerfully as he worked the handle up and down a little, then he shoved it home. For a split second nothing happened; then the rock seemed to heave up, there came the dull roar of an explosion, and the rock went up and out in a blast of flame.

As the electrician shoved the handle clear down, every man in the party, himself included, as soon as he felt it hit, started from where he stood. They had not got ten feet before the rock heaved, and not twenty before she went up. It was down-hill and they were all, as Red said afterward, "making a hundred yards in nothin'."

As it was, two or three of them got rolled down the slope by the rush of wind. But no man was hurt. The rock had a good many fissures and at least some of the guncotton was not fully nitrated. Some of the holes were too straight up and down, and the gases generated went up as if from a gun barrel. In any explosion the gases follow the line of least resistance and in this one there were a lot of lines—which saved the running men from a worse rock bombardment than they got. As it was, the rock was shattered and torn away for two-thirds its length. Before the roar of the blast died away, the water rushed in, forced by the pressure of the South China Sea behind it.

The valley was fairly wide, and the slope that led up to the rock barrier ran steeply. The first rush of water picked up the men in its way and rolled them over and over. Then at the bottom, when it began to stretch out across the valley, the force grew less. Jimmie, Red, the electrician, and the crew got on their feet, the water about up to their knees. The Chinese who had been on the rock and just over it had disappeared. Those in the valley turned and ran.

When the party reached the sand dunes some of them were swimming, the rest, the taller ones like Red and the electrician, were half swimming, half walking.

"And that's that," Jimmie said, as he came on board. "Now if the water will get deep enough to float this hooker, we will sail into Mr. Warrenne's headquarters."

The valley was gradually filling, though a good deal of the water was roaring on down the cañon, as the tidal wave had done. But this time the trough in the middle of the island could not drain off all the water—with the whole sea as a supply.

"Are you set to go, Bean?" asked Grigsby, as the water lapped at the keel of the yacht.

"Yeah, boy. Scotty is waiting till he feels her lift."

The hum of a plane's motor was heard clearly, and every one looked up. Over the top of the hills came two planes, still climbing to gain altitude. Jimmie Cordie brought his glasses to bear, as did the rest who had them.

"New type bombers," Jimmie said. "Soviet for a guess." He lowered his glasses and went on quietly: "Get those anti-aircraft guns in action, Codfish. They're going to bomb us."

Both planes had climbed high and now both swooped down, one following the other. The first came over the yacht about five hundred yards up and as it did, dropped a bomb. The plane was greeted with every gun on the yacht that could be brought to bear, but it flashed by unhit. The bomb landed on the quarterdeck aft and blew the stern of the yacht to pieces. There had been two guns and their crews on the quarterdeck. Guns and men disappeared as the flames shot up after the detonation. The Chinese captain Tzu-kung, confined in the yacht's brig, died also.

When the explosion came the yacht had already lifted in the water and cleared the sand dunes. But she was sinking by the time the second plane roared overhead. The bomb dropped by this one missed.

The black gang, headed by Scotty, made the deck just as the two life rafts carried on the superstructure went into the water.

"JUMP, CODFISH," Jimmie ordered. "Red, lower Katherine to him. Get down, Yid. Overboard, everybody. Come on, Paulet! Never mind that 'The captain with the ship went down' stuff."

The first plane had circled and was coming back. The flyer tried to hit one of the life rafts but missed. The second plane swooped lower and opened up with a machine gun, but the bullets went high. Both rafts were being carried by the rising water toward the mouth of the cañon.

On one was Katherine, Ming Li and some of the wounded. Clinging to its sides were Grigsby, the Bean and Yid, with some of the crew who were not strong swimmers. On the other were the rest of the wounded, with Scotty, Red, Jimmie Cordie and Paulet and the rest of the crew swimming close beside it. Both rafts were fairly close together.

"Get Katherine into the water," Jimmie shouted. "Less chance of being hit there. Try to land this side of the—"

"Look! Look!" called Katherine, as she pointed up, trying to stand on the slippery platform of the life raft.

Coming over the hills from the direction of the sea was a third plane. It was coming fast, also.

"You needn't hurry, feller," Jimmie Cordie said grimly, looking up at it. "Your buddies have already attended to the matter, very efficiently…. When the planes come again, everybody go under, deep!"

The two Soviet planes had just started to come down on an angle that would permit accurate shooting at the swimming refugees. They both heard and saw the other plane, and instantly flattened out and, it seemed from below, almost hesitated a moment. Then they both started to climb.

The Fighting Yid had been more than half drowned three or four times as the raft tilted, his back hurt him, and he felt the cold of the water creeping up, yet he ran true to form:

"Oi, Jimmie," he called, "all de vork mit de guncotton goes it for noddings, ain't it?"

Jimmie heard him and laughed. "Look at the fun you're having, Yid," he called back.

"Oh! Look! He's climbing higher than they are! Oh, my goodness! He's—he's—" Katherine realized that no one was listening to her and that they could see as well as she could, so she stopped announcing.

The third plane was much faster than either of the two bombers and gained height so rapidly that it looked as if the two Soviet planes were standing still.

Up it went, straightened out, and then came down on the tail of the nearest plane like a hawk swooping on a chicken. The Russian tried to loop, but as he brought the nose of his plane up, a stream of machine gun bullets almost cut him in two. The young Chinese officer had not lied when he told Yen Yuan that he had fought the "little guns."

The plane burst into flames and went down, plunging into the water nose first.

"Laugh that off, ye scut," Red said as the water closed over it. "How do ye like them machine gun bullets?"

The other Soviet flyer tried hard to get away. He used every trick he knew, but inside of three minutes, down on his tail zoomed the pursuit plane that had come over the hills. Another burst of fire and he went to join his comrade under the water.

By now the rafts had been carried close to the mouth of the cañon and much closer to where the foot of a hill rose from the water.

"Push 'em! Push!" yelled the Yid. "Everybody swim und push."

A minute later the rafts both grounded and all on them or in the water splashed up to solid footing on dry land. The wounded were picked up and carried.

"To the top!" Jimmie Cordie shouted, drawing his Colt .45.

NOT A man of them had more than a Colt, and a good many of the crew did not even have that, particularly those of the engine room force. As Jimmie spoke, there was a rush of Chinese down the hill. Warrenne had seen what had happened and now was literally crazy. All thought of taking Katherine was gone from his mind. The one and only thing in the world at the moment was the killing of the men who had cost him so dearly.

Grigsby, Jimmie Cordie, Red Dolan, the Bean, the Fighting Yid, and Captain Paulet stepped in front of the rest, forming a half circle. There was no fear in their eyes or in their hearts as they raised their Colts.

It was a merciless, accurate fire that went up to meet the oncoming Chinese and men dropped, but this was a charge that could not be stopped with Colts. It came closer and closer, and as it did, more pirates poured over the top of the hill.

"If I can get the hands av me on a sword—" Red said, but the rest was drowned out by the roar of a plane and the staccato hammering of machine guns. Over their heads came the plane, so close that afterward the Yid said, "I got it a close haircut, no foolink."

Over, up to the top, a loop, back and across the fighting plane went, its machine guns full on the Chinese who scattered to get out of the way—back and to the sides, like rats at the sight of a cat.

"Now drop it us annoder yacht," the Yid called up, "und ve go und get us Mistair Varrenne for de yardarm."

"Be content with what you've had already," Jimmie answered with a grin. *"Allons, mes enfants! Vive la France!"*

Once in a while Jimmie reverted back to his days in the *Régiments étrangers*.

"Full speed ahead mit dis back?" grunted the Yid. "How can I did it?"

"I'll carry ye, Abie darlin'," Red answered, picking up the Yid as if he were a baby. "Up ye go, ye Hester Street gossoon."

The plane was roaring back and forth over the top of the hill as if saying, "Come on up. I got 'em."

The wounded had to be carried and the hill was steep, but they made it. It was not as lofty as the highest one the guns had been placed on, but it rose high enough for them to see the Chinese fleeing in all directions from the plane's fire.

"Dig in," ordered Jimmie. "That bird can't cover us forever. Bring those loose rocks over here."

The plane went up, made a half circle, came down on a glide, side slipped to reduce speed, and landed on the side of the hill toward Warrenne's headquarters. As it landed, one wing crumpled and the under carriage tore away. It looked like a bad washout, but right after it hit the side of the hill, two men popped out of it, as Red said, "like bats shot out of hell."

The ignition was evidently shut off because the plane didn't catch on fire. Both of the newcomers started promptly up the hill, and from where the yacht's party stood mostly with open mouths, the grins on their faces could be plainly seen.

"Jimmie!" yelled Red. " 'Tis the little banty, Carewe!" and Red ran to meet the flyers.

"Hullo, Jonathan," Jimmie said as he shook hands. "We're glad to see you."

"My word! We got here in the jolly nick of time, didn't we? You don't know how glad I am to see you chaps."

"You did that. What did you land for?"

"Why, I wanted to be in at the finish, old dear."

"Ye would, ye scut," said Red. "For the size av ye, 'tis a good man ye are, ye shrimp av the world."

Carewe laughed. He knew that when Red talked like that, he was talking to one whom he had accepted as a buddy.

"There's nothing in size, Mr. Dolan," he answered. "If there were, a cow could catch a rabbit. This is Captain Wen Chih, of your giddy old friend Yen Yuan's army, Jimmie."

"We are honored by your presence, captain," Jimmie addressed the T'aip'ing. "Tell us about it later, Jonathan. We'd better be getting set for Mr. Warrenne. He probably knows that your plane is down, and will start some of that 'up and over' stuff darned quick."

CHAPTER XV

THE LAST ACT

WARRENNE HAD SEEN the plane land and crack up. He turned to Radischev, who had flown over from Hanoi with the flyers. "Now," he said, "we will wipe them out.... What is the matter with you, Radischev?"

"Enough," answered Radischev, his face pale. "Do you realize that the Soviet planes sent to the War Lord Fokien have been destroyed with two of our best flyers?"

"Best flyers? My hat! They let one man shoot them down like— Sorry, old chap. It is done now."

"I do not dare to go back. If Fokien did not flay me alive, the Soviets would place my back to a wall."

"Stay here with me," Warrenne said, as he studied the hill through his glasses, "They are fortifying the hill. Can't allow that, old dears." He lowered his glasses and called to an officer who stood with a group a little way back.

"Ch'en! Deploy your men around the hill and go up and take the dogs who have bitten us. Take all alive if possible, especially the woman."

A messenger ran up to Warrenne, panting from the long run from headquarters. "Lord, I bear news."

"Tell it swiftly," answered Warrenne.

"It is this, Lord. That water has flooded the middle of the island, and has covered the guns in the city square. The vessels have put out into the harbor and wait orders. And Wang-sun is dead."

"Dead? He had recovered consciousness after we recaptured his house. What killed him?"

"His throat contracted, Lord. The foreign devil squeezed tight. Before he died Wang-sun ordered that you be told he had seen—"

"I do not care what he saw. Get back with my order that the vessels remain in the harbor. I will sink any that disobey. Lead your regiment forward, Ch'en."

"My men would not obey that command if I were to give it," answered the old pirate. "They have seen the T'aip'ing fight for the foreign devils."

"The T'aip'ing? What rot! Give the order, O Ch'en." Warrenne's hand went to his Webley.

"Do not draw, Warrenne," Ch'en warned. "My war brother Hui has you covered from where he stands. The man who worked the machine guns in the small plane that shot down the Soviet flyers was recognized by our men when it came close to the ground. He is Captain Wen Chih, one of the war captains of the T'aip'ing. I have no men who will attack a man of that mighty society, O elder brother."

"I am not afraid of the T'aip'ing," Warrenne snapped. "Are you and your men, Yi-yin?" turning to another officer.

"No," answered Yi-yin. "I am old and have no loved ones to

think of. My men are still back near the place where the rock was blown up, and without doubt they do not know about the T'aip'ing. They would follow me, even if they did know, being men of my clan. You and I have been together since the start, Lord. I will order my men up the hill and lead them also."

"Ch'en, move your regiment back to headquarters. We will go into the matter later. Will you come with us, Radischev?"

"With you? I do not understand."

"I lead with Yi-yin."

Radischev laughed. "What does it matter? I will come, Warrenne."

As they walked away, Ch'en said to the officers who were with him: "I will lead my men back to headquarters—and there I will seize a ship and sail away. It is better to die on our ships than await the T'aip'ing hunting that will surely come."

"I also, with all my men."

"And I. Command us, O Ch'en."

"And I!" chorused the rest.

"It may be," Ch'en went on, "that we can make our peace with the all-powerful society when we explain that we did not know that the yacht and its people were under protection."

WARRENNE, AFTER he arrived at the place where Yi-yin's men awaited, looked them over. "Three, four, about five hundred. Yi-yin, take half of them and get to the right of the hill. Swing them around it as far as possible. I will take the rest and skirt the valley, coming up from that side. Do not start up until you hear three rifle shots, then a pause, then two. If you gain the top before I do, try to take as many as possible alive. We will instruct them, in the torture chamber."

Yi-yin bowed an order to his officers who had come up to where he was with Warrenne and Radischev.

Warrenne watched the troops led by Yi-yin start at the double for the base of the hill. There was a smile on his lips. "The curtain rises on the last act. I hope the Boston Bean remains alive."

Radischev raised his hands, shrugging his shoulders in a typical Russian gesture of resignation. "You have lost many men and all your guns; you have lost for me everything—yet you smile, What have you gained? You have sunk a yacht and now you go to destroy a few men and perhaps gain a woman. And you smile!"

Warrenne laughed as he motioned to an officer to start. "One thing leads to another, old chap. There are more men and more guns and more women in the world; and for you there are many times what you have lost. From the first firing of the yacht's machine guns it became a game to be played; and I always play through to the finish. Shall we start?"

ONE OF the plane's machine guns had been put out of commission by the crash, but the other was unharmed. It was taken from the scarf yoke and brought up the hill with about five hundred rounds of ammunition. Now it was in place on the breastworks, and the Yid and the Bean were lovingly adjusting it. It was the only weapon the party had, outside of ten Colt .45s and the automatics that Carewe and Captain Wen Chih wore strapped around their waists. For the Colts, Jimmie Cordie, the Bean, the Yid, Red and Grigsby each had a belt half full of shells. Captain Paulet and four of the crew had practically full belts.

Carewe sat with Katherine, Jimmie, Red and Grigsby on top of the breastworks, looking toward the water in the valley. Carewe had told them what had happened since he sat in the restaurant with the Chinese flyer, finishing with: "So Captain Wen Chih and I started out to do the jolly old rescue thing, old dears. I saw the Russian planes come over the hills when I was quite a ways out. I say, what was it that went up like a giddy young volcano just before I arrived?"

Jimmie laughed. "We made some guncotton, John, and blew up the ledge that was holding the sea back. We figured that we might be able to sail down on Mr. Warrenne and smack him, then steam back out. My gosh, when I think of the work I put in on that darned thing, and all for nothing!"

"Think that over, Jeems," Grigsby said. "The water cleared the valley of Warrenne's men. After the bombing, how far would we have got across the valley if it had been dry? He would have knocked us off long before we could make the hill. So you see, Jeems me lad, your guncotton got us here."

"Explain that to the Yid. Did you hear what he yelled over to me? Carewe, that T'aip'ing lad sitting over with Paulet is no amateur with a machine gun, if you are asking my opinion."

"My word! I should say he isn't, Jimmie. Captain Wen Chih can make them lie down and wag the jolly old paws, what, what?"

"He can," Jimmie answered gravely. "And he had to do 'er, with the rotten flying you did, Jonathan old kid. I never saw any one handle a plane worse."

"Why, Jimmie Cordie!" Katherine protested hotly; then as they all laughed, she had made a little girl's face at Jimmie. She looked at the slim, reckless young English flyer, then at the five adventurers. "Why—why—you all like him, too," she announced firmly. "He's—he's English, and I'm English; and we are glad you like us. Aren't we, Carewe?"

"My word, yes," Carewe went on. "You don't know how I missed you chaps. I made up the totterin' old mind that if I found you again I'd hang around—that is, if you chaps would let me."

RED DOLAN looked at Carewe, his frosty blue eyes getting warmer as Carewe smiled at him. "Oh, ye did, did ye? And what would the likes av ye be doin' around wid us? Maybe-so if ye stuck around, 'twould make a man outa ye at that." Red's hand went to the butt of the Colt .45 in his holster.

Carewe's eyes widened a little as he saw it, but his smile remained. A little puzzled frown came on Katherine's brow as she observed the gesture.

"How about it, Jimmie?" Red asked.

"Suits me," Jimmie answered.

"How about it, George?" Red asked Grigsby.

"Yes, Red," Grigsby answered very quietly and solemnly.

"Ye hear that?" Red demanded of Carewe.

"Why—yes, I hear it, Red. I say, what are you driving at?"

"This," answered Red Dolan, drawing the Colt and handing it butt first to Carewe. "Take this. 'Tis yours from now on." As Carewe took it, Red asked, "Do ye know whose Colt it was?"

Carewe looked at the "P" burned into the butt of the gun, then drew a long breath. "Oh, my word! It's—it's Putney's gun!"

"It is," Red answered. "It is the gun that was worn by a good man, God rest his soul in Paradise. I have carried it always since he went ahead av us. Now 'tis yours and wid it ye take the place av him wid us—that is, as far as ye can, ye spridhouge."

"Heads up!" shouted the Yid. "Here comes it Mistair Varrenne und everythink."

As it did, there came faintly a distant dull *boom!* and then another, and still another.

"What the heck is goin' on over at headquarters?" Jimmie asked as he stood with ready Colt waiting for the charge to get within revolver-range.

"It sounds as if the T'aip'ing war fleet had arrived," Carewe answered. "My word! I forgot to tell you that Yen Yuan said that their fleet would sail at once."

The men in the charge must have heard the firing also, but they paid no attention to it. Yi-yin went down within a hundred yards of the top, a bullet from Grigsby's Colt in his brain. Radischev, running about even with Warrenne but a little to the left, was almost torn in two by machine gun bullets from the Yid's gun. The Yid was swinging over to get Warrenne.

"Lay off of *him!*" shouted the Boston Bean. "Lay off Warrenne, everybody. Jimmie! Red! Keep off Warrenne! He's my meat!"

Warrenne was running lightly, his lips tight. His Webley was in his hand, but he had not fired it yet. He came up against machine gun fire and the deadly leaden sleet of the Colt .45s as if bending a little against a summer rain.

The Chinese wavered a moment when Yi-yin fell, then rallied and came on. Now it was to avenge the fall of their leader and fellow-clansman. Another hundred feet and the charge began to bunch in to hit the breastworks.

As they did, Chinese streamed over the side of the hill, fleeing inland from the pirate city. One, frantic with terror, ran closer and yelled, "Run! Run, brothers! The T'aip'ing war fleet is closing in. A hundred ships! We are destroyed! Run! Run!" The charge wavered, scattered.

"THAT WILL be all," Jimmie Cordie said, lowering his Colt. "Let them run."

"Not quite all," the Boston Bean said, as he lifted a long leg over the breastworks.

"Come back here, ye long-legged beanpole," Red yelled. "What the—"

"Pipe down, Red," Jimmie ordered. "The Bean is going after his meat."

Warrenne had stopped and was standing as if frozen as his Chinese ran. He had his Webley in his hand, and as he saw the Boston Bean walk down the hill toward him, he raised it.

The Bean halted when within about twenty feet of Warrenne, his Colt held seemingly loose in his hand.

For a moment both men looked calmly at each other, then the Bean said, "Regarding that matter of the Colt—"

Both Colt and Webley went into action. Warrenne was a good shot and a fast one—but the Bean was a better shot and a faster. His first bullet hit Warrenne just above the heart and got there in time to make him jerk a little. Enough to send his bullet a bit high. The Bean's second bullet hit Warrenne squarely in the chest and sent him down as if hit by a giant hammer.

The Bean stood for a moment, looking at the body of the man who had stolen Katherine; then walked away.

"Vell," said the Yid, as Katherine started out to meet the Bean, "ve have had it a nice, quiet time at your yachting party, Mrs. Admiral Vinthrop."

JADES AND AFGHANS

No man marches with safety into the hills
of mid-Asia; and it did not make traveling
any easier for Jimmie Cordie and his
fellow soldiers of fortune to have it known
they sought Genghis Khan's treasure

CHAPTER I

SMOKE OF BATTLE

THE FIGHTING YID came up to where Jimmie Cordie sat on an ammunition box.

"Vell," he said sociably as he sat down on another box, "all is quiet on de vestern front, ain't it?"

"I hope it keeps that way," Jimmie answered with a grin, as he looked over his orderly camp established at the base of one of the foothills of the Karakoram Range, Chinese Turkestan. "One or two more jazzings around like we got yesterday and the day before and there will be some new faces in the angel chorus, Mr. Cohen. All it needs now is for the Afghans to hop us."

The roly-poly Hebrew adventurer smiled cheerfully. "After Tartars und Uzbegs und mixed pickles of Chinks, Cossacks, Kirghiz und vat-not have all taken it a crack at us, vot do ve care?"

"If they will limit the callers to a few, it will be all right. Have you ever taken an Afghan charge, my distinguished friend from Jerusalem?"

"Hester Street, New York, not Jerusalem," corrected the Yid. "Vonce, ven I vas vid de Boston Bean, ve got it caught between some Afghanders und some Tartars. Und dare vas some Chink bandits on de left."

"Yeah? Which did you choose?"

"Oi—ve run like heck to de right!"

Jimmie laughed. "Good idea, Yid. Maybe we'll have to do the same thing—only I hope we get the jades first. I suspect, though, that Shih-kai and his swordsmen would rather die than run, as long as there's a chance of getting back the T'aip'ing jades."

"Ain't it!" agreed the Yid. "I never see it—"

"Holy cats!" broke in Jimmie Cordie. "Look at them come!"

The Afghan charge came fast, from several passes that led into

The gunners knew they could expect no mercy— so they offered none.

the little valley through which a stream meandered toward the fertile plains below. But the defense from the camp was equally fast. Before the first Afghans had reached the river, two machine guns from the top of the hill opened up. As the horses splashed through the shallow water, three more machine guns added to the staccato scolding.

Then between the machine guns at the camp there appeared, as if by magic, long lines of swordsmen of the T'aip'ing secret society who stood about two feet apart, their swords resting across their left forearms. There was no flurry, no confusion, no shouted commands nor running around. The camp struck at its foes as quickly as a rattler strikes at a foot or paw suddenly appearing above it.

It was the instant defense of hardbitten veterans. The men at

the machine guns shot the Afghans coldly, accurately and merci-
lessly. They knew they could expect no mercy from the invaders,
and so they offered none.

Up in the hills where War Lord fought War Lord and the
tribes fought any and all they thought they were strong enough
to whip, any fight meant kill or get killed.

Five machine guns and a target of onrushing men and horses
coming over a level space. The sleet of steel-jacketed bullets
would have stopped any body of men in the world but Afghans.
When Afghans charge, the only thing that can stop them is
death—and it generally takes more than one bullet to bring
that. Man after man went down as his horse was shot out from
under him, but the moment he hit the ground he was up, sword
still in hand and continuing the charge on foot.

Saddle after saddle was emptied, and yet the rest did not even
slacken speed. Jimmie Cordie, the Fighting Yid, Red Dolan
and George Grigsby were mentioned first whenever machine
gunners were spoken of by soldiers of fortune in the Orient, and

the Englishman Carewe, who made the fifth man aiming a gun at the invaders, was not far behind.

The two who had been posted at the top of the hill—Grigsby and Carewe—took the center of the charge. Jimmie Cordie took the left front and Red Dolan the right. The Yid, being more or less of a sharpshooter even with a Browning, brought his gun to bear on isolated groups which had issued from the passes after the main body. Red Dolan and Jimmie Cordie, after a second's pause to watch how far on either side the two guns on the hill were reaching, picked the line up from there and went left and right.

In spite of the deadly fire, the Afghans, those on their feet and those who still were in the saddle, cleared the river and with wild yells of triumph started across the last hundred yards. In all, they were about one hundred and fifty—not a fifth of those who had left the passes. The rest lay in tangled heaps of horses and men.

AT A touch on his shoulder Jimmie Cordie looked up as a keen, alert-looking Chinese boy hooked another belt on the Browning.

"Give order, lord, that the swordsmen meet them," a young, impassive-faced Manchu said.

"Hop to it, Shih-kai," Jimmie answered, standing up and drawing his Colt forty-five. "We can't hold them."

Red Dolan and the Yid, seeing Jimmie stand, also got up from their guns and drew their revolvers.

As they did it, the lines of swordsmen ran forward. Red hesitated for a split second, reholstered his Colt, stooped and picked up a thirty-thirty Winchester that lay beside the Browning, clubbed it, and went with the swordsmen.

"Come back here, you big ape!" Jimmie shouted. Then, as he saw Red paid no attention to him, he jumped up on a full case of ammunition and began using his Colt. There were few men in the Orient who could equal Jimmie Cordie with a forty-five.

The Yid ran over and stood beside him.

"Shoot 'em away from Red!" Jimmie commanded between the *pow-pow—pow-pow* of the heavy service revolver.

The two machine guns on the hill were silent. Now the high-pitched *zing* of rifle bullets propelled by smokeless powder blended in with the coarser detonations of the revolvers. Grigsby and Carewe were using their rifles.

The Afghans, when they saw the swordsmen charge out, yelled in scorn and derision at what they thought were Chinese luggage bearers who had the courage to attack Afghans with swords. The yells were quickly hushed, as the horses went down from the quick slashing cut that hamstrung them; and the men on foot met swords that equaled theirs. Here were no clumsy, slow bearers for the Afghans to play with before slaying. These were master swordsmen.

But the Afghans closed with the same swift fierceness they had shown in the charge. They were all big men, heavily bearded, dressed mostly in dirty sheepskins. The men that met them were slim and boyish-looking, much smaller. To a man they were stripped to the waist, and the swords they wielded looked much lighter than the heavy Afghan blades. It was like a wolverine attacking a big brown bear. It was, as the Yid said afterward, "Von hell of a fine fight to vatch."

The Afghans would cut directly down or slash in from the side. Nine times out of ten the lighter sword would seem to be pressed far out or down. Then suddenly the Afghan blade was out or up and the smaller man would sway in, his blade darting in ahead of him.

Not always, however. Many a slim swordsman was beaten down by sheer strength by the Afghan opposing him. When two Afghans reached the same man, he always went down.

Red Dolan had dropped the rifle to pick up a sword and was fighting beside Shih-kai. Jimmie, as best he could, was making the odds even for him. If more than two Afghans reached Red and Shih-kai, and Jimmie had a clear path to send a bullet down, only two Afghans closed. But in the mad swirl of the fighting, it was not always possible. A milling crowd of both Afghans and Chinese swordsmen got in between, and when Jimmie and the Yid could see through to Red and Shih-kai, Red was down and Shih-kai stood over him.

WITHOUT A word, Jimmie and the Yid started for them, shooting out of their way any Afghan that got in it. Halfway to where Shih-kai stood, four Afghans ran up. The Yid had his eyes on Shih-kai and, as the attackers came up on Jimmie's side, did not see them for a second. Jimmie halted and killed the first two with bullets put squarely between the eyes. As he swung his gun in line with the third, the fourth Afghan arrived. He had run out a little and come in behind Jimmie.

The Yid, as Jimmie shot, had turned a little, just in time to see the third Afghan's sword coming down at his head. The Yid grunted "Oi!" and threw up his Colt barrel to guard his head. He got in there just in time to take the keen edge on the blued-steel barrel. But the force of the blow was more than sufficient to drop the Yid like a poled ox. It was like taking a hammer blow on the head.

The fourth Afghan crouched as Jimmie pulled trigger and the bullet lifted a strip of skin from the top of the Afghan's head instead of going where Jimmie meant it to go. Yet it dazed the Afghan for a second, long enough for Jimmie to drop his empty Colt and grasp the sword wrist. The Afghan grunted, and his left hand went to his belt where a dagger was sheathed.

Jimmie reached for the left wrist with his left hand and missed. The Afghan, a big burly man, yelled loudly and the dagger flashed up. Jimmie Cordie knew that he could not stop that dagger falling; but the smile remained on his lips and in his eyes.

His shoulder came under the Afghan's arm and he tried to raise the descending arm by pushing up. All he could do was to delay it a little. Jimmie Cordie was a strong man, but the Afghan was much stronger. His dirty face, bearded to the eyes, covered with blood from the furrow on his head, was working with animal-like ferocity as he forced the dagger down. As Jimmie twisted his body trying to get a jujutsu hold, his right ear felt as if some one had laid a red-hot poker along the top. He heard a dull thud and then the Afghan fell away, the dagger dropping to the ground.

Jimmie straightened up to see the Afghan who had reached the Yid lying across the Yid's body and Shih-kai stooping to drag the Yid out from under. Red stood a little distance away, swaying back and forth. Over the field of battle there stood groups of the swordsmen. No Afghans were on their feet. Jimmie's eyes took it all in and also saw Grigsby and Carewe coming down from the top of the hill, some fifteen or twenty swordsmen with them. He saw it all, and yet he did not see it with understanding eyes.

"I was facing the camp," he said aloud. "He was facing the hills. That bullet grazed my ear and got him through the forehead. Who in hell could have—"

Shih-kai came up to him. "You are wounded, honorable elder brother?"

Jimmie came to at the question and smiled. "No, master swordsman."

"There is blood running down your ear."

"A bullet grazed me. The bullet came from the hills."

"Many Afghans have guns, resplendent one."

"Not guns that carry from here to the nearest hill, war brother. Send men to find out who it—" Jimmie stopped talking and ran to Red Dolan, who had fallen again while trying to walk to where Jimmie and Shih-kai were standing. Shih-kai went over to a group of swordsmen who were looking down on the Afghan slain. He pointed to the hills and was about to issue an order when he stopped. Instead, he stared at a little procession marching calmly down the hill from which Jimmie thought the bullet had come. First a tall man dressed in European whites, carrying a rifle, then three Chinese strutting proudly along with a machine gun, then several more Chinese with boxes, then four with rifles.

Shih-kai walked over to where Jimmie knelt trying to staunch the flow of blood from Red's wounds. He touched Jimmie on the shoulder, and as Jimmie looked up, said:

"The one who shot the bullet comes, elder brother."

Jimmie looked over his shoulder. "Well, for Pete's sake! The Boston Bean is arriving. I'm darn glad that he sent his calling card in ahead of him. Go and meet him, Shih-kai."

Carewe, a slim young Englishman, who had been up on the hill with George Grigsby, came up.

"Is Red badly hurt, Jimmie?"

"He's cut up pretty badly and lost a lot of blood. Is George attending to the Yid?"

"Yes. My word, I should say Red is cut up! Are you wounded yourself? There's blood all over your ear."

"No. Tear your shirt up; I've used all of mine. A bullet grazed my ear, sent by the Boston Bean."

"What? Where is he?"

"Coming down the hill. Tear it into bandage lengths. That's it."

"I say, he came close, didn't he?"

"Closeness never makes any difference to the Codfish duke. Give me a hand with Red. I think we can pack him to a tent."

CHAPTER II

BLOOD FEUD

THREE HOURS LATER, Jimmie, as he came out of the tent that had been made into a hospital, met George Grigsby at the entrance.

"I was just coming in to see how they were," Grigsby said.

He was a big man, almost as big as Red Dolan, but not as heavy. He had served in the Foreign Legion with Jimmie Cordie and the big Irishman, and afterward in the A.E.F. as a major in the infantry. Since the war, with Jimmie and Red and one other— Arthur Putney, who had died defending a pass so that the others might live—he had been in the Orient.

Born in Breathitt County, Kentucky, Grigsby looked the typical mountaineer of pure Anglo-Saxon stock. Slow in movement and speech until roused, he went into action with the suddenness of T.N.T. He fought always with a little frozen smile on his firm lips. To the rest of the reckless, quicker-tempered soldiers, Grigsby was, as Jimmie Cordie said once, "a sheet anchor to windward."

"Red and the Yid are in bad shape," answered Jimmie, who was much slighter than Grigsby, with black eyes, high cheek bones and a bony "Duke of Wellington" nose. Jimmie Cordie moved with the grace and ease of a black leopard, and was just about as fast. "Red has all of a pint of blood left. I don't think any of his wounds are infected, but one thing is dead open and shut, George. He can't be moved for some time. The Yid's skull isn't cracked, at least I can't find one, but he can't move his right side at all and is raving like a drunk. I've got him strapped down to the cot and two T'aip'ing watching him. Where is the Bean? I haven't had a chance to ask him the how-come of his showing up."

"Over there with Carewe," waved Grigsby.

"Let's sit down a minute," Jimmie nodded. "When I twisted to get at that gentle little playmate, I guess I sprained my side." They walked over to a pile of boxes and sat down.

"I've been checking up," Grigsby said. "There are three thousand rounds left for the Brownings. About enough to last half a minute with six guns in action."

"You can make it four guns for a long time," Jimmie answered. "Red and the Yid will shoot no machine guns for some time."

"There is plenty of rifle ammunition and also plenty for our

Colts—given that we don't stick around here very long. Shih-kai tells me that there are one hundred T'aip'ing unwounded. Fifty or fifty-five wounded. We started in with five hundred men a week ago, Jimmie. We've still got a hundred miles to go before we even see the waterfall."

"Well, if we get much more of what has been handed us every day since we crossed the Indian border, we won't have to worry about mileage. From where I sit the only thing I can see to do is to take the chance that it won't kill Red and the Yid and pack them up to the top of the hill where you and Carewe had the Brownings. You say there is water up there?"

"Yes, a good spring and a lot of big bowlders that can be made into a stockade. I don't see it, though. If we hole up we'll have to fight all the time and get nowhere. The moment our ammunition is gone a fresh bunch will come along and mop up on us. Why not— But you say that Red and the Yid can't be packed."

"Not for any distance, George. My idea was to hole the outfit up and take one man with me plus some of the T'aip'ing and go in after the jade. As far as exhausting the ammunition goes we are up against what old Colonel Watson used to call a frozen fact. If we started back Red and the Yid would die. Here or up on the hill they have a chance, as long as we can keep the neighbors off them. And with the T'aip'ing swords and rifles, to say nothing of the Colts, it will be a long time before any hostiles crash the stockade. We might get a break."

Grigsby smiled, "Breaks don't happen very often, Jimmie."

"I got a break when the Bean's bullet arrived," Jimmie pointed out. "Two seconds later and Mr. Cordie's son Jimmie would have been climbing the golden stairs."

"Well, when our numbers are called it won't make any difference where we are. Better start the moving up. Some of the wounded Afghans have made the hills, and it won't be long before all the kinfolks arrive. We've collected a blood feud, Jimmie."

RED AND the Yid were very carefully carried up the hill in improvised litters. The Yid had sunk into a coma, his breathing slow and hoarse. Red was conscious, but too weak to do more than move his head. Jimmie Cordie's first aid had saved Red's life.

The Boston Bean came over to Jimmie who walked beside the litters.

"I haven't had time to ask how come you appeared in the well-known nick of time," Jimmie said, "and before I do I want to ask you a favor. The next time you crack down on whoever I'm playing with, give my ear more clearance, Mr. Winthrop."

"Tuck your ears in when you begin hugging your partner," answered the Bean gravely, as Jimmie eased in between the bearers to hold Red's head.

The Boston Bean, or Codfish or any other name that called attention to the fact that he had been born in Boston, was listed in the Massachusetts Blue Book as John Cabot Winthrop. Through several relations he was a multi-millionaire. He had town and country houses, yachts and all that goes with unlimited money, and his one idea of a perfect day was to be in a tight corner where swords and bullets were singing the song of death. Tall, lanky, broad-shouldered and lean-flanked, the Bean fought with a bored "you-be-damned" expression on his face. He had been a Legionnaire with Jimmie, Red and Grigsby, and a lieutenant in the A.E.F.

After France the Bean, as Jimmie Cordie said, had "stuck closer than ten dollars' worth of glue." If the Bean couldn't find Jimmie Cordie and Grigsby and Red Dolan at the moment, he would try for the Fighting Yid who was generally going somewhere for something. Failing in that, the Codfish duke would organize his own expedition and start anywhere for anything. Most of the time he managed to be along with Jimmie Cordie.

Once on top of the hill it did not take the experienced fighting men very long to make, with the aid of loose bowlders, a place that would be very hard to take. Red and the Yid were placed on cots made from tent canvas and supports taken from the scrub timber.

Finally Jimmie Cordie sat down beside the Boston Bean who was lying flat on his back, his hands under his head, looking up at the brilliant stars.

"You may proceed to explain why you came uninvited to the party, Mr. Winthrop. First, where is Katherine?"

"The last I saw of my fair young wife, she was in Peking visiting some of the Nevilles, please, sir."

"Yeah?" Jimmie grinned. "How come you got let out of school, Codfish?"

"Well, General Niuchwang wanted some information about what the northern War Lords were doing about holding the Turkestan passes. He knew that I had met two or three of them and he asked me to go up and take a look-see. Her Royal Highness announced that she was going along, but with the aid of all the Nevilles in China and points west, I succeeded in persuading her to stay at home."

"You mean you got a chance to sneak out. All right, you left Mrs. John Cabot Winthrop in Peking and went up in the Irenkha-birga. How come you got so far off the track?"

"Well, me good man, if you must know I thought that inasmuch as I was out, I might as well see something of the country. And also I heard of some jades that—"

"Some jades? By any chance were they—no, they couldn't be. Go on, Brownbread."

"Where? I can answer your first question. Yes, some jades. The second one—'by any chance were they?'—I'll have to refer to my attorneys, I'm afraid."

"We are after some jades, also. I thought for a minute that you had heard of them."

"I see. Well, instead of heading for Peking by going due east I started south. When I left I had quite a few more bearers and—er—implements of war than I have now. Instead of the quiet and peace my soul craves, I got a running fight all the way.

On arriving at the top of the hill over there I not only heard but saw the party being staged in the valley. I was too far away to recognize any one, but I made out that one of the two gents doing the bunny hug was white—so I cracked down on the other on the theory that a dead Afghan was a good one... Now what about you?"

JIMMIE LAUGHED. "Well, in Hong Kong about two months ago the Yid was fussing around in a place he had no business being, as usual. It was on the Street of Ten Thousand Delights. Out of a shop there came a white man. He was wounded in several places and very much all in. Right after him came nine million Chinese, according to the Yid. Three guesses what the Yid did, Beaneater."

"I don't need any guesses. The Yid declared war. Go ahead."

"He did—with his Colt forty-five. The man made it to the Yid and passed temporarily out of the picture. The Yid backed to the wall and reloaded. You savvy the Street of Ten Thousand Delights, Bean?"

"I've heard about it. I didn't think that any European had ever been on it. It's supposed to be the hang-out of the river and bay pirates, isn't it?"

"Yes. The Yid would have had as much chance as a lame dog in a running race if Shih-kai had not happened to be within sound of the shots. He and the Yid took the wounded man to George's apartment. The man was practically cut to pieces and died about four hours after old Dr. Martin sewed him up. In his pocket there was a little jade statuette of a man holding a sword.

"Shih-kai had left after he helped the Yid get the man to George's apartment, but came back all fussed up just as we were looking at the statuette. He had gone back to the shop to get the how-come of the attack, and had been told that the man was trying to sell the jade.

"That jade is one of three statuettes made in the reign of the Emperor Wu-ting, 1324 B.C., each an image of one of the three brothers who started the T'aip'ing Society. Until Genghis Khan captured the city of Chenang in 1200 or so A.D., all oaths taken by T'aip'ing officers were made in front of the statuettes."

"I've heard of the lost statuettes of the T'aip'ing," the Bean said. "So the one the man had was one of them?"

"Yeah. This bird, whose name was Wilson, told us a story just before he died about being up near Samarkand with a partner. It rambled a lot, but we got the main facts. He said that behind a waterfall there was a tunnel, and at the end of the tunnel there was a room full of the loot that Genghis Khan had taken north with him. On a shelf there sat three jade figures. He had one of them in his hand when he and his buddy were attacked by a lot of big snakes. His—"

"What kind of snakes, for Pete's sake? There are no cobras so far north—"

"How do I know? Rock pythons, maybe. His story is that his buddy got bitten and he had a hard time getting out of the room and tunnel with him. It seems that in the excitement he stuck the little statuette in his pocket. Well, he finally made it to Hong Kong and tried to sell the jade because that was all he had. He don't know why he was so suddenly jumped in the shop."

"Maybe some of your highbinder friends recognized the statuette and—"

"Easy on my friends, feller. No, it was nobody belonging to the T'aip'ing Society who attacked him. As soon as Shih-kai saw the jade on the table, he went down on his knees."

"I wish I could have been there to see it," the Bean said, lazily changing his position. "To see a war captain of the T'aip'ing unbend is something to see, Jeems."

"It was the first time I ever saw him even bat an eye, and I've been with him a lot. Well, after he got up from his knees he asked me to take the jade to Yen Yuan, saying that he wouldn't dare to touch one of the Three.

"I took the jade to Yen Yuan, and darned if he didn't act almost as emotional as Shih-kai. I told him what Wilson had told us, and promised to go up and hunt for the two other statuettes for him. We left with some five hundred T'aip'ing swordsmen and plenty of ammunition to take the average amount of fighting we thought we'd get. Well, from the time we got six inches over the border we've been busy entertaining the neighbors day and night. You can get a report on what we've got left from Quartermaster-General Carewe if the matter interests you."

"It doesn't," answered the Bean, looking at his wrist watch. "Well, I have a few minutes before I meet Mrs. Winthrop for tea, so I'll stick around."

Jimmie laughed. All of them knew the Boston Bean's lovely English wife. She had been Katherine Neville, and the Bean and the Yid had, two years before, rescued her from the hands of a Chinese War Lord.

Through great danger Katherine had shown that she ran true to her name, one of the proudest in England.

CHAPTER III

THE INVALID GARRISON

RED DOLAN SAT on his cot, propped up with some of the blankets. The color was beginning to come in his cheeks and lips. "Give me another wan of them beef cubes, Jimmie darlin'," he coaxed.

"I will not, you big ape," Jimmie answered firmly from where he sat beside the Yid's cot. "You get a glass of water at three o'clock and some mutton and rice broth at six. Ease down on that cot and go to sleep, you hear me?"

"Sure I hear ye, shrimp. Who couldn't? Just wan, Jimmie? A half wan, then?"

"What you'll get is a wallop on the jaw if you don't stop fussing about something to eat. You'll get food at the right time."

"And who is going to give me that punch on the jaw?"

demanded Red, beginning to enjoy himself. "Not ye, me half-pint-sized bucko. As weak as I am, wan—"

"I know. One Dolan can lick six Cordies, and as weak as you are you can lick sixty. I'll admit it. Are you going to get down on that cot and go to sleep or do you want me to come over there and put you to sleep?"

"Sing that song to me, Jimmie alanna."

"What song? My gosh, are you goofy, you red-headed chimpanzee? You darn near scared me to death when I saw—"

"You know. The wan, 'Rock Me to Sleep with a Sock in the Jaw.'"

"Listen, Red: the Yid has got a foot on the one-way trail, and I don't feel like singing. Keep as quiet as you can—please."

"He has? May the good saints in heaven help ye take the foot away! I'm still, Jimmie."

Terrence Aloysius Dolan weighed some two hundred and thirty pounds, and it was all bone and muscle. His hair was a fiery red, his eyes a frosty blue, and he would fight anything, anywhere. Odds never made any difference to him. His answer to any objection about closing in was, "Aw, slap 'em outta the way!"

Jimmie Cordie took the place of a patron saint with the big brawny Irishman. Red had two loves: one for Jimmie Cordie and the other for a sword. Red would drop a gun any time to use a sword. And incidentally, any woman or child could take one look at Red Dolan and know they had found a willing slave.

JIMMIE PUT a hand on the Yid's forehead. The two T'aip'ing who had been detailed as assistant nurses had been dismissed by Jimmie, and he was alone in the tent with the patients. The Yid's bonds had been removed when he went into the coma, and now his hands lay quiet on top of the blanket. As Jimmie spoke to Red, the Yid's eyes opened and he looked up at Jimmie.

"Steady, Yid," Jimmie said distinctly, as he saw the expression in the glaring eyes. "It's Jimmie, old kid. You're all right, Abie. Don't move. It's Jimmie Cordie."

The Yid pushed Jimmie's restraining arm away as if it had been a baby's. Jimmie had put his right arm across the Yid's chest and pressed down with it as he spoke.

"Dis time I get you, vild man," the Yid snarled. He was no longer the good-natured, joking Yid. Jimmie tried to hold him down on the cot, but the Yid threw him off and got to his feet. Red sat up and then tried to get up, but couldn't make it. The Yid was crouching to spring at Jimmie, his great hands outstretched like the claws of a tiger, his broad shoulders and back arched like a bow, when Red's movement attracted his attention for a moment.

"Vot? Anodder? Vait, Mr. Vild Man, I get you also."

Then he launched himself straight at Jimmie. Instead of trying to evade him, Jimmie Cordie, as fast as a dancing shadow, went down below the hands reaching out for him, and when he came up he was between them. With every ounce of strength he had in it, his right fist crashed on the Yid's chin. As low-hung and heavy-set as the Yid was, the blow literally lifted him off his feet and hurled him back to the wall of the tent. As he fell to the ground, his head hit the side of the Red Cross box.

Jimmie Cordie swayed a minute, then as his right hand went to his side just below his ribs he sat down on the edge of Red's cot.

Red, who had remained sitting up, said, "Well, for the love av Mary Mother!" as Grigsby and the Boston Bean came into the tent.

"Watch the Yid," Jimmie said, through lips twisted with pain. "He's crazy again."

"We've got the deck, Jimmie," answered Grigsby quietly. "Take it easy."

A moment later as he and the Bean lifted the Yid to the cot, Grigsby said, "You knocked him out, Jimmie. His head is bleeding again."

Jimmie stood up. "I was afraid he would go through me and get to Red." He walked over and looked down at the Yid. "He wasn't hurt there before. If I haven't killed him the rap he got against the box may have jarred free whatever was making him crazy. Something happened inside of his head. He was paralyzed on one side an hour ago."

"What's the matter with your side?" asked the Boston Bean.

"I wrenched it fooling around with the Afghan you killed, and when I tried to knock the Yid cold I must have wrenched it some more."

"You mean when you did knock the Yid cold, don't you? I didn't think the Yid could be stopped with a punch."

"Neither did I. I must have caught him just right. Also, his head being in the condition it is may have helped the good work along. I only hope that I haven't put him out for good."

The Fighting Yid opened his eyes and then grinned up at Jimmie. "Oi, Jimmie, did you see me use de Colt for a sword to guard mit?"

Jimmie Cordie drew a long breath, then smiled down at the sane Yid.

"Yes, I saw it, Yid."

The Yid gingerly felt his head, then raised himself slowly on an elbow. He looked at the Bean and Grigsby and then over at Red.

"Vot happened?"

"You guarded all right, but the force of the blow knocked you out, Yid," Jimmie answered. "It cut your head open a little. Lie down and rest. We mopped up on them, old kid. How does your head feel?"

"Sore, und my jaw also. I vish I had been it dare at de finish."

"You were. It finished right after you went to sleep. Get me some fresh bandages, George."

"I'll fix the Yid up," Grigsby answered. "Get out and take a rest, Jimmie."

"Vot happened it to de big red-headed loafer?" the Yid asked as Grigsby was bathing the wound.

Red heard him and sat up. He had got down on the cot as Jimmie left the tent. "Well, ye Hester Street pup," he started, bitterly, "Do ye know what ye tried to do?"

"No, vat? Oi, George, easy mit de hair pullings, I esk you!"

"Why, ye goofy ape, ye tried to—" Red saw Grigsby's eye, and ended the sentence with, "lick all the wild men by yeself."

"SUCH A business?" sighed the Yid, whose real name was Abraham Cohen. He had earned the name of the Fighting Yid in the A.E.F., where he had been one of Jimmie Cordie's sergeants, and afterward in the Orient where he fought for War Lord or potentate.

He fully lived up to his name. The Yid was short, stocky and looked roly-poly with fat. But it was very deceiving, that look of fatness. The Yid had no fat on him at all; it was all bone and muscle, as on Red Dolan's frame. His eyes were china blue and always seemed to be popping out of his head with surprise at such naughty doings in a sad old world. That also was not so. The Yid was never surprised at anything. He had no morals, no ethics and absolutely no fear of anything.

Like the Bean he tried to be with Jimmie Cordie and the others as much as possible. And like them all, what nerves he had were chilled steel. If the Yid were fighting for some War Lord and suddenly found out that his friends were on the other side, he would promptly desert and turn his machine gun on his former employer.

CHAPTER IV

THE CAVE OF THE JADES

A WEEK LATER Jimmie, Carewe and Shih-kai stood close to where a little river came tumbling down some thirty feet from the cañon above. Back of them stood ten of the T'aip'ing swordsmen. Jimmie and Carewe were armed with thirty-thirty

rifles and holstered Colts swung from cartridge belts. The
T'aip'ing had thrown off any attempt to pass as luggage bearers
and now stood as what they were, the best swords of the dreaded
secret society.

Jimmie's side still hurt him a little. Red and the Yid had been
getting better when the little party had left the camp on top of
the hill; and Red, who wanted badly to come, had to be threatened with being strapped down before he would quit trying to
prove how strong he was.

It had been decided that a quick dash to the cave of the jades
by a small party had the best chance to succeed. So, lightly
outfitted and armed, traveling at night, Jimmie, Carewe and the
T'aip'ing had made it. The Boston Bean, Grigsby and the rest of
the T'aip'ing remained to "make the world safe for Mr. Dolan
and Mr. Cohen to remain in," as the Bean said.

"Well," Jimmie announced at last, "here we are. Wilson said
that to the left one could get behind the falls, and about in the
middle of the rock ledge is the opening of the tunnel. Let's go,
Carewe. Shih-kai, you stay here with the swords. We'll go as far
as the tunnel mouth and in a little way, then come out."

Jimmie was right about coming out after they got in a little
way. It was no trouble getting behind the water or locating the
tunnel mouth. The opening was about as high as a tall man and
fully four feet wide. It was also dry underfoot and along the side
walls. They advanced slowly, throwing their powerful flash lights
ahead and on the walls and roof.

"I don't see anything of the snakes," Jimmie said. "It may be
that Wilson—"

Something that looked like a thick green and gold rope swung
down from the roof. It started from beyond the light thrown by
the flashes, and came with the speed of an arrow.

Both Jimmie and Carewe had their forty-five Colts in their
hands and as the thing swung down at them, both Colts went
into action. Jimmie shot from his hip. Carewe raised his revolver
to the level of his shoulder. Six heavy, soft-nosed lead bullets

tore the head of the serpent to pieces, and the rest of it began thrashing around in the tunnel.

"Speaking of snakes," Jimmie said, slipping three fresh shells into his Colt, "that baby must have been all of—"

Then their flash lights picked up two more flat, deadly-looking heads with coils beneath them as thick as a man's body. Jimmie shot four times and Carewe emptied his Colt. The tunnel was filled with the noise of great bodies twisting and throwing themselves about. Through the writhing mass there came three more of the heads.

"Outside!" Jimmie shouted, backing toward the tunnel mouth, firing as he went. Carewe went with him, his Colt roaring at every step. Two of the heads disappeared. The third came steadily on, the sinuous body behind it seemingly endless.

Jimmie Cordie laughed. "That baby must be bullet-proof, Jonathan."

"My word!" Carewe answered calmly. "It looks like it. No—there it goes at last. I say, how are we going to get through to the old treasure?"

"Let's get out, first. Throw your light straight up. I'd hate to have one of those little worms drop on my hat."

The roof was solid rock as far as the mouth of the tunnel, and they got out from behind the falls without hearing or seeing anything else.

Shih-kai was waiting for them anxiously. "I was coming in, honorable elder brother," he said. "The shots came to my ears."

"We met some darn' big snakes and they ran us out," Jimmie explained with a smile. "I don't know how many there are in there, but those we saw were no infants. We'll hole up somewhere and see if we can think up something to make them do a little of the running."

"There is a large cave, resplendent one, up on the side of the hill. There you may rest and be unseen."

THAT NIGHT Carewe said to Jimmie, "I don't want to be a

Nosey Walker, old chap, but I really would like to know how you can make the T'aip'ing lie down and wag the good old tail."

Jimmie smiled at the slim, boyish-looking young flyer who had won his way into the outfit as well as to their hearts. Carewe had commanded a flying squadron during the war and after it had flown in China where plenty of nerve was required as well as flying skill. He looked as different from Red as any two men could, yet, he and Red were as alike as two peas in the pod.

"There isn't any mystery about this T'aip'ing business," Jimmie answered. "A long while ago I was a student at Boston Tech. I heard one day that a young Chinese student whom I liked had contracted a contagious fever, and would be taken to a hospital. I went over to see him and found out that he was more scared of the hospital than the fever. I went with him and to cut a long story short, I kidded him back to health.

"When I left Boston Tech I lost track of him and did not see him again until twelve years later in China. He fell on my neck and insisted on taking me to see his pa. Three guesses who his pa was—and is."

"His pa is Yen Yuan, the absolute head of the T'aip'ing, eh?"

"Correct. Well, I couldn't persuade him that I had not saved the life of his only son, and I can't to this day. I have a suspicion that an order went out through the T'aip'ing that I was Yen Yuan's honorable elder brother and to be treated as such by all who wish to live and enjoy good health."

"So that's it!"

"Sure. Several times I have been able to do things for Yen Yuan that a European could do better than a Chinese, in England and other places, and the T'aip'ing have done twice as much for me. I'm not a member of the T'aip'ing, though. None but Chinese are... And now if you are going to continue favoring me with your company, figure out some way to remove those big snakes long enough for us to go in and get the jade statuettes—and a handful of old Genghis Khan's loot."

Carewe grinned and lighted a cigarette. Five minutes went by.

Finally Jimmie shook his head. "Darned if I can figure it. There may be an underground crack opening into the tunnel from *le bon Dieu* knows where. Or there may be a bigger cave opening from the tunnel, and the tunnel is the only way into their den."

"There must be some opening in the roof," Carewe reasoned. "The first two or three swung down at us; remember?"

"That's right. But the tunnel may have been timbered and a space left between the timbers and the rock above. They could have been up there, and when they swung down on us, used some old upright for a tail hold,"

"That's quite possible, Jimmie. If the tunnel only ended at the room and wasn't too long and we could plug up the entrance and then use—"

"Too many 'ands,' young feller," Jimmie laughed. "We'll take another look in the morning."

CHAPTER V

THE SNAKE WAR

AS THE ENGLISHMAN and Jimmie were eating breakfast the next morning, Carewe made a suggestion.

"I say, did you have any idea of gassing the giddy old pythons, or whatever they are?"

"Yes, I did," Cordie answered. "After Wilson told us about the tunnel and the snakes I had a faint idea of doing it, but I didn't figure on the tunnel being so long or meeting that special brand of snakes. I packed several cans of formaldehyde and four gas masks along from Hong Kong."

"My sainted Aunt Maria! If it is only a tunnel and a room we can seal up the opening."

Jimmie grinned. "First try and place the cans far enough inside to do the dirty work at the crossroads, Mr. Leftenant-Commander Carewe. The pythons may think the cans are some new kind of prepared snake food. Let's go down and see if we can find out how long the tunnel is."

They passed behind the waterfall, advancing very cautiously, throwing their flash lights straight ahead. Before they had taken ten steps in the tunnel a coiled snake struck viciously at them from the rock floor. Jimmie and Carewe were both ready for just that happening, and both shot. The big, flat head which looked to be at least a foot wide, disappeared under the impact of the heavy bullets. As it did, another head came into the beam of light from Carewe's flash light. Then another and another.

"Outside, old kid!" Jimmie shouted. "It would take a machine gun to shoot the road clear."

Once out and beyond the falls, Carewe asked, "Did you see what looked like a turn to the left, Jimmie?"

"Yes. About fifty feet, I guess. Maybe-so it's the entrance to the treasure room. What I don't understand is how Wilson and his buddy could get all the way in, as he says they did. He also said that his buddy got bitten. A python generally smashes against his kill with his head and then squeezes the life out by coiling around."

"Perhaps there are other, smaller snakes in there, and that the jolly old pythons were away taking tea at the time, what, what?"

Jimmie looked at the game young Englishman and laughed. "Well, we can try out the formaldehyde, anyway."

He called Shih-kai over.

"This we will do, Shih-kai: Wall up the entrance to the tunnel, using rocks and wet earth. In the wall we will leave a hole large enough for a man to crawl through. After the man has gone in and placed the cans which hold a deadly vapor, the man will crawl back through the hole, and then the hole will be sealed." He went on to explain more fully what he hoped to do with the formaldehyde.

At the finish Shih-kai bowed. "This I ask, honorable elder

brother. That I may be the one to go in with the cans. My insignificant head rests on my shoulders only as long as you are safe."

"You can go in with me and light the cans while I hold off the snakes."

An hour later first Shih-kai and then Jimmie Cordie crawled out of the hole left in the lower right hand corner of the wall built at the opening. They had got in about twenty feet before attack came from the pythons. Jimmie had managed to shoot them back long enough for Shih-kai to place and light the cans which had been prepared outside.

As the T'aip'ing closed up the hole, Jimmie said, "Well, that's that. If she works we'll walk right in, get what we're after and walk right out again. If she doesn't the only thing I can think of is to tunnel in from the side of the hill and take a chance of hitting the room."

"How long before we go in, Jimmie?" asked Carewe.

"Darned if I know, Jonathan. Five or six hours, at least."

THEY WALKED up on the side of the hill toward their camp and sat down. The. T'aip'ing, all except Shih-kai and two others, started out to patrol the surrounding hills.

"There don't seem to be any fumes escaping up," Carewe said, finally. "Maybe we've— Look, Jimmie." He pointed to the left above the falls and about a hundred yards away from them. From the ground there was coming a steady little column of gray-yellow smoke.

Jimmie turned and saw it. "There goes the ball game," he said, rising. "Let's go over and take a look-see."

The fumes were coming from a hole that looked as if it extended downward at a forty-five degree angle. The hole was a little bigger than an average-sized man's body, and the inside looked smooth as glass, composed entirely of black rock.

"Sit on her, Carewe," Jimmie said gravely, "while I go and find a cork."

"But I say! The blooming thing is too wide for me to do that, and besides—" Then he saw Jimmie's grin and changed his sentence to: "You giddy Yanks are hard to take, sometimes."

"Well, then, help me rustle some branches. We can pack it with mud."

With the aid of Shih-kai and the two T'aip'ing a covering was made that seemed to hold in a lot of the fumes. Not all, but the column became much smaller.

"If there is one hole like this, there are probably forty more," Jimmie remarked, "but enough gas may have lingered in the tunnel to make our little playmates good and sick, anyway."

Suddenly the Englishman snapped alert. "I say—don't you suppose this hole was meant as a passage into the treasure room? After the snakes were put in there, whoever did it knew that he couldn't get in through them, what, what? That is, if the snakes stayed in there and bred. So he dug this hole. It goes down on an angle of at least forty-five degrees and is too smooth to have just happened that way."

Jimmie looked at the hole, at the falls, at the side of the hill, trying to figure the slant. Then he smiled.

"You are no longer a high private in the rear ranks of my army, but a proud and haughty corporal. When the smoke clears away you and I will shoot the chutes. Shih-kai, do you think that you and the little brothers could make a rope, say a hundred and fifty feet long, out of vines and creepers strong enough to bear the weight of two men?"

"Yes, honorable one, given time. Many times have we made ropes in the hills. Is it your intention to descend into the earth with the Lord Carewe?"

"Yes, with you holding the rope. It may be that we only need it to hold onto going down and coming up."

"You will tie the rope around you, smiling one who is our elder brother?"

"No. There might not be room to turn. We will hold with our hands."

LONG BEFORE the rope was finished the fumes had ceased coming out of the hole. Some of the T'aip'ing had come in from the hills and helped braid it, which hastened matters. But it was growing dusk when Jimmie Cordie and Carewe started down in gas masks, Jimmie first, each holding the rope in his left hand. In their right hands were the Colt forty-fives.

Shih-kai and four of the T'aip'ing had hold of the rope and paid it out. Jimmie had instructed that two quick pulls at the rope meant "pull up." Shih-kai and the others on top did not think much of the operation and stood with tensed muscles, their eyes on the hole. They were all strong, active men in the prime of life, and each of them had made up his mind that if the tugs came there would be no delay in bringing their honorable elder brother and his friend to the top.

The circumference of the hole did not get any smaller nor any larger, and Jimmie and Carewe slipped down as easily as oil down a gun barrel. It was dark, and because their hands were on the rope they could not use the flash lights. The lights would not have done much good, anyway, because of the vapor that still remained in the hole, which fogged up the glass in the masks.

It was not a thing that the average man would have cared to do, sliding down a hole to where big snakes waited in case the formaldehyde had not stupefied them. But both Jimmie and Carewe were firm believers that "what is written is written"; and both of them slipped down through the darkness without the beat of their hearts quickening a stroke.

Jimmie felt his feet go out into space at last. How far he had come or how much rope there was left, he did not know. He judged they were about a hundred and twenty or thirty feet down. His entire body left the hole then, and he went down through space, hanging by his left hand to the rope. A moment later his feet rested on solid ground. He released the rope, and in another moment Carewe landed beside him. Drawing their flash lights from their belts, both turned to locate the hole above. It was about ten feet over their heads, the rope reaching down to their knees.

Whether they were in the tunnel or a room they could not see. The vapor was so thick that the powerful flash lights could not penetrate it for more than a couple of feet.

Jimmie touched Carewe on the arm and then backed to the wall. Carewe followed him, and once their backs had come against the rock Jimmie began easing his way along it, feeling ahead of him with the Colt barrel.

Before they had gone five feet, Carewe made a sudden movement and bumped against Jimmie, who turned. Carewe was throwing his light on the ground at his feet. Jimmie put his light down also, and with the two beams they could dimly see that Carewe had stepped on a small snake which was trying to coil but doing it very slowly. Jimmie reached down and struck the snake's head with the barrel of his Colt and they went on.

Twelve steps more and they came to a corner and turned with the wall. Jimmie stumbled over something, and again the two beams were brought to bear. It was a box, bound with brass rings. They stepped over it and then over another. Then they came to an opening. Here the vapor seemed less thick, and as their flash lights played over it they could see that it was heavily bulkheaded with timbers. Jimmie stood for a moment, undecided.

Wilson had told of a shelf on which sat three of the jade figures. But whether the shelf was inside the room or just out of it at the entrance, he had not been able to say as he lay dying. As Jimmie hesitated, Carewe touched his arm. He had thrown his light up to the left. Jimmie turned his head and saw Carewe pointing up.

On one of the timbers that projected a little way beyond the others, sat two small statuettes.

JIMMIE'S LIGHT played over them for a moment as he satisfied himself that they were the ones he was after. Then he reached up and got them. They were small enough so that he could tuck them both inside his soft flannel shirt without any trouble.

Carewe's light had followed Jimmie's hands, and as the right came out from the shirt front, Carewe again touched Jimmie's arm and played his light on a chest under the timbers.

Jimmie stepped over to the chest and knelt in front of it. He tried a massive lock, but could not even move it from the much-corroded links of copper chain that almost covered the strong box. Finally he stood up and shook his head. Carewe could dimly see him do it, and he nodded his understanding that the chest could not be opened.

There was a slithering sound back of them. Both men whirled about. Their lights picked up the vine rope by which they had dropped into the treasure chamber just as the upper end of it slid down through the hole to the stone floor of the room. Their means of escape upward was cut off.

Neither Jimmie or Carewe showed the slightest uncertainty. There was only one way out, and they took it. With flash lights pointed dead ahead and slanting down, they stepped through the opening into the tunnel of the snakes.

That walk to where the mouth had been sealed up was like a walk in a nightmare. Great pythons lay with bodies twisted and coiled together. From the roof there hung the bodies of those who had struck at the men who had entered the tunnel before, the great heads torn and shattered. On the floor were others that had been hit. The vapor was very thick. More than one of the pythons were moving sluggishly. Twice both Jimmie and Carewe had narrow escapes from being caught in coils that were still trying to contract, but at last they made the wall of mud and stones. Carewe knelt at the corner that had been closed after Jimmie and Shih-kai came out, and began to force the stones out of the hardened mud, using the barrel of his Colt for a chisel and pry. Jimmie stood facing the tunnel, his Colt ready to stop any snake still with life enough to attack. It took Carewe five minutes to make the hole large enough for them to crawl through. When he did he stood up and motioned Jimmie through. Jimmie pointed to him and to the hole. Carewe promptly went down on his hands and knees and went through, with Jimmie at his heels. They kept their gas masks on until they had cleared the falls, both knowing that there would be a rush of vapor through the hole.

ONCE OUT and on the bank, Jimmie took off his mask and started to turn and help Carewe remove his. Abruptly he stopped. Within five feet of them stood a Chinese officer with the insignia of a colonel on his natty khaki uniform.

Back of the colonel a few feet were six other officers. Fifty feet back of them was lined up a full infantry company, their rifles at order arms. Up on the hill where the T'aip'ing had been at the rope there was lined up another company, and up at the cave where they had camped and at the mouth of the pass to the north there were several more companies.

"I will take the jades, Captain Coldie," the Chinese colonel said, blandly. There is no "r" in the Chinese language, and few Chinese can make a sound anywhere near it. Those educated abroad or who have spent years in England or America can sometimes come close, but most Chinese who speak English cannot.

"I am more than glad that I was able to get them for you," Jimmie said, as he handed over the statuettes. "You are—?"

"Colonel Tzu-lu, commanding a legiment of the Wal Lold Chung's almy, Captain Coldie."

Cordie nodded; he had heard of the War Lord Chung.

Carewe had taken off his mask and was looking around as if he could not believe the evidence of his own eyes. As Jimmie handed the statuettes to Tzu-lu, Carewe spoke.

"I say! Can't we—"

"Look around you, Jonathan!" Jimmie interrupted. "Look very carefully up at the hole. Do you see—what I do not?"

"What you do not? I see— My word, talk about pulling the giddy old chestnuts out of the fire, what, what? We are a flaming fine pair of cat's-paws, aren't we, old thing?"

Colonel Tzu-lu smiled. "We have an old saying, Lieutenant-Commandel Calewe. It is, 'Man makes a thousand plans and God makes but one.'"

"Which is a good one for all men to remember," Jimmie remarked with a grim smile. "Go ahead with the second act, colonel. My side is hurting me quite a little and I will be glad if you make it as short as possible."

Tzu-lu laughed as did two or three of the officers who understood English. "I have been told much of you, Captain Coldie. The second act, as you call it, will open by tlying to make both you and Lieutenant-Commandel Calewe comfoltable on the way to Mengtze. If you will both undelstand that I am acting as an official undel instluctions and that thele is nothing pelsonal in the taking of the jades and the blinging you to the city of Chung, it will be much easiel fol—us all."

"I speak for Lieutenant-Commander Carewe as well as for myself," Jimmie answered promptly, smiling at the trim young colonel, "when I answer that we both fully understand it—and will remember it when the time comes that we retake the jades."

Tzu-lu smiled. "It may be, Captain Coldie. Allow me to plesent my staff," and he beckoned the officers forward.

CHAPTER VI

A MANCHU SWORDSMAN

THE BOSTON BEAN rose from the machine gun he was operating and began using a thirty-thirty rifle. Grigsby had already risen from his gun. The Afghans had done as Gribsby had said they would do. They had come back with all their relatives. The morning after Jimmie, Carewe and Shih-kai had left there had been a direct attack up the hill from all sides.

It had been just as directly met with two machine guns. Both Red and the Fighting Yid staggered out of the hospital tent at the first yell and started for guns. Grigsby saw them come out and curtly ordered them both back into the tent.

"Like fun I'll go back!" Red shouted defiantly.

The Yid protested, "Oi, George? I am vell as anything. I shoot it a thirty-thirty, ain't it?"

"It ain't. You heard me. Get back in that tent and make it snappy." It was Major Grigsby talking, and the Yid and Red both knew it. Grigsby paid no more attention to them, running to the Browning set up in the northeast angle.

" 'Tis the fault av ye, ye Yid ape," said Red bitterly, as he sat down at the entrance of the tent, not inside.

"My fault?" The Yid sat down beside Red. "Vat did it I have to do mit, Irish loafer? Is it my fault dot ve are back in de army all of a sudden? Vat did it I have to do mit, I esk you?" The Yid was considerably peeved.

"It is the fault av ye," insisted Red, as the machine guns began their *rat-tat-tat-tat-tat*. If the Yid was peeved, Dolan was doubly peeved. His cuts had been sewed up and his naturally healthy body was responding with new blood to the beef cubes and the nourishing broth. "If ye hadn't been slower than the second coming ye could have killed that wild man that walloped ye over the head. Bad luck to the scut he didn't brain ye once for all. Ye could have got him and then taken wan av the sixty-nine off av me. Then I wouldn't have got cut and would be out there at a gun."

"Oi, my persecuted race! So dot is vy it is my fault? Listen, gonnif. In de first place, vy did it you grab a sword und run out to play mit guys vot vas veaned on swords? Could it you stand up to dem, I esk you?"

"Could I— Here they come over the wall!"

"Sit down," the Yid ordered. "De T'aip'ing have got 'em. Sit down und vatch some regular swords go it to vork. See! Dare is no more vild men left for you to play mit."

The first charge was driven back, and the second and the third, and finally the Afghans stopped coming in a body. They had lost too many men, and were waiting for reinforcements. But there was a steady try for the hill by isolated groups who wanted the glory that would be theirs if they wiped out the little stone fortress. It took ammunition and eternal vigilance to stop them. They came day and night, more of them at night after the fighting priests had stirred them up.

WHEN THE Bean at last lowered his thirty-thirty, the attack was nine days old. Nine days and ten nights, during which more Afghans had arrived who at once started out to show those already there how good men could take a hill. Each and every time any considerable body of them joined, there came a charge in force and just as many times they were stopped before they got to the breast-high wall.

After the third charge an old Khan had ridden up under a flag of truce and asked that hostilities cease while the wounded were removed.

The Boston Bean and Grigsby agreed, and then asked the Khan to come in and have a cup of tea or whatever else he would like. The Khan glared at them for a moment and then, as his eyes plainly showed, thought it would be a good chance to find out how much ammunition the defenders had left, and grunted acquiescence.

He saw plenty—at least he thought he saw plenty. Out of piles of ammunition boxes, or rather out of the top boxes of neatly arranged piles near each machine gun, he saw belts hanging, ready for use. He saw rifles, revolvers, and cases of ammunition for them and also an orderly pile of foodstuffs near a stone oven. He had crossed a little stream on the way up which he knew came from a spring on the top of the hill, so he did not need to look for a water supply. He knew they had it.

Once inside the fortress he refused scornfully any food or drink from the ones with whom he had a blood feud. But he did not refuse the food until it had been cooked. In the meantime his eyes had been busy. As he rose to go back down the hill, he said in Pushtu:

"If you English dogs surrender I will make your death an easy one. Do it now before all the bullets for the little guns of death are shot away. If you make me take this hill I will empale any that are left alive." He cast longing eyes at the trim Brownings. If he had them and ammunition to go with them he could make himself Lord of the Hills.

Both Grigsby and the Bean read his mind and smiled: "We are not English," the Bean answered. "We are of another race, Americans. You know of Americans, O mighty ruler of the world?"

"No!" snarled the Khan. "Why do you lie to me? You are English, the same as those dogs who hold the border against us. Will you surrender?"

"You tell men that they lie while you stand under a flag of truce, shameless one? Go, before you do or say something that withdraws the protection."

"That is true," the old Khan answered promptly. "I am under a flag of truce and I withdraw the lie. I have never heard of Americans before. I go—to return with all my men." He stalked proudly away, through a little opening in the wall and down the hill.

"He wants the guns pretty bad," Grigsby said, as he and the Bean watched the old Khan.

When the Bean lowered his Winchester there were no more Afghans on their feet to shoot at. He couldn't have shot at them with the rifle, anyway, because he had used his last shell.

Grigsby came over. "Did she jam on you?"

"No. I used the last belt. From now on the war will be conducted with Colts." As the Bean spoke he drew his and raised it up over his shoulder to "throw down" on a long shot. Then he lowered it as one of the T'aip'ing shouted. What looked like an Afghan had suddenly run out from a clump of second growth on the left, at the base of the hill. He was followed by two more men who gained on him rapidly.

The runner kept on for fifty or sixty yards, then as he heard the thud of running feet close to him, stopped, whirled around and drew a sword. The two pursuers had their swords out and both closed in on him. There was a flurry of blades, one of the two fell away, the runner staggered back, then went at the remaining man, who had raised his sword for a cut.

"Holy cats, that was fast!" the Boston Bean gasped as the runner stepped back from his opponent, who was falling. "I didn't even see his sword move. Who—" The Bean stopped. Afghans had run out from their shelter all over the left side of the hill, while the T'aip'ing swords, some fifty men, had cleared the stone wall and were running down the hill.

"It's Shih-kai," Grigsby said. "We better—put a fence up for him, Codfish! Take the right!" His Colt went into action. The Boston Bean's joined in the *pow-pow-pow* before Grigsby stopped talking.

The nearest Afghans dropped, and before any of the rest could reach the swaying man, the T'aip'ing had arrived. Two of them stopped and picked up Shih-kai. The rest charged straight on past, to where the oncoming Afghans were thickest. Shih-kai had fallen just before the T'aip'ing got to him.

THE TWO men who had picked him up turned and carried him up the hill and into the fortress. For a long time there was the tossing of blades and the yell of combat down where the Afghans worried and snarled around the ring formed by the T'aip'ing swords. Shih-kai had come to as he was being put down, and had snarled an order that kept the few remaining T'aip'ing inside the wall. They had been ready to die with him if necessary.

"Our brothers down there die in defense of the Black-eyed Smiling One," he added. "What better death? Remain here until it is your turn to die."

Grigsby, the Bean, the Yid and Red, who had come to the stone wall, watched the fight. There was no more machine gun and rifle ammunition. With their Colts they sent many an Afghan to the Afghan heaven, but the range was a long one.

Finally there was a surge forward and the Afghans met across
what had been a ring of good T'aip'ing swords. But it had been
a very costly victory, and the old Khan cursed and raved as he
looked down upon the bodies of his kinsmen.

"He'll come with all he's got now," Grigsby said, as he started
to bandage up Shih-kai. "Do you feel able to talk a little, Shih-
kai?"

"Yes—if—I talk slowly. Did the pariah cur's sword bite deep?"

"Not so deep as long. It laid your ribs open. If it hurts you to
talk, don't do it."

"The Black-eyed Smiling One and the Lord Carewe were
taken at the waterfall. A Chinese regiment came. I ordered
my little brothers to stay and guard the rope by which we had
lowered the two into the cave of the treasure, and then I escaped
into the hills to bring you to the rescue."

"Are either of them hurt?"

"No. The Chinese colonel remains at the falls to get the treasure of Genghis Khan. I remained close until I saw that my
honorable elder brother and the Lord Carewe were being held
as prisoners. On the way I slew an Afghan and took his clothes
so that I might get—" He closed his eyes.

Grigsby felt Shih-kai's heart. "Still beating. Carry him into
the tent."

Three of the T'aip'ing lifted Shih-kai carefully, and Grigsby
followed them to do what he could to make the brave Manchu,
whom they all classed as one of them, comfortable.

CHAPTER VII

A WAR LORD'S GREED

COLONEL TZU-LU STOOD with Jimmie Cordie watching
about two-thirds of his regiment digging into the side of the hill.
The men were using their bayonets and makeshift wooden shov-

els and anything else they had that would loosen and remove dirt. He was speaking in Pushtu now, having found that Jimmie understood and could talk it.

"And so the Lord Chung learned that a man was offering one of the lost jades of the T'aip'ing for sale. The Lord Chung knew that if he could secure it he could force the T'aip'ing to support his plans in return for the jade. So he sent men to take the jade."

Jimmie laughed. "Why did not the Lord Chung send for the man and buy the statuette?"

Tzu-lu smiled. "That I do not know, Captain Cordie. This though I do know: the Lord Chung takes—when and where he can. It was his men that your friend who is called the Fighting Yid killed at the shop. The Lord Chung learned that the wounded man was taken to Major Grigsby's apartment. His watchers reported that Shih-kai, one of the war captains of the T'aip'ing, and Captain Cordie left the apartment and entered the palace of Yen Yuan. So the Lord Chung knew that he had lost the jade forever. But he hoped that from the wounded man you have learned where the other jades were and his watchers remained close. The expedition was followed and after the Afghan attack your leaving the camp was also reported. I was ordered to take my regiment and once you had secured the jades, bring them and you with them to Mengtze, the city of the Lord Chung."

"Thank you for the explanation," Jimmie answered, courteously, "The Lord Chung rushes in where wise men would fear to tread lightly."

"You mean by insulting the mighty T'aip'ing? The Lord Chung is Manchu, Captain Cordie and fears no man. He plays boldly and puts all on one turn of the cards. He has won again. With the jades in his possession, he can make the T'aip'ing do his bidding. I am Chinese, and—that is why I spoke plainly to you at the waterfall. I am an officer obeying orders and have no quarrel with the all-powerful society—and do not wish to have."

"I'll call Yen Yuan's attention to that fact," Jimmie answered, "when I take the two statuettes to him."

Tzu-lu smiled also. "It may be—but I doubt that you will be able to do so. This I will tell you: the Lord Chung hates all foreigners and in Mengtze the platform is being built on which you and Lieutenant-Commander Carewe will be given the death of a thousand cuts." Tzu-lu spoke as calmly and indifferently as if he were telling of an escort of honor being arranged to take Jimmie and Carewe to the border.

"That will no doubt help a lot in his subsequent negotiations with the T'aip'ing," Jimmie answered, cheerfully. "Why don't you take the treasure of Genghis Khan, provided there is any, and come to Peking or Hong Kong with us and present the statuettes to Yen Yuan personally? Your reward would be much greater than any Chung can or will give you, and the T'aip'ing can fully protect you there."

Tzu-lu smiled. "I could not if I wished, Captain Cordie. Among the officers of this regiment are the men of the Lord Chung's House. Many of the rank and file are vassals whose ancestors have served the House of Chung for centuries."

"I see. If you will pardon me, colonel, I will rejoin Commander Carewe in the tent you have so kindly set aside for us. My side is still painful and I find that remaining on my feet any length of time makes it worse."

"Certainly, Captain Cordie. But this I tell you in all frankness: Do not try to escape. It is impossible. If you do I will be forced to use harsh measures to insure your presence in Mengtze."

"You spoke not long ago of man's one thousand plans and God's one. It may-be that God's plan will be shown us, Colonel Tzu-lu."

"It may be. In the meantime, may I suggest that you and Lieutenant-Commander Carewe do not attempt to put any of man's plans into action?"

Jimmie smiled as he saluted the young Chinese officer in whose eyes there twinkled a little glint of humor.

AS JIMMIE entered the tent, Carewe looked up. He had been trying to fix one of the straps on his leather puttees.

"Well, old bean, have you got started on what you Yanks call the giddy old frame?"

"You have that wrong, Jonathan. No Yank ever said 'giddy' unless to describe how he felt in the cold gray dawn of the morning after."

"After what? I say, that's another thing—why don't you finish a sentence?"

"All fooling aside," said Jimmie, quickly sobering, "We're in a darn tight box. It's on the program that you and I grace a platform in the city of the Lord Chung and get Ling-chi."

"My sainted aunt! The death of the thousand cuts! I say, old chap we'd better take it on the lam, what, what?"

"I tried to get Tzu-lu to do that very thing with us, and present the statuettes to Yen Yuan."

"And he wouldn't? My hat, he is the first Chinese I ever—"

An officer came to the entrance of the tent and saluted. "Colonel Tzu-lu's compliments and will Captain Coldie and Commandel Calewe join him at lunch?"

That night about eleven Carewe, as he was getting ready to sleep, asked Jimmie: "If we get the chance to take it on the lam—will we try for the statuettes?"

"Yeah, boy! Tzu-lu packs them on him. I'm trying to figure out some way to decoy him over to one side."

"When you asked me to look very carefully up at the hole, did you mean for me to see that Shih-kai was not among the T'aip'ing dead?"

"That was it. He got away, and if he lasted long enough to make G.H.Q. there are some other brilliant minds on the subject of jarring us loose. That's why I don't want to start anything that might fog us all up."

Carewe laughed. "In the meantime what becomes of the jolly Afghans?"

"It is up to the said brilliant minds to dispose of them, Jonathan. Go to sleep."

THE FIGHTING Yid, who was oiling his Colt, looked down the hill and announced cheerfully: "Here comes it company. Poppa has got it grandpa mit, dis time."

The old Afghan Khan was coming up, once more under a flag of truce. With him was a much older Afghan. So old, that as he stepped over a low place in the wall of stones, Grigsby and the Boston Bean who met them could see that his fierce old face was a network of wrinkled skin that looked like a mummy's. Evidently he outranked the other and had taken command.

"I am Kaju Khan," he snarled, "of the Asmar, and just come. What are you doing here in the hills?" As he spoke, his eyes, still keen and full of fight, were taking in the entire camp.

The Bean answered in Pushtu: "We are peaceable men and go about attending strictly to our own business, O Kaju Khan of the Asmar. We do not attack, only defend our—"

Kaju Khan interrupted. "Truly, from what I see you are peaceable men! Is it not known to all that peaceable men can withstand Afghan charges for days? Why lie to me? You are men of war, and"—here the old fighter smiled grimly as he looked down the hill where the bodies of the men who fell in the last charge lay—"you have played the game for a long time. Once more, what is the business that brings you to the hills? You can tell me, because you will not live to attend to it."

The Boston Bean laughed scornfully. "When speaking of Afghans, say 'braggarts'; then all men will know. We are men who hunt for fights with such as you so that we may eat our breakfast afterward with hearty appetites. In our land, O mighty Khan of the Asmar, we count death as the greatest thing—provided we can take plenty of pure breeds such as Afghans with us, to fight with them again in the lands beyond the sky. If you can take us so easily, why waste time in coming up to make idle talk?"

The Khan looked at the Bean, at Grigsby, then as Red and

the Yid came up, at them. He stared at them, starting at their feet and going up to their eyes.

Then he smiled, a tight-lipped little smile, more of a grin of recognition.

"Go back!" he said curtly to the other Afghan.

"I? Go back? Why—I am Chahar Khan of the Darweza."

"Go back, I said! I am Kaju Khan of the Asmar. I wish to talk to these men."

The Afghan is without question one of the most suspicious men on earth. An expert framer himself, he thinks, naturally, that all others are trying to frame him.

"It is true that you are the Kaju Khan of the Asmar, but I have done the fighting and taken the loss. Now you come and—"

"Fight some more—with five times as many men as you have left of the Darweza!" snorted the older chief. "Go down the hill. I will hold your interest in the matter sacred."

Chahar Khan did not like it at all, but the remark about the five to one started him down the hill. He did not need any teacher to tell him that old Kaju would promptly use the five to mop up the one if he decided to do it—kin or no kin.

AFTER CHAHAR got thirty or forty feet down the hill, Kaju said: "Now we talk man to man. There is no blood feud between you and the Asmar."

"That is right," answered the Bean gravely. "Come and sit down."

As the old Khan stalked toward a pile of ammunition cases, going close to one of the Brownings as he went, Grigsby said softly to the Boston Bean:

"Tell him you are going after Genghis Khan's treasure. Refuse to make a deal of any kind with him."

The Bean grinned, "Very good, me lud," then walked over to where Kaju Khan sat, his eyes still on the machine gun.

"Now," the Bean said, "let us talk man's talk. You have asked what we do in the hills. Why should we not tell you, mighty one? When we are rested we will go where we wish, brushing all aside that attempt to stop us."

"How many of the machine guns have you?" asked Kaju.

"Five and spare parts," answered the Bean.

"And bullets for them?"

"Charge up the hill at us and count the bullets we send you."

Kaju gave vent to a dry, amused little chuckle. "What do you want in the hills? Tell me truly this time. It may be that you and I can trade."

"Who trades with an Afghan loses shirt and skin," quoted the Bean gravely. "I will tell you. We go for the treasure of Genghis Khan."

The old man nearly fell off the box. For many hundreds of years the Afghans had hunted for Genghis Khan's treasure—and found several caches of it, too. He recovered himself promptly and asked as indifferently as he could:

"You know where it is?"

"Yes, we know."

"Where?"

The Bean smiled, "Where the woodbine twineth, mighty leader of the Asmar."

"Where the— You dare jest with me? Soon you will be sitting on a sharpened post!"

The Bean rose and pointed down the hill.

The Khan started to rise, looked at the Browning, at the Bean's face, then relaxed.

"I withdraw the threat," he grunted. "Tell me and we will go together and get it, dividing equally."

The Bean laughed. "Who believes an Afghan? Are we men to get within a week's journey of Genghis Khan's treasure and then share it because others come snarling threats? No, we will not tell you."

Kaju Khan rose. "I waste time, as you said. Know this, foolish one: I go to bring my men up the hill to take you and the guns. Once I have you—you will tell under torture."

"It may be. Will you lead your men up, O boaster? If you do, I will sent a bullet into your ear to whisper where the treasure is."

Kaju smiled. He was no more afraid of death than was the Boston Bean, and they both knew the other knew it.

"No. I am too old to lead a charge. Once I would have, when as young as you, and at the finish buried my sword into your heart."

"That," answered the Bean courteously, "you did not need to tell me, mighty one. I know a man."

The Afghan grunted and without another word went down the hill.

CHAPTER VIII

THE BEAN'S STRATEGY

"WELL," THE BEAN said as he rejoined Grigsby, Red and the Yid. "I told the old gent all about it, going into details about the rooms full of pearls and diamonds and rubies as big as cabbages. He wanted to go fifty-fifty with us. I refused him, proud and haughty. Now he has gone to get his outfit and mop up this time, no foolin'. What's the idea, George? There's no chance of them getting tired and going home."

"Oi, Beaneater, vait till you hear it de frame-up ve got. All ve got it to do is to hold dem off until night."

"Well, if that's all I'm going to take a nap. You birds can attend to a simple little thing like that without my help."

"Here it is, Codfish," Grigsby said. "I don't think they will attack for a little while, anyway. They won't until after the old boy gets all through explaining why he sent the other Khan down. His explanation won't be believed, and there will be a lot of wah-wah. Also, he will want to get his own outfit hooked up to block the others off of us, so he won't have to divide. It's going to be like a convention down there."

"I don't doubt that. But why tell him about the treasure? That's what my poor, feeble brain can't grasp."

"What would a long-legged scut the likes av ye be doin' wid a brain?" Red asked. "No wan that ever came from—"

"Pipe down, Red," Grigsby said. "Here comes Shih-kai with the man he's picked out. Stick around, Brownbread; your poor feeble brain may grasp part of the idea."

Grigsby was right about there not being any further attack that day. The first Afghan chief got back to his tribesmen and announced hotly that Kaju Khan was up there making a trade in which there was no doubt but what the Darweza would come out the little end of the horn.

That started trouble right away. The Darweza began figuring their chances of cleaning up on the Asmar, or at least cutting out the machine guns for themselves once they were taken.

When Kaju arrived at his camp he called in his top men and told them about the treasure. One of them immediately proposed sending the Darweza, their rivals now, up the hill so they could be wiped out. Others scorned that suggestion and wanted to go up themselves, ignoring the Darweza.

All in all, as Grigsby said, it became very much like a political convention.

That night, about midnight, two of the Asmar came into Kaju's tent, bringing with them a very scared-looking Chinaman. "This cur," one announced as he roughly pushed the Chinaman forward, "came to us at the outpost and called out that he wished to be brought into your presence. Here he is."

Kaju looked at the cringing man. It was very natural that the man should fear: to be alone with Afghans was like being alone with hungry tigers for a man of any race.

"I am Kaju Khan. Why do you want to see me?"

"I am a poor man, O ruler of the world, and—"

"You will also be a dead one, jackal, unless you talk and to the point. Why do you come to me?"

"I—if I tell you—will you give me a share, lord of the hills?"

"Give you a share? Of what? Am I one to be bargained with by a dog of a Chinese? Yes, I will give you your share. Tell me, or—" The old Khan's dagger flashed from the sheath. The Chinaman gave a little squawk of terror and dropped to his knees.

Kaju sheathed the dagger and grunted. "Tell—if you wish to live."

"This then, resplendent one. I am one of the bearers of the foreign devils. After the one who joined them on the hill came, I overheard them tell—"

"You overheard? How did you, a bearer, get close enough to hear?"

"I was trying to get one of the little hand guns, magnificent one, and was on the ground behind the tent."

"A thief!" Kaju said scornfully. There is no bigger thief in the world than an Afghan, but he likes to pretend he isn't and that he scorns all other thieves.

"Yes, lord," the Chinaman answered humbly. "I heard them... You will give me my share?"

"Yes, as I have promised, you will receive your share. You heard what?"

"The foreign devils told the one who came about the treasure of Genghis Khan and where they were going to get it."

That was a natural thing, and it was also natural that any Chinaman who overheard it would at once figure his chances to get some of it—even if he had to go to Afghans. The old Khan knew that a Chinaman would take any risk to gain a fortune, so he promptly demanded:

"Where is it?"

The Chinaman told just where it was, describing the waterfall, the tunnel, and the jade statuettes. The Afghan paid no attention to the jades; he was after gold and jewels, not jades. Finally

Kaju Khan stood up, his eyes shining. The treasure of Genghis Khan was enough to make any man's eyes shine, no matter how old he was.

"Take this dog out and guard him well. I will question him further at the waterfall. He may know more than he has told. Send the chiefs to me—of the Asmar only. This is a matter for our clan alone. Remember that, and see that all tongues are bridled. Wait, have the word passed to the other tribes that I am sick and going home to rest, leaving the guns for them."

The Afghans laughed. "We will attend to it, Kaju Khan."

AN HOUR later the Asmar mounted their horses and rode away.

Chahar Khan watched them, a frown on his face.

"Kaju Khan has not tricked us, as he thinks," he snarled to several of his clan who stood with him. "He rides for what the English dogs came for, having dealt with them. Whatever it is, it is worth more than the guns he leaves for us. We will follow in an hour, leaving enough behind to hold those mongrels behind their stone walls. Shall we of the Darweza be given candy like a child while the Asmar get something of value?"

One of his men came up, rubbing his wrists which were still red from ropes that had bound them.

"What happened to you?" asked Chahar Khan, sourly.

"This. I was over by the Asmar and they caught me listening. They bound me and threw me to one side like a dog. Truly I have a blood feud with Durani and Ghilzai of the Asmar. They are the ones who bound me and laughed. I come to tell you that I ride at once with my brothers and kinsmen."

"You are riding also! What did you hear? You will do no riding, by the beard of the prophet! Unless you tell me—and remember to speak true words."

The Afghan knew his chief meant what he said. Once Chahar Khan's suspicions were aroused, no one would do anything unless he knew what it was all about, if he and the swords of his family could stop them. So the Afghan told what he had overheard the two Asmars saying, which was, "We ride for the treasure of Genghis Khan—we of the Asmar alone."

The old Khan's order for bridled tongues had been obeyed as far as outsiders were concerned, but among themselves, they had talked. The two that were already quarreling over their share of the loot had not noticed the Darweza clansman standing behind them until too late. When they did see him they had promptly disarmed him, tied him with ropes and tossed him aside, as he reported.

The moment he got to the words: "We ride for the treasure of Genghis Khan," the Darweza camp became like a town in the mining country when news of a rich gold strike comes. There was a mad rush for horses. No one would stay as guards over the hill.

Blood feuds and all other things were forgotten. They were going to be in on the treasure or know the reason why.

Grigsby had figured that once the news reached the Afghans it could not be kept a secret, and he smiled a little later as the T'aip'ing who had been sent to Kaju Khan stood in front of him.

"I told him, lord. Then I escaped as all ran for their horses. The way is clear." The speech was in Pushtu, and Grigsby got enough of it to know that his plan had succeeded, though he was sure it had when he had seen the Afghans ride away.

"Und now," the Yid said to Red, "ve go und get it de bone vile de two big dogs is fighting for it. Stick mit a Colt dis time, you no-good Irish loafer."

"Stay behind me, Yid omadhaun, wid the coco av ye. Ye cannot guard it for yeself."

CHAPTER IX

ENEMIES MEET

"THE QUESTION IS," Carewe said sleepily as he tried for a more comfortable position on the blanket that served him for a bed, "whether the Afghans will wait until the brilliant minds begin to—"

He left the blanket like the bullet from a gun barrel. Jimmie Cordie was just as fast, and they both crouched, ready to hurl themselves at the body of the man whose right arm and shoulder was already under the tent wall at the rear. When the head appeared, they both relaxed. Jimmie laughed softly. If was the T'aip'ing second in command to Shih-kai. He made no attempt to come farther into the tent.

"Speak, little brother," Jimmie said, quietly.

"The Afghans attack within an houl. The Lold Gligsby also comes to get you and youl fliend, Black-eyed Smiling One. Whele ale the jades?"

"On Colonel Tzu-lu's person. His tent is the highest one in the middle of the row facing this tent. How did you get here ahead of the Afghans, who must have ridden?"

"We cut off a palty that tlied fol a sholt cut and slew them, taking theil holses. Then we caught a man of the hills who led us ovel a pass high up."

"Fair enough. What are we to do?"

"The Lold Gligsby oldels that when the Afghans come you both hide in tent. As they attack he will come and get you." The T'aip'ing smiled as he saw both Jimmie and Carewe grin cheerfully.

"You have my permission to go, little brother. Tell the Lord Grigsby his orders will be obeyed to the letter." The T'aip'ing withdrew from the tent, and as he did Jimmie said, "Short, sweet and to the point."

"I say, how could they get away from the giddy old Afghans and—"

"Wait until I open my office as a fortune teller who knows both past and present, Jonathan, then cross my palm with silver. Get busy, old kid."

"On what? Where can we hide in a tent this size? We can get a sword or a gun as soon as the flaming fight starts."

"Orders is orders," Jimmie answered cheerfully. "Start digging a funk hole, Lieutenant-Commander Carewe. Just long enough and wide enough to get into. Then cover it and you with your blanket and trust in the luck that never deserts the British army and navy."

"What to dig with, Jimmie? They've taken every bit of metal off—"

"Hands, heels, nose and head. Get busy, old-timer. The Afghans may arrive before Grigsby, and I would hate like heck to get caught by those gents without anything in my hands."

"You and me both," answered Carewe, getting to work.

It was well for them both that they did not strike any rocks. They both finished at the same time and both lay down in the trenches to see if they were deep enough to make the blankets look as if they were stretched out on the ground with nothing under them.

As they reached for their blankets, there came the wild, eerie yell that starts the Afghan charge. Jimmie and Carewe both pulled the blankets over them without any more testing of anything. They heard the cries of the Chinese, the sound of shots, and then there arose the noise of ten thousand cat-fights going all at once. Mingling with it was the ring of steel on steel, and ragged volleys.

Then the sound changed. Cries for mercy began to go up, and most of the yelling took on a triumphant tenor. Twice Jimmie and Carewe sensed that the tent flap had been drawn aside.

Suddenly there was a lull for a split second. Then they both heard the *pow-pow-pow-pow* of Colt forty-fives, and the yells once more changed into cries of surprise.

Jimmie held up the edge of his blanket a little and said: "The Lold Gligsby is alliving," and put the blanket down. Neither he nor Carewe made any attempt to get up. They knew that until the users of the Colts arrived in person, or the T'aip'ing swords, any Afghan would kill them on sight.

IT WAS not until they heard Red Dolan's voice shouting, "Jimmie! Jimmie, ye scut! Where are ye?" that they threw off the blankets and sat up. Red was within three feet of the trenches, and stepped back as they came up like twin jacks-in-the-box.

"For the love av— Are ye buried?"

"Buried, no!" answered Jimmie, as he and Carewe got to their feet. "Hand me something, you big ape."

"Here, I brought it for ye." Red handed Jimmie a Colt forty-five and belt of cartridges. Then he unbuckled another and handed it to Carewe. "And here is wan for ye, banty."

The Boston Bean appeared at the entrance. "Let's go!"

"Go, nothing!" answered Jimmie. "I'm going after the statuettes and by gosh, I'm—"

"The matter has been attended to, me good man. We have the statuettes and your boy friend the colonel with them. Come on, Jimmie. It's getting darn' good and thick outside, and—"

Grigsby shouted from outside the tent. "Come on!"

The moon had come out a little, and it was fairly light. The Chinese camp was still an indescribable swirl of mad fighting. The Chinese outnumbered the Afghans five and six to one, but were not near the fighters and had been surprised, besides.

But several units had rallied, and were giving the Afghans a stiff fight. There were rings of Chinese fending off the Afghan attack with their bayonets, around which the Afghans crowded and pushed to get a chance to strike a blow. At other places the

Afghans had been surrounded and two or three Chinese companies were trying to mop up. The tent lines were mostly down.

Just in front of the tent stood Grigsby and the Fighting Yid. In back of them, facing the mix-up, was a line of about thirty T'aip'ing swordsmen, two deep. At the Yid's feet lay Colonel Tzu-Ju, unconscious. With the T'aip'ing was Shih-kai, sitting between two of them on a seat they had made by clasping each other's wrists. He held his sword in his hand and his scarred young face was as impassive as ever.

When he saw Jimmie and Carewe, he stood up and snarled an order. The T'aip'ing came in and formed a wedge, still facing the camp.

"Start toward the right, Shih-kai," Grigsby said calmly, "swing well out. We will take care of any rush from the left. Do you want this colonel, Jimmie? The Yid knocked him out and then felt the jades on him, so he brought him jades and all."

"No, I don't want him. Wait until I get the— Yes, I do want him. Can you pack him, Yid?"

"Sure—und three more like him."

"All right. *Allons, mes enfants!*"

As they started they attracted the attention of several Afghans, who charged promptly. They did not live to get to the T'aip'ing wedge. Jimmie Cordie, Carewe, Grigsby, Red and the Boston Bean stepped out and formed a line. They stood with heels together, their heads up and shoulders back. Five of the most deadly guns in the Orient. The Afghans went down like leaves blown from the trees in the fall. Other Afghans heard the sustained firing and started toward that deadly line without the slightest hesitation. But a Chinese company came running up and the Afghans had to stop and fight.

AN HOUR later Jimmie Cordie held up his right arm, signalling a halt. They were in the hills three miles away from what Red called regretfully, "wan damn' fine Donnybrook Fair."

"What is it, Jimmie?" asked Grigsby.

"I'll have to take it slower. My side is giving me hell and high water."

"It is?" demanded Red. "Why the heck didn't ye say so, ye poor half-pint av nothin'? Get on the back av me, Jimmie darlin'. 'Tis a feather ye are."

"I will not. I can walk if I take it slow. George, we better be hunting a hole, pronto. The Afghans will come right after us as soon as they mop up on the Chinese. From what I saw they won't be long doing it, either. How much ammunition have we?"

"What is in our belts and Colts. Shih-kai knows a pass that will take us in about three hours to a city a T'aip'ing War Lord holds. The Afghans will stick around trying for the treasure before they start after us. Better let Red or me carry you, old kid."

"No, I can make it. My side seems easing up."

Red came up. "Jimmie, how about the gold and diamonds and jewels and all? Have we lost them?"

"Did we ever have them, Mr. Dolan?" asked Jimmie, gravely.

"We did not—and well ye know it, ye scut."

"Well then, can one lose what one never had? Think that over."

Red walked along for a minute or so, then announced, " 'Tis right ye are, Jimmie alanna."

Less than three hour later, coming out of the pass, they saw a regiment leaving a walled city on the double. One of the T'aip'ing had gone ahead and told the War Lord, who was approaching.

Colonel Tzu-lu had been carried in a litter alongside of the one that bore Shih-kai. The blow that had knocked him out had been a hard one delivered by the Yid's forty-five, but he was in good physical trim, hard as nails and young. As the litter was put down on the ground he got up and stood swaying a little, regaining his clearness of brain.

Jimmie Cordie saw him and came over. The young colonel tried hard to click his heels together and straighten his shoulders back, but could not quite make it.

"God's plan, Captain Coldie," he said, with a little smile.

"Quite right. I will take the jades, Colonel Tzu-lu."

"I am mole than glad that I was able to keep them fol you." He handed the statuettes to Jimmie. Now he had full control of himself, and as he handed them over, he bowed.

"Thank you." Jimmie took them. "If you go back to what was once your regiment, what will happen to you, Colonel Tzu-lu?"

Tzu-lu laughed, a real little laugh. There was no fear in his eyes.

"I doubt if I have a legiment to go back to, Captain Coldie."

"And if you went back to the city of Mengtze and reported the loss of the regiment as well as the jades and the treasure?"

"I much plefel going back to the Afghans, Captain Coldie. The Lold Chung is melciless to failule. I would be boiled in oil, ol given the death of the thousand cuts."

"Then—once I suggested that you carry the jades to Yen Yuan, the T'aip'ing chief. Again I suggest that you make a personal presentation of them to him, coming with us to do it." As he spoke, Jimmie handed the statuettes back to Tzu-lu.

The young colonel drew a long breath as his hand went out for the jades. A few hours before he had been a man about to die by Afghan swords or by torture. Now this smiling, black-eyed soldier of fortune had given him back his life, and with it the protection and friendship of the powerful T'aip'ing society, with which he could rise high in any service, if not in theirs.

He tucked the jades back under his tunic as Jimmie said, "This for treating Lieutenant-Commander Carewe and me—as you would wish to be treated."

"You have given me mole than I can evel lepay, and flom now on—"

Jimmie grinned and held up his hand. "I think the Command-er-in-Chief of us all, whose one plan takes precedence, is the One who should be offered thanks, Colonel Tzu-lu."

AZTEC TREASURE

Temple riches beckoned to Jimmie Cordie and his fellow adventurers—yet they knew a Guatemalan jungle trap awaited them

"**I SAW IT,** I tell you! At the top of the temple. A room five times as big as this cabin, full of gold things and jewels! I had some of them in my hands when— Look out for the jaguar men! The swamp came up and—and— Heads up, Winton! There's a snake! Kill it quick. I—I—"

The delirious man fell back in the bed to which he had been carried after being rescued from a raft in the Gulf of Honduras off the coast of Guatemala.

The lookout of a yacht off Bonacca Island, en route for Belize, had picked up the raft and half an hour later the man on it had been put to bed after first aid treatment. He needed the first aid badly. There were two unhealed wounds, one on his right leg and the other on his head. His skin was burned black, his body frightfully emaciated.

"Is he dead, Jimmie?" asked a big red-headed man standing by the bed.

A slim, black-eyed man leaned over and felt the heart of the derelict, who for an hour had been raving about Aztec and Mayan temples that were surrounded by swamps, about big snakes, men who were jaguars, and treasure carried from Mexico City on *La Noche Triste*.

"No," answered Jimmie Cordie. "His heart is still beating but he's darn near it. Hand me that brandy. I'll see if I can get some of it down his—wait a minute. Put it down, Red. He's gone west."

159

*The jaguar
men attacked
fanatically.*

Jimmie Cordie straightened up and looked down at the skeleton-like face of the dead man. "Sorry, old-timer," he said, gently. "We did the best we could for you, but your number was up."

"Jimmie," asked Red Dolan, "what the hell is this *La Noche Triste* thing he was wah wahin' about?"

"*La Noche Triste?* That means the sad night, Red. The night the Aztecs were driven out of Mexico City by the Spaniards. Quite a long while before our time."

"Yeah? And what is all this stuff about gold plates and jewels? Was he goofy, Jimmie?"

"I guess he was, Red. Partly, anyway. From the looks of him he went through enough to make any one that way."

Jimmie covered the body with the top sheet and as he was doing it, Red Dolan picked up a cured skin bag that had been tied around the man's neck with a sinew cord. Jimmie Cordie had taken it off and put it on a little table by the bed while giving first aid.

"What do you think is in it, Jimmie?" Red asked.

"I don't know, Red. Maybe-so something he found. Wait till we get on deck. Do you remember what he said about an old stone fort at the mouth of the river he came down? I was too darn busy holding him down to pay much attention."

"He said they chased him all the way down the river and where it opened up in some damn gulf the current swept him in close to an old stone fort where they almost got him. And who

the hell 'they' are, I dunno."

"I don't either, Red," Jimmie answered, absently. "Let's go."

SIX MEN sat on the quarter deck of the yacht. The bag rested on a table, and what it had contained was beside it. A chunky little gold figurine, intricately carved. All of the men were smooth shaven and dressed in immaculate yachting linens. All were deeply bronzed by sun and wind. As they sat lazily in their deck chairs, at first glance they looked much the same as any group of well groomed men of leisure who were guests on a palatial private yacht would look.

A second glance would have disclosed that there was something about the eyes and the hard bitten faces of the men that promptly put them out of the leisure class. Jimmie Cordie, their admitted leader, was typical—ex-sergeant, Foreign Legion; captain of machine gun company, A.E.F., and since the war, fighter in the far places where bullets and steel make and execute the laws.

Beside him sat John Cabot Winthrop, who owned the yacht. Foreign Legion; lieutenant of Jimmie Cordie's company, A.E.F., and soldier of fortune in the Orient. Known as the Boston Bean, or Codfish, or Beaneater, or by any other name that could even remotely suggest Boston.

Next to the Boston Bean there sat The Fighting Yid, who had been born on Hester Street in New York, and named Abraham Cohen. The Yid had fought as a machine gun sergeant in the A.E.F., and since for any war lord or potentate who needed his services. If the Yid could not find one that did, he would try to make contact with the Boston Bean and go somewhere for whatever they thought they wanted.

There was Red Dolan—two hundred and thirty pounds of fighting Irish and none of it fat. Foreign Legion, lieutenant of M.P. during the war, and as close to Jimmie Cordie as was possible since the day he saw him in the Legion. Red had a simple rule of life. He would ask Jimmie, "How about that, Jimmie?" or "What now, ye scut?" The answer always satisfied Red. Terrence Aloysius Dolan, born in Cork, Ireland, would fight anything at any time. Mr. Dolan, outside of the two questions he would ask Jimmie Cordie, had a suggestion he would always make irrespective of odds. It was: "Aw, let's slap 'em the hell outta the way."

There was John Cecil Carewe—Englishman, ex-commander of the Royal Essex Flight Squadron. Slim and boyish-looking with clean cut, aristocratic features—a simon-pure, natural born flyer. On the outside, no two men could be more different than Red Dolan and John Cecil Carewe. Inside, they were as alike as two peas in a pod so far as love of fighting and absolute disregard for odds against them went.

Sitting at Jimmie's right was a big man with broad shoulders and lean flanks. George Kenneth Grigsby, Breathitt County, Kentucky. Foreign Legion, major of infantry, A.E.F., and known in the Orient among soldiers of fortune as "a damn good man to be with." To the rest of the reckless adventurers, Grigsby was as a sheet anchor to windward. He fought as he lived, silently and with a little smile on his lips and in his eyes.

The Boston Bean's yacht was the third or fourth that he had owned, the others having been lost in Chinese waters while the Bean, as he put it, was "fussin' around." The Bean was a millionaire several times over, thanks to various relations who had left him their money, and he bought yachts whenever he thought he needed one. He also lost them with the same air of indifference. About all he ever said was, "Well, I never liked her anyway."

The yacht had cleared for Belize, British Honduras, where Mrs. John Cabot Winthrop was visiting relations in the English service stationed there.

In Hong Kong, the Bean had received the order: "Come and get me, John." By dint of much persuasion he had managed to get the rest of "Jimmie Cordie's Outfit" to make the trip with him by way of Panama Canal.

Tired of Oriental fighting and intrigue, they had agreed to be the Boston Bean's guests. The Fighting Yid announced, though, "Vonce I get it on board I do nothing but sit und reach for high vons. I took it von trip for a rest mit you und Mrs. Admiral, und met it mit a typhoon and pirates und everything. Dis time, no matter vot happens, I am de rester of de gang."

The Yid referred to Mrs. John Cabot Winthrop when he spoke of "Mrs. Admiral," and a trip they had made when one of the Bean's yachts had been carried onto an island by a tidal wave.

JIMMIE CORDIE spoke. "And that was what Red and I got out of his ravings. No question but what he was crazy. But how much of it was truth and how much was goofiness?"

The Boston Bean picked up the figurine.

"It's the Aztec Wind God. That much is true, anyway, Jimmie."

"Well—personally I think that he found an Aztec treasure, and there is no doubt but what he got chased away from it by some outfit. The question is—will we, won't we, will we?"

The Boston Bean grinned and called to a sailor who was polishing brass work at the rail near the stern. "My compliments to Captain Paulet, and will he report to me here?"

"My word," Carewe said. "You seem to be able to translate that giddy 'will we, won't we, will we' thing, Beaneater. I say, Jimmie, are we going to take a shot at the jolly old treasure, what, what?"

Jimmie grinned. "I don't know, Jonathan. Far be it from me to drag you gents off a perfectly good yacht to go treasure hunting in Guatemalan swamps. But if it is the Aztec treasure, I'd sure like to see it."

"You know it dot country?" demanded the Yid. "Vell, I do. Vonce me and anodder guy goes broke on de Pacific side und ve decides to valk across to de Atlantic. Oi, vot didn't happen to us. In de rivers dare is alligators mit mouths a yard long mit sharp teeth all over dem, und dare is de *corali*, de *toboba*, de *culebra de sangre* and odder snakes, all vorse dan de rattler, und plenty of rattlers to go mit dem. And den dare is snakes as long as dis hooker und as big around as Red. Und bugs—oi, forty-nine million of dem, und all vid stickers as long as a dagger. In de swamps dare is—"

"Stop and take another breath, Yid," Jimmie advised. "We have gathered so far that you don't care much for Guatemala."

"I don't," answered the Yid firmly. "Und I have lost it nothing dare to go und hunt for. Poppa stays mit de ship."

"Well, ye Yid, flat-faced duck," Red said scornfully, "have I lived to see the day that ye are scared to go anywhere? Stay here, then, and Jimmie and me will go and get the treasure. And divil a smell av it will ye have, ye—"

"Find it first, Irish goniff," the Yid interrupted with a smirk.

Captain Paulet arrived from the bridge, and Red decided that the Yid could wait. Red wanted to hear the orders given the captain.

"Has the body been prepared for burial, captain?" the Bean asked.

"Yes, sir."

"We will hold the service here, then. Afterward we will turn, and— Have you the position we were in when we picked up the raft?"

"Yes, sir. It is logged."

"Very good. After the burial, get back on it."

Captain Paulet, a calm, blue-eyed Englishman who had commanded a mine sweeper in the North Sea, smiled as he went back to the bridge. He had also commanded other yachts for the Boston Bean.

CHAPTER II

A SPY REPORTS

THE AZTEC TEMPLE stood in the middle of a cleared space about half a mile square. From the edge of the jungle there was a slight depression of the ground on all sides of the square. If seen from the air, the temple would give the impression of sitting in the middle of a big saucer.

It stood on a base of stone, two hundred feet long and about seventy-five feet high, approached by stone stairways on all four sides. Wide steps, fifty feet long and two feet high led up to the square cut temple. The roof was supported by pillars carved as serpents. The temple looked to be very old, but in a perfect state of repair.

At the top of the east stairs there stood a man, whose statue-like figure was naked save for a short skirt made of brilliantly dyed feathers. The man's face was eagle-like in its arrogant fierceness, his skin a golden bronze.

At the man's feet knelt an Indian, who was also naked except for a loin cloth. Beside the Indian there lay the skin of a jaguar, the head and body perfectly preserved.

"You may speak," the standing man said coldly.

"The one we pursued escaped us, lord."

There was no change in the questioner's eyes as he asked, "How?"

"We came on him at the river just as he was getting on a raft that he had built. He killed the first of us to reach him, and then, twice wounded, he got on the raft and floated down the river. We had to stop and build—"

"Silence. At the stone fort that the Spaniards built? Why was he not finished there?"

"Those of us that went along the banks reached there before he did, mighty priest, and the current bore him in. But a wind came and swept the raft out into the shoreless waters."

"How badly was he wounded?"

"He could not have lived until the sun went down, lord."

"So now," the standing man, who was the high priest of the temple, said, a cold menace in his voice, "the time has come when the jaguar men come and tell of escapes from their claws! Many things have happened since the temple of the great emperor was guarded by a thousand priests and thousands of dogs like you, but this is the first time the jaguar men have failed."

"We only came on him at the river bank, lord," the kneeling Indian answered. "Word was not brought us until—"

"There is no explanation," interrupted the high priest. "Come with me and ask Ah Puch, Lord of Death, to decide your punishment."

The Indian rose, his eyes and face showing a deadly fear. He knew what that, "Ask the Lord of Death" meant.

"WAIT, MIGHTY one," he stammered. "It may be that I can still serve the lord and that the all-powerful one will forget my having once failed. Many years have I served, and—" He saw by the expression in the priest's eyes that he was wasting his breath in pleading. He stopped talking and knelt again. "I have news, lord. And only I know where they are. If my life is spared I can—"

"Where they are? Where who are, dog?"

"The other white men. They came up—"

"Other white men? Rise and tell me. It may be that it will not be necessary for you to ask the lord to decide your punishment. Start at the beginning and tell me."

The Indian, a sub-chief of the jaguar men, rose. "Word was brought to me that a boat was coming up the river containing white men, many of them. I went to where the water comes down over rocks, where no boat may go, and waited to see if they came that far. They did, lord, and then the boat turned—"

"How many of them?"

"Eight, lord. But two remained with the boat and took it down the river."

"How are the men who remained armed?"

"With rifles and small guns, mighty one."

"What did they do after the small boat went away?"

"They made camp there on the river bank."

"Then what?"

"Then they searched along the banks, on both sides."

"How did they get across the river?"

"They made a raft and poled it across. Two of them. A big man with hair that flamed in the sun and a smaller man with hair the color of night. But the rest found what they were seeking near where the small boat landed them."

"What was it?"

"The place where the one who escaped made his raft."

"Then," the high priest said slowly, "he lived—and told them. Then what did they do?"

"They circled and acted as hunting dogs act when trying to pick up the scent."

"They circled? And no snakes struck at them?"

"Many snakes struck, lord, but none of them lived to bury their fangs. The white men shot with the little guns without aiming and the snakes died."

"They circled—then what?"

"Then one of them cried out and the rest ran to him. He pointed to something on the ground and they talked about it. I was too far away to hear, lord, or to see what they pointed at. They went back to their camp and rolled the hammocks they slept in, put them on their backs and started into the jungle."

"They carry nothing more than hammocks?"

"No, lord. Unless they carry other things in the packs on their backs. They wear many belts full of cartridges."

"Where are they now?"

"This morning at dawn they had reached the three trees that fork where the swamp begins. They made camp there last night."

"The one who escaped must have left a broad path, that they follow easily. Why did not the jaguar men attack?"

"Lord, there were only ten of us. Many more have been sent for—"

"Why did not the ten attack?"

"Because, lord, the white men are never unguarded. Two always stand on watch. Their guns are always ready."

"You are afraid of the white men. Wait until those you have sent for come, then attack. See that you are not afraid any more, or those with you. Take them alive if possible and bring them to me."

"We will attack to-night, lord. There will be enough of us to take them alive."

"Go, then. I will intercede with Ah Puch, the Lord of Death, for you—but if you fail this time, Ah Puch will demand that you be punished."

THE INDIAN bowed his head to the feet of the high priest, then ran down the stairs.

The high priest watched him until he disappeared into the jungle, then turned and walked into the temple. Once inside, he went up a short flight of stairs and into a room that opened onto a balcony.

He faced an old man, dressed as the high priest was, with the exception of a fillet of gold around his head, from which rose two golden serpents, their bodies twined, their heads apart with mouths open, showing fangs of some white metal.

This formidable patriarch looked up and asked, "What was it, Tuxtl-Xiu?"

"One of the chiefs of the jaguar men," answered the priest curtly, sitting down on a three-legged stool. "He told that the one who escaped from the temple also escaped on a raft. He told of six white men who are following the tracks made by the one who escaped. They are already at the swamp on the west."

"What of it?" snarled the old man. "Many white men have got that far—and farther—and never have any of them gone back to where they came from—save the one who escaped eight suns ago. How did he get through the water? The other who was with him could not."

"I do not know," answered the high priest. "You, who are my uncle, and very wise, should know. This I do know. The jaguar men are not as they were in other days. Who could have escaped their claws then? Now they are weak, as we are. Once the temple held a thousand priests. Now, you and I and two others guard the sacred trust. I have been thinking that it would be better if we released the water and let it cover the—"

"No," interrupted the old man, rising. "No! I, Xolotl of the royal line, say it. Never! As long as there remains one to work the levers, never! When there is but one left, he may, according to the order of the emperor. Never in four hundred years have the Lord of the World's orders been disobeyed by the loyal ones. What if the jaguar men are weak? You are strong—and so are we, the old ones, when need arises. You are high priest, but I—I am Xolotl! Remember that, high priest."

"I remember it, royal one," answered the high priest humbly.

"See that you do. Go and see that the levers work smoothly."

CHAPTER III

THE ATTACK

"**VELL,**" **SAID THE** Fighting Yid, as he looked around at
the camp made on a little knoll in the jungle, "it is vot I call neat
but not gaudy, ain't it, Jimmie?"

Jimmie Cordie looked at the six hammocks, swung from
poles cut a few minutes before, and then at the little fire. "Well,
it's neat, anyway, Yid. You were right about one thing, Old Kid
Cohen, and that was about the ten million and six bugs."

"Vait," the Yid answered. "You ain't seen no bugs yet. Vait till
ve get it deeper in de swamp."

"I will," promised Jimmie as he rolled a cigarette. "Why don't
you try to scrape some of that mud off yourself?"

"Vot? Scrape it de mud off! Oi, vot a suggestion. I vish I had
about a foot more of it on me. De more mud, de less I get it
bitten."

"Who is biting you, Mr. Cohen?" asked the Boston Bean,
sitting down beside Jimmie Cordie.

"Who ain't? My, I vish I stayed on de yacht."

Jimmie and the Boston Bean laughed. They knew that the
only thing that could have held the Fighting Yid on the yacht
would have been chains.

Red Dolan, hearing Jimmie laugh, walked over from the fire.
"What was that about the yacht?" he asked.

"I said dot I vished dot I had stayed mit," the Yid answered.

"Well, why the hell didn't ye?" Red demanded, sitting down.

"Vell, I thought, 'My, my, dare goes it Mrs. Dolan's little boy,
Red, out to de snakes und de vild cats und everything. I better
go mit und hold his hand so dot de bad pussycats don't scratch
him.' Now you know de how come, Mistaire Dolan."

"Is that so?" Red asked. "Well, let me tell ye something. Any time a Dolan needs the likes av a Yid gibboon like ye to—"

Jimmie laughed and rose. "Tell it to him plainly, Red, so that he will understand. I've heard it before, so I'll go and visit with George."

Grigsby smiled as Jimmie sat down near the fire. "Still enthused about the end of the rainbow, Jeems?"

"Same as ever," Jimmie answered with a grin. "What's a few snakes and a little mud compared to the treasure of the Aztecs?"

"Nothing at all," Grigsby agreed. "But, at that, Jimmie, it doesn't sound good to me."

"What doesn't sound good to you?" Jimmie answered lazily. "We found the old fort, we tested out the current and found that it would bring a raft in close, we got up to the rapids and found where he had built a raft and up to date we haven't had a darn bit of trouble in following the path he made through the jungle. If the rest is as easy, we'll hit the temple right smack in the eye pretty soon."

Grigsby laughed. "That's the boy, James. Keep the rose-colored glasses on as long as you can. I didn't mean what we had done. I meant that this talk about Aztec temples way down here in Guatemala containing treasure doesn't sound so hot to me."

"Why?"

"Well, figure it out, Jimmie. In the first place, it is all of seven hundred miles from here to Mexico City. Why should the Aztecs bring treasure way down here to hide it? Within a radius of fifty miles from the city there are hundreds of places where they could have hidden all the treasure they ever had."

"That's right, George. But here's a couple of things to think about. In the first place, there was a system of perfect roads running from Mexico City in all directions and still a perfect system farther away than this neck of the woods. I remember that in history."

"That's right, Jimmie. They had perfect roads. Go ahead."

"The Aztecs also had unlimited man power, George. Cortez writes that the natives were as thick as bees around a honey-pot."

"That's right, they did."

"Well, given perfect roads and unlimited man power, distance did not enter into their calculations. Here is another thing, George. Some of their temples may have been more sacred than others and also more safe at the moment as far as loyal Indian tribes went. The Spaniards had got to a lot of the tribes who turned on the Aztecs as soon as they saw the Spaniards had a chance. So, all in all, I don't think it is so darn much of a wild-goose chase. Given we can find the temple, I'll bet we'll find treasure."

Grigsby laughed. "We've tried to catch wild geese before, Jimmie. What are you going to do with your share of Montezuma's treasure?"

"Buy me a place on Long Island and raise little white ducks," Jimmie answered with a grin. "I've always wanted to— Heads up!"

AS HE spoke, his .30-30 detonated. The instant reaction of the soldiers of fortune was automatic. Red, the Yid and the Bean rose and ran in a little, then turned and faced out. Carewe, who had been dozing by the fire, was on his feet as quickly. He saw Grigsby step aside and then go around Jimmie Cordie and turn. Carewe took three steps and the tight little circle was complete. It had need to be done swiftly, for from the dense jungle all around the knoll, there came the hurtling charge of what looked like great jaguars. Jaguars that ran on two legs.

And as they charged, the body of one of them was falling from a tree where Jimmie Cordie's eyes had picked him out. The long black body was perfectly crouched on the limb, but the man the skin concealed had got just a little bit careless. A three-pronged knife protruded a little from beneath the jaguar skin. Enough for the prongs to be seen. Jimmie Cordie's keen eyes, trained to note the slightest variation from normal, saw the prongs and the next instant the man paid for his carelessness with his life.

The sub-chief had not intended to attack before dark, but as the shot came, knowing that all chances of surprise had gone, he ordered the jaguar men to close in.

There were many of them, enough to form a large circle, three or four deep, and they came in fast. Many of them tossed the jaguar skins to one side and charged naked save for their loin cloths, the three-pronged knives their only weapons. Others kept the skins on, the forepaws hooked together around the neck, the head just over the wearer's.

The attack was fast and silent, but it was met with a sleet of steel-jacketed bullets from six Winchesters in the hands of men who could all qualify for the Distinguished Marksman medal and who were absolutely unafraid.

The Yid, who generally talked as he fought, began, "Oi, von for you—und von for you—und von for you—und—vat, am I missing? Dot's de boy, fall down for poppa. Red, here is de pussy-cats come to scratch you. Und von for—" and so on.

Before the charge had got halfway it slackened, wavered and broke, then became a retreat. The sub-chief had not been hit and had run with the rest. But once in the shelter of the jungle, remembering what the high priest had said about the Lord of Death, he succeeded in forcing the jaguar men to charge again.

"What the hell kind av wild men are they, Jimmie?" asked Red during the pause.

"Just ordinary men, Red," Jimmie answered, "wearing jaguar skins. Like the leopard men in Africa. That pronged knife they're packing is meant to be the jaguar's claws. Not much good against rifles. At close quarters it would be a nasty thing to try and ward—here they come!"

THIS TIME the charge was much slower and made by little units of two or three jaguar men, with quite a lot of space between units. But that formation made it worse for them. It gave the circle of rifles time to destroy unit after unit, as method-ically and accurately as a machine cuts out patterns.

The Boston Bean stood with a bored expression on his face

and a "you be damned" look in his eyes. It was the Boston Bean's usual expression when he was having an extra pleasant time. His Winchester was going *bang, bang, bang,* like the tick of a clock.

Red Dolan was attending strictly to business, which he always did when fighting, his cheek against rifle stock, a cold fire in his blue eyes.

Carewe, Jimmie Cordie and George Grigsby stood as if on the target range, their deadly rifles almost as fast as machine guns.

The jaguar men did not get halfway in the second charge before they broke and ran. The anger of the high priest and the Lord of Death's punishment was to be dreaded, but here was death close at hand reaching out for them. This time, after they gained the shelter of the jungle, those of the jaguar men who reached it kept right on running—and in the opposite direction from the temple.

The sub-chief had been hit by a bullet from Carewe's rifle but not killed. It had smashed his collar bone on the right side and knocked him off his feet. As the rout came past him he got up on his knees and tried to get to his feet, but could not make it. A smashed collar bone makes the body very sick and the sub-chief sank back to the ground.

"Let 'em run," Jimmie Cordie said, lowering his rifle. "I'll go and bring one of our new boy friends in. Maybe-so we can get a line on the temple. You gents cover me."

"I'll go wid ye, Jimmie," Red said promptly.

"Come on. We'll get the one who tried to get up."

The sub-chief saw them coming and again tried for his feet, this time to fight. But he was too sick to make it and fell back in a faint.

"Vy didn't you get it a live von?" asked the Yid, as Red eased the sub-chief to the ground.

"We didn't see any," Jimmie answered. "This bird has only passed out of the picture for a little while. Break out that first aid kit, Codfish. Yid, get that flask of brandy I know darn well you have stacked somewhere."

A half hour later the sub-chief sat with his back to a tree. His shoulder had been given first aid and he had two big drinks of brandy in him which made him feel much less sick. After he had regained consciousness he had submitted to the first aid without a struggle and had swallowed the brandy, yet all the time his black eyes were like those of the beast whose skin had covered him.

Now, as he sat against the tree, he glared at the white men who sat in a half circle in front of him. He looked at them all, one after the other, at their weapons and at the heavy belts of ammunition, and each of the white men, as the sub-chief's eyes met theirs, knew that he was not afraid of them.

FINALLY, JIMMIE Cordie spoke. "Why do you attack us, O man who wears the skin of a jaguar?" It was in perfect Spanish.

The sub-chief answered promptly. "We attack all who come unasked into our country, white man. You have driven off a few of us, but there are many more. As many as the leaves on this tree. Soon your bullets will be all shot and then you will feel the jaguar's claws."

"It may be," Jimmie answered. "We have many bullets to shoot, O jaguar man. We go to the temple in the swamp. Where is it?"

"I know of no temple."

"That is too bad," Jimmie answered, slowly drawing his Colt. "If you did, and could guide us to it, you would not have to go into the cold darkness. Can the jaguar men who are as the leaves of this tree ward off from you the bullet that will come from this gun to tear through your heart when I reach the count of three?"

"No," the sub-chief answered calmly. "Shoot, white man. I am not afraid to go into the cold darkness."

Jimmie Cordie brought the Colt up on a line with the sub-chief's heart and began a slow count, "One—two—"

The Indian's eyes were as steady as ever as he looked straight into Jimmie's. Jimmie Cordie laughed and holstered the Colt.

"You win, old kid."

And as he said it, the Boston Bean's Colt detonated. He was sitting crosslegged at the right end of the semicircle. For a split second every one, even the sub-chief, thought that the Bean had shot at the man who had called Jimmie Cordie's bluff. The Bean's gun looked to be on a line with the sub-chief's stomach.

Then they saw what the Bean had shot at. The headless body of a *culebra de sangre*, one of the most deadly smaller snakes of Central America, was twisting and writhing within six inches of the sub-chief's left leg. The *culebra de sangre* bite is death—and a frightful one—no matter what is done for the person bitten.

The sub-chief glanced down at the snake, his face as impassive and Indian-like as when he was looking at Jimmie Cordie—but he could not keep his eyes that way. Jimmie Cordie saw the look of fear which lasted the infinitesimal part of a second.

"He was coiled to strike," the Bean said. "Sorry if I startled you gentlemen. There wasn't time to explain that I thought I had better shoot. He may have been harmless, at that."

"Vot?" the Yid demanded. "Harmless? Oi, Codfisher, dot vos a *culebra de sangre*. Von bite from dot baby und Mary bar it de door. Und how you die. Mit de bends und mit froth at de—"

"Never mind the symptoms, Mr. Cohen," Jimmie said, rising. "I think I'll keep on my feet if they sneak up on you that way. Are there many of them here?" The question was to the sub-chief, who had edged away from the still twitching body.

"Yes," answered the sub-chief. "Many of them, white man."

"Und vare dare is von, dare is more. Dey hunt it in packs like dogs. Und dey strike at anything dot is on de ground vot is alive. Red, come close to poppa. I von't let de—"

"Cut it, Yid," Jimmie said curtly. So curtly that the rest looked at him in surprise. All but the sub-chief, who was looking at the body of the snake. "Let's be getting out of here," Jimmie went on, in Spanish. "We will leave this jaguar man here. It may be that his friends will come and carry him to safety."

The Yid translated for the Bean and Red who stood close, and added: "Jimmie is making a play."

Grigsby understood Spanish and said to Carewe, "Jimmie says we pull out. He's seen something we haven't."

THE SUB-CHIEF sat against the tree and watched the white men go to their hammocks, roll them, adjust their packs and pick up their rifles. Once he tried to get on his feet but sank back.

Jimmie Cordie came over to him. "Good-by, man who wears the jaguar skin. We go to the temple. Do not disturb the bandages around your shoulder for three days. Then take them off and wash the wound in fresh, clean water."

The sub-chief looked up at him, opened his mouth as if to speak, then shut it.

Jimmie grinned down at him and walked away. The sub-chief watched the little column start down the knoll and then looked around at the ground. Suddenly he yelled. "White men! Quick! Come back! Another comes! Quick or I am a dead man!" Another *culebra de sangre* was almost to the body of the first one.

Jimmie Cordie turned and looked at the live snake. "Why should we kill for you, jaguar man?" he called.

That broke the Indian's courage. He had seen men die after being bitten by a *culebra de sangre*. That and his wound and his sickness. He had faced Jimmie Cordie's gun bravely. But he had always been afraid of the *culebra de sangre*. Always since the day when he, as a child of six, had seen his father die from the bite of one.

"Kill!" he yelled. "I will tell you! Kill, white man!"

Jimmie Cordie's right hand flashed to the butt of his Colt .45 and the gun roared as the muzzle cleared the holster. It was a hip shot and one that demonstrated why Jimmie Cordie was noted wherever soldiers of fortune gather.

The snake had coiled, and the vicious head was poised for the forward dart when Jimmie Cordie started the draw. It was so fast that the snake's head never got started. A second headless body twisted and jerked on the ground.

"You gents stay here," Jimmie said, holstering his Colt. "I'll go up and talk to him. I thought that would break him.

"Well, jaguar man," he said, as he reached the tree, "we killed for you. But we cannot stay here and do it until you are able to walk. Do you want us to put you up in the tree?"

"No. There are tree snakes who would— Why do you seek the temple of the Aztecs, white man?"

"To take the treasure away from those who have guarded it for many hundreds of years," Jimmie answered calmly. "You are not Aztec. Why should you take the bite of a *culebra de sangre* for a people who are no more?"

Now, in the days long gone past, that would have had no effect on one of the jaguar men. In those days, when the Aztecs ruled all of Central America, which was all the world as far as the Indians knew, all natives firmly believed that Aztec vengeance could and would reach out to the end of the world for them.

But to the sub-chief the Aztecs were, after all, only a tradition, as was the former glory of the jaguar men. He had been in Belize and in Guatemala City, this sub-chief, and had seen white men and their way of living. He knew that instead of a thousand priests at the temple, there were only four, and those, three of them, old men. No regiments of plumed soldiers, no inner and outer ring of thousands of native warriors. Only a few jaguar men who had heard what their fathers told of past glories.

So the sub-chief, who wanted to live, answered Jimmie Cordie, American soldier of fortune. "If I direct you to the temple, white man, what will you do for me?"

"What do you want done for you?"

"This. I am to be taken to the river and there a raft is to be made for me. I am to be given one of the small guns and food. I am to be placed on the raft and the raft sent out in the current. I will take care of myself after that. Down the river there are people who will take care of me. People who do not fear the high priest."

"How will I know that you have given me the right directions, jaguar man?"

"There is a road of stone, built many years ago, that leads to it. It is not far from here. Not through the swamps, but along high ground. I will tell you how to reach it. Send some of the other white men to find it. Once on it, follow it to the temple. In places it is deep in the jungle growth, but it can be traced."

"All right," Jimmie answered. "There are other small guns in the packs, and we will give you one with a belt of ammunition. We will do as you ask—after we have seen the road of stone."

"I do this because I know that if I go back and tell of failure the high priest will cast me to the Lord of Death."

"You are wise, jaguar man. Tell me how to get to the road."

The sub-chief told him. As a matter of fact, he, the sub-chief, did not think it made much difference whether the white men reached the temple or not. He knew what the priests would do.

CHAPTER IV

THIS TRAP IS SPRUNG

"**VELL,**" **THE VID** said, three days later, as he parted the undergrowth and looked through the hole at the temple, "he vasn't stringing us. Dare she is."

The three-day journey along the stone road had been a comparatively easy one for the six adventurers who were trained to the minute and used to worse places. They advanced slowly with alert eyes and ready guns. There were plenty of snakes, and more than once the snarling charge of jungle cats had been stopped by bullets. At times they had to leave the roadbed and go around the thick impassable tangle of jungle growth, but they always got back on it.

The snakes were bad and, as the Yid said, the bugs were "badder," but at last they made it to the saucer-like depression and, doing as the Yid had done, saw the temple.

"That's right, Mr. Cohen," the Boston Bean answered. "Without doubt, there she is."

"What are you waiting for, Jeems?" asked Grigsby, as Jimmie showed no evidence of being in a hurry to cross the cleared space.

"No likee," Jimmie answered with a grin. "It isn't according to Hoyle, if you're asking me. That left-hand end of the clearing is a darn sight higher than the right, George."

"And what has that got to do wid us goin' across?" went on Red. "There she is, and here we are. Come on."

"Wait a minute, Mr. Dolan. It has too much of 'will you walk into my parlor, said the spider to the fly,' to suit Mr. Cordie's son Jimmie. In all the stories I ever read about this treasure hunting thing down in this man's country, we ought to see eight million priests buzzing around."

"What is it, Jimmie?" Grigsby asked. "You think it is a trap?"

"I don't know, George. It's been too darn easy up to date. It is a cinch that the treasure, if it is there, is guarded by more than a few jaguar men."

"Well," the Boston Bean said, "there is one never-failing way to find out, and that is to go ahead and spring the said trap."

"For wance ye have said something, Beaney," Red approved. "Are ye sick, Jimmie darlin'?"

Jimmie laughed. "Far from it, Old Kid Dolan. Let's go. Spread out a little and heads up."

They walked across the cleared space to the temple steps without anything happening. The jungle and the temple seemed asleep in the hot sun and as if they had been that way for a thousand years. The Yid, in avoiding the rotting trunk of a tree, stepped into what seemed to be a mud hole, but it was not a deep one, and he said nothing about it.

At the beginning of the steps Jimmie halted. "Yid, go in and wake the sleeping beauty up."

"Let Red go und do it. I don't vant it no beauties, sleeping or oddervise."

"I'll go and wake her up," Red answered. "Her or whatever else is up there. Come on, Jimmie."

THEY CLIMBED the stairs, all of them with Winchesters at the ready, and then walked slowly across the stone paved court and into the temple.

"You know something, Beaneater?" the Yid asked.

"No. What?"

"I have got it a feeling dot ve are already in de trap."

"What you feel is cold feet, Mr. Cohen," answered the Boston Bean.

The Yid grinned and was about to say something when Red Dolan, who was on the extreme left of the line, using his flash light, shouted:

"Jimmie! Here it is! Mary Mother! A room full av gold!"

It wasn't a room, in the strict meaning of the word. It was more of an alcove just to the right of a great idol which sat on a polished black stone base. There was no door, and no attempt had been made to hide the treasure. It lay piled up like loosely thrown wood. Some of it was still in the skin bags it had been carried in. Most of the bags had rotted away and the contents spilled.

"The pot of gold at the end of the rainbow," Jimmie Cordie said softly, as the flash lights played on the almost incalculable wealth.

It was fully half an hour later that he laughed and put down a golden mask of Xipe, the Corn Goddess. The eyes were immense opals.

Grigsby saw Jimmie do it and straightened up. He laughed also.

"Let's get outside and clear our heads," Jimmie said. "Get all the gold plates ready, Red. George and I are going to cook dinner out on the balcony."

There were a great many idols along the walls of the temple, and the two men stopped to look at some of them.

"Some made of wood," Jimmie said, "and some are metal. Darned if I know what metal the Aztecs had besides gold and silver. Maybe-so they— Listen, doesn't that sound like running water to you?"

"It is, Jimmie. Outside the temple. Better go back and get the others. I think the trap is being sprung."

"I'll get 'em," Jimmie answered with a grin. He drew his Colt and fired a shot at the stone roof.

The shot did get Red, Carewe, the Yid and the Bean. Nothing else would. The sound registered in their brains and they came back from a golden world. As one man they dropped what they had in their hands, rose, drew their Colts and came out of the alcove like four torpedoes from the tubes of a submarine.

"What now, ye scut?" demanded Red as they reached Jimmie.

"Sorry to have to disturb you gentlemen in the counting of your wealth, but—listen."

"What the hell is it, Jimmie?"

"Darn good way to find out is to go and look. Sounds like Niagara Falls."

HURRIEDLY THEY went out of the temple, across the court and to the top of the steps. Jimmie looked as far around the clearing as he could, then said, quietly, "Well, they've sprung the trap."

The entire depression was covered with dark, slimy water in which floated dead trees and the rot of the jungle. In it swam great alligators and snakes that looked as big as the ones the Yid had told about: "as long as dis hooker und as big around as Red."

On the dead trees there were jaguars and wild cats, *tigrilos*, monkeys, lizards and scorpions, all mixed together. The alligators and big snakes were so thick that the tree trunks were being constantly turned over, throwing the occupants into the already crowded water.

"It looks," the Boston Bean said calmly, "like a cross section of hell."

"What now, Jimmie?" demanded Red.

"I can't think of anything, Red. Unless it is to see if she goes all the way around the temple." Jimmie knew that it did, even as he spoke. And it did, all the way around the temple and to the very edge of the depression. They walked around the broad balcony that circled the temple and saw that it was the same on all four sides.

"How deep, Jimmie?" asked Carewe. "I should say about five feet."

Jimmie Cordie grinned. "What matter, Jonathan? No can swim and no can wade with those babies fussing around. We'll have to wait until she goes down."

"Oi," the Fighting Yid said, "vot vill ve did for fresh vater und eats? My, I vish I had stayed it on de yacht."

The rest laughed and the Bean said, "Don't worry, Mr. Cohen. As soon as we run out of iron rations we will dine on Hester Street Yid. You are the fattest and will be the first to go."

"Go down and get ye a drink," Red added. "See all the nice water that's—that tree is going to touch the steps! Jimmie, the tree!" They had come back to the stairs they had climbed up.

As Red shouted, he unslung his Winchester. A tree had floated in and touched the stairs, and the living cargo—two black jaguars—had promptly unloaded. They started in the only open direction—up the stairs—but died before they had taken three bounds.

"If one tree can do that, so can others," Jimmie said. "Six men and four stairways. One man for each and two as roundsmen. Take this one, Red. Get to the right, Carewe. Bean, you take the next and you the other, Yid. George and I will make the rounds. Snap into it, gents. If many cargoes like that land we'll

be playing pussy-in-the-corner with everything but the mort-
gage before long."

Not many minutes later, the Yid's rifle began to speak, after a
lusty yell of, "Corporal of de guard! Post number four! Corporal
of de guard! Quick mit de reserves. Two of dem has touched!"

Jimmie Cordie and George Grigsby were at the Bean's stair-
way when the Yid yelled and they got to him just in time. The
Kid, in trying to fill an immense boa constrictor so full of lead
that he could not climb stairs, had let two *tigrilos* get past him.
Not altogether past, but up to the step he was standing on. Both
of them were now crouched to spring.

"Oi, such a business," the Yid said, with a dour grin, as two
rifles were lowered. "I vas knocking off dot big beggar down dare
und dose two hellcats snuck it up on me from de side."

Jimmie Cordie laughed. "Well, Mr. Cohen, you better not
let 'em do much snucking up on you. If George and I had been
on the other side the hellcats would have been having Fighting
Yid for lunch about now."

"Und dare is more truth than poetry in dot," the Fighting Yid
answered cheerfully. "Go ahead, corporal of de guard. Poppa can
handle it now."

CHAPTER V

A MAD VENTURE

AS THEY WALKED along, Grigsby said, "Not so good,
Jimmie. We can't stop 'em at night, even if our flash lights hold
out."

"I know it. But if we hole up in the temple—what then? It
will be a madhouse when the snakes and what not get over their
fright and begin on each other. See the trap, George? Walk right
in, gentlemen, and take a look at the treasure—and then try to
walk out, with or without it."

Grigsby looked out over the teeming water and smiled, "Think of some other way, Jeems. The walking does not look very good—either with or without."

Jimmie studied the water. "It comes in between those two big trees at the left—about a hundred feet wide—and it's backing up at the right. There is higher ground to the left where there is a swamp held back by some kind of a dam. This place is on a slant, George. The Aztecs were engineers and knew all about hydraulics. They've got some kind of floodgates they can open and let the swamp in—and it's a cinch they've got other gates to the right that let it out. Holy cats, look at that tree. It's a young zoo. The priests must have a game preserve that they turn loose with the water."

"All of which is very interesting, Mr. Cordie, but does not get us out of here. No can stay, Jimmie."

Jimmie laughed. "We're between the well known devil and the deep sea, Mr. Grigsby. No can stay and no can go. I wonder how in heck the gent that we picked up got away. Maybe he did not get as far as the temple and—that's wrong. He said that he saw the treasure. If he got away, we ought to be—" They were passing a door as Jimmie got to the "ought to be." They had passed it before but as Jimmie spoke he stopped and looked in.

Despite the approaching darkness it was light enough to see without using flash lights and what Jimmie saw made him stop talking. Grigsby stepped to his side and looked in also. On the floor lay the bodies of two men, both white men. The bodies were wasted away and it was plain that the men had died of starvation quite recently.

"The fellow who got away spoke of a man named Winton," Jimmie said, "warning him to look out for a snake. These may be the men who were with him. But how he made it and they didn't is—"

"They can't tell us, Jimmie. Better get on with our own getting away."

"I'll see if they've got anything on them that will tell who they were. Maybe they have people who—"

Red's voice came to them: "Jimmie! George! Gimme a hand! The whole damn menagerie is coming up the stairs!"

Jimmie grinned. "Go ahead, George. I'll be there in a minute."

Red had exaggerated a little as to what was coming up the stairs, but, at that, there was plenty. Grigsby's rifle helped put up a steel-jacketed fence and when Jimmie Cordie arrived, his rifle finished it.

"One of the men was Winton," Jimmie said, as he sat down for a minute. "The other was named Carlington. They were—"

"What men?" demanded Red.

"We found two bodies in a room, Red," Jimmie answered, "and were looking them over when you hollered uncle."

"And so would ye have hollered, ye scut, if ye saw what I saw."

"I don't doubt, it. Here's the papers they had on 'em. Winton kept a diary. The last entry is: 'Bates is going to try it. There's not one chance in a thousand that he can make it. Carlington and I had rather die here. We can keep the beasts and snakes out of a room we have found.'"

"They didn't have the nerve to try it," Red announced. "What was 'it,' Jimmie?"

"Darned if I know, Red. I wish I did."

"And so do I. Wance night comes we'll be huntin' rooms ourselves. If the likes av him could—"

"Red," Jimmie interrupted, "you were listening to him while I was first aiding. Think back, old kid."

" 'Twas a lot of gibberish, Jimmie darlin'. Wance he thought he was talking to some other lads. Maybe-so the wans ye found. He was telling them that some damn thing was big enough to hold them all and he was bawlin' them out for not—"

"Well, for the love of Pete! It's about time my feeble brain began to squeak. I'll bet that's what he did. If they are—"

"Tell us, ye shrimp av the world," demanded Red. "Do ye

think we are mind readers? You wid the 'I'll bet that's what' and the 'they are.'"

JIMMIE LAUGHED as he rose, "It's a wild guess, Red, but here it is for you. Some of those big idols are made of wood and no doubt are hollow. My guess is that he rolled one of them down to the water, got in it and then floated across."

"Why wouldn't the water come in and drown him and how did he know he would float across or some big snake wouldn't come in and—"

"If I knew that I'd be the mind reader, Mr. Dolan. Keep your steps clear like a good housekeeper while George and I go and do a little inspecting of idols."

They stopped in front of one of the biggest idols, the full figure of a man, standing with folded arms, about ten feet high not counting the base and at least four feet broad from the hips up. Jimmie dug with his knife for a minute, then said, "Wood, all right, and I think—" He climbed up on the base and rapped the idol with his fist. "Yeah, hollow. The priests used to get in 'em and make talk for the natives. Let's see if we can up-end him, George."

They tried, but could only sway it. "I've got about as much strength as a jack rabbit," Jimmie finally announced. "I'll go and relieve Red. The two of you can do 'er."

A little later, Red came back to where Jimmie sat on the top step.

" 'Tis hollow," he said, "wid an open place in the back big enough for a man to get into."

"Any trapdoor or what not to the opening?"

"No. It was back to the wall. What the hell is seethin' in the mind av ye, Jimmie?"

"I'm going to get in and float across."

"Ye are what? Ye are like hell. If ye do, I'm going wid ye, ye black-muzzled omadhaun. Supposin' it don't ride high and—"

"Quit supposing and take this post. If I can make any kind

of a door that will fit tight enough to hold water out for a little while, I'm going."

"And me right along wid ye," interrupted Red firmly as he sat down. "After ye get across—I mean now, after we get across, what then, Jimmie darlin'?"

"We'll find their hydraulic plant and wreck it," Jimmie answered with a grin. "Wait until we get that thing across."

Jimmie went back to the idol which now was lying face down on the floor. In the back, just above the buttocks, there was a square-cut opening, large enough for a medium-sized man to get through.

Jimmie looked at it and laughed. "That lets Red out. He couldn't get one shoulder through."

"What's the idea, Jimmie?" Grigsby asked, quietly.

"Well, here it is, George. If we stay here we will be all washed up darn soon after dark. I'm going to whittle out a bulkhead for that opening and pack it with my shirt tail—no, that's wrong. After the bulkhead is made I'll get in and you gents can put the bulkhead on and pack it with your shirt tails so as to make her water-tight. A couple of holes can be drilled for air.

"Then you and Red carry Mr. Cordie and the idol down to the water and shove us off. If I make it to shore, I'll go and call on the priests or whoever is at the dingus that operates this trap. I may be able to persuade them or him to pull the switch. Then I'll stick around on the other side until you gents walk across with all the treasure you can pack. Simple, isn't it, Mr. Grigsby?"

"Very simple, Jeems. So very simple that it isn't worth a damn. Given that the idol will float with you in it—how do you figure it will float promptly to the shore line?"

"I don't figure it," Jimmie answered with a grin, "that's the beauty and simplicity of my plan. No figuring is required. I take it for granted."

GRIGSBY LAUGHED. "I see you still retain all of your well known carefulness, Jeems. What if five or six of those big alligators or snakes decided to play a little football with you and the idol out there or you get foul of a tree?"

"In either case," Jimmie answered solemnly, "it would be just too bad for old man Cordie's son Jimmie."

"No question about that. Another thing, Mr. Cordie. Given that you get to shore—do you think that you alone can, as you say, persuade the priests to pull the switch? All joking to one side, Jimmie, there are too many chances against you."

Jimmie Cordie grinned. " 'Man makes a thousand plans and God makes but one,' " he quoted an old Chinese saying. "Maybe God's plan is that I make 'er."

"Maybe-so, Jimmie," Grigsby said. "Let's go and put it up to the rest."

Ten minutes later, the six men sat in a little circle, at the top of the temple. The Fighting Yid was talking.

"Vot I don't see is vy we can't all take it idols und float over. Vot de hell is de use of—vait, I got it. I go mit Jimmie und den—"

"For Pete's sake!" Jimmie interrupted. "Don't start that again. Any one would think I was going to a—"

"I have an idea," Red interrupted in turn. "Take all the idols and put them wan on top av the other, makin' a raft. Load all the gold on it and pole it across. 'Tis an idea worthy av Saint Patrick."

"Darn right it is, Red," Jimmie answered. "Only trouble is that there are only three of the wooden idols and they'd sink under our weight. And there is no more wood around. The bases are all metal."

"Well, then, ye and—"

"Don't you start again either. My gosh, it's darn near dark, right now. If I don't make it, then Carewe can try in another idol. He's light enough to float high."

"All right, Jimmie," Grigsby said. "Let's get it settled. You go and take Carewe with you. Both of you can get in the idol. We'll shove you off and if you make the shore two of you can do a lot more than one."

"My word," Carewe said, his eyes shining. "I say, old thing, I'll never be able to thank you enough for giving me the chance. Jimmie and I will trail the giddy old rotters to their den, won't we, Jimmie? And then we'll—"

" 'Tis what I get for bein' a full-sized man," Red Dolan mourned. "Wan av me would make two scuts like—"

"Und vot about me?" demanded the Yid, peevishly. "If I vasn't built like de back of a sea-going hack I could—"

The Boston Bean laughed scornfully. He, too, would have gone unhesitatingly. "How about me? Because I'm six foot two and can't double up like a jack-knife, I'm counted out before I get a chance to—"

"Cut some off," Jimmie interrupted. "I'll take Jonathan with me if you insist. And if we get hung up on a tree, I'll feed him to the alligators and while they're eating him, swim for home."

Carewe laughed. "Right, old topper. I say, let's get started."

"That's a good suggestion, Mr Carewe," Jimmie said. "Yid, you and the Codfish Duke stay here and keep the stairs swept. Red and George can tuck us in and wish us *bon voyage*. We'll pack the idol down the stairs to the right and get on board there. The rest of you gents can shoot anything away from us as long as you can see."

CHAPTER VI

THE SECRET OF THE LAKE

TUTUL, THE HIGH priest, sat in a little stone house built about fifty feet back from the depression, at the left. With him sat Xolotl of the royal line. At the wall to the rear of them two polished wood levers jutted out for about four feet. They were heavy, rounded shafts of some dark wood.

"The wings worked easily as they always do," Xolotl said, his voice holding an illy concealed sneer. "What more is needed to guard the treasure? Could a thousand priests do it better, O high priest?"

"No," answered Tutul. "And yet, the water that comes to force them open and again to shut them, runs more slowly than it did. It took two hours to fill the chamber that in turn—"

"What is two hours? When you have lived as long as I, you will know that— Still they shoot—hear it? The fools, do they think they can destroy all the helpers of the Lord of Death that float and swim down on them? I had thought by now that they would be dead."

"It may be that they have barricaded themselves in a room, as others have done. That they can last until the God of Hunger comes for them."

"It may be. Have you enough of the sacred smoke ready to drive the little helpers of the Lord of Death from the temple after the water is released?"

"Yes, plenty of it. And I am very tired. Have I your permission to sleep for a little while?"

"You have. Although I am old, I do not need sleep like you do. Go and—"

The door opened and two of the white men Xolotl had called fools stepped into the room. Jimmie Cordie and Carewe had made the shore.

The back of another idol had been used to make a covering for the square hole and after Jimmie and Carewe were inside, the cracks had been packed and tamped with canvas from one of the knapsacks. Four small holes had been dug out between the shoulders, for air. It was a tight fit, but once inside, both of the reckless adventurers had grinned cheerfully after Jimmie ordered, "Seal 'er up, gents."

Grigsby and Red Dolan shoved the idol out into the water and then stood and watched it. The heavy part of the idol was the front of the god it represented and so, once in the water with that part down, the idol rode fairly high in spite of the weight of the two men.

"If they get into that jam to the right, they're done for," Grigsby had said and Red Dolan had answered, "I should have gone wid Jimmie."

As Red said it, the "little helpers of the Lord of Death," as Xolotl had called the beasts and reptiles, seemed to suddenly make up their minds to take a hand in the game. A big alligator nosed the idol, then tried to climb up on it, but it bobbed away from him. A snake, swimming toward the stairs, brushed against it and then struck at it with a head that looked to be as big as a suitcase. The idol tipped and almost went under, but righted itself.

"Them holes we dug," Red said. "The water will come in and drown—Mary Mother, take care av—"

"It's going to brush that tree," Grigsby interrupted, raising his rifle. "Clear it, Red."

The idol was drifting toward a tree that had recently been felled, as the limbs and branches were thick with leaves. On the trunk and the limbs and among the leaves were several big cats and three or four great snakes. The cats, as the idol came close, crouched to jump on what to them was a log on which they would have more room.

As Grigsby and Red opened fire, the Yid and the Bean did also from the temple top. One of the cats jumped and made the idol, only to fall off into the water. He hit with enough force to send the idol clear of the tree.

INSIDE THE idol, Jimmie Cordie laughed, then asked, "All right, Jonathan?"

"Quite, old dear. Except that the giddy old ship is leaking a little. I say, when we decide to come out do you think we can kick the jolly old trapdoor open?"

"If we can't," Jimmie answered, as he eased his right arm into a more comfortable position, "we are liable to stay in here for a long while. How would you like to be in that so dear Essex just about now?"

Carewe laughed. "I'd have a little more room there, anyway. It's quite all right here, old thing, if it weren't for the water coming in against my ear."

The idol floated along, every once in a while coming to rest beside a tree trunk or in a little backwater. And every time some reptile or beast sent it along. It may be that God's plan made the little helpers of the Lord of Death do as they did and it may have been just luck. Either way, half an hour after it was launched, the idol drifted head first into shallow water about a hundred yards up from where there seemed to be a jam, and grounded in shallow water.

And there was not, within a hundred feet, any beast or snake.

"We've arrived," Jimmie Cordie said, as he felt the scrape. "Turn over, Carewe, and try to get your knees up. We'll open the door and take a look see."

A minute later, Jimmie Cordie, with his Colt .45 in his hand, stepped out of the idol into about two feet of water, and right behind him came Carewe. It was getting dark and they could see the temple, but not clearly enough to distinguish objects.

"I'll tell them that we arrived," Jimmie said, raising his Colt. "Red is having nine hundred different kinds of fits."

He fired one shot, then two more. Before the echo died away, there came the sound of three shots from the temple.

"That's that," Jimmie said, as he put three fresh shells in the Colt. "Now, the way I figure it, the plant that operates the what-nots that control the so beautiful lake we have been boating on, must be close to the shore. We'll circle it, Jonathan, old kid. Are you all right?"

Carewe laughed. "Lead on, Yank," he answered.

It was a journey few men would have cared to take, even in the daytime. But Jimmie Cordie and John Carewe, Yank and Johnny Bull, started with grins on their faces, ready to face the music.

JIMMIE CORDIE, as he entered the candle-lit stone house, ordered in Spanish, "Hands up!"

Neither Xolotl nor Tutul obeyed. The high priest, with the quickness of an uncoiling spring, sprang straight at Jimmie Cordie's throat, absolutely ignoring the menace of the leveled gun.

He was stopped in mid-air by the two .45 caliber bullets that hit him in the heart and he went down against the stool he had been sitting on, dead before he reached it.

Xolotl's hand had reached the hilt of a dagger and half drawn it when Carewe fired, killing him.

"Not so good," Jimmie said, looking down at the bodies. "We've shut off the information tap."

"There didn't seem to be much time for questions, old bean," Carewe answered calmly. "I say, look at the levers."

Jimmie went over to them and threw his flash into the hole through which one came. "It ties on to another one that goes to the left," he said, "I can see water below it. It's some kind of hydraulic mechanism." He shut off his flash and faced Carewe. "Darned if I know which one to pull—or shove," he added.

"This one seems out a little farther," Carewe answered. "It may be that if we—" He pushed on the lever. "My word, it's going in, Jimmie. I say, I heard water either running in or going out."

"Let's get out and see if we can find the dam or whatever it is they control. This probably brings it back in place."

A hundred feet beyond the stone house they came to the edge of a swamp, and at a narrow place between two ridges made of stone, they saw two wide walls that in the darkness looked like the sides of a ship, that were slowly coming up and shutting off the flow of water and jungle debris into the depression.

"I say, it must take plenty of power to send those—"

"It does," answered Jimmie. "Come on, we've got to find the one that lets it out. I'll explain the principles of hydraulics to you on the way, young feller—if I don't step on a snake."

They circled the depression and found another little stone

house within two hundred feet of where the idol had landed. This one had the same kind of levers and was empty. The two old, very old, priests who had been there had heard the shots fired by Jimmie and Carewe on landing, and had crept cautiously out to see what they meant.

They saw Jimmie and Carewe start around the rim and at once had turned and started the other way around to notify the high priest that two of the white men had escaped from the temple. On the way, one of them was bitten by a corali and died in two minutes. The other, old and weak, had staggered on.

"These must work with reverse English," Jimmie said, as he took hold of one of the levers. "Try yours in, Jonathan."

"No can do, Jimmie," Carewe announced after a moment. "I'll pull out and you push down. My sainted Aunt Maria, that's doing it, Jimmie!" The levers went home and again the sound of running water was heard.

"As treasure hunters we are a couple of fine hydraulic engineers," Jimmie said with a grin. "Let's go and see what is happening."

THEY COULD not see well, even with the flash lights, when they reached the place where the depression fell away sharply, but they could make out the same kind of a ship's side slowly disappearing.

Jimmie looked across and said, "It will take until morning and then some to empty the saucer. There goes the water over. Holy cats, what a mess. I think I'll climb a tree back at the power plant for the rest of the night. Some of those babies are going to get crowded on shore."

Carewe laughed. "I think I will also, Jimmie. And a tall one. My word, it sounds like a madhouse, doesn't it?"

"And looks it," Jimmie answered. "A madhouse of beasts and snakes. Holy mackinaw! Did you see that jaguar rip that snake up? Let's go, Jonathan. I think your idea of a tall tree a darn good one."

At the door of the little stone house Carewe said, "Why not

stay here until dawn, Jimmie? We can barricade the door and the window and—"

There was a sound in the jungle like the snap of a rotten limb. Jimmie and Carewe turned, their flash lights lit. The beams of light picked up jaguar men, charging in, the three-pronged knives held out in front.

The old priest had met the jaguar men, not those who had run at the knoll but others, coming back from some expedition, and told them of the white men.

Jimmie and Carewe had their flash lights in their left hands, away from their bodies, which without question, saved their lives. As it was, their Colts stopped the charge long enough for them to back into the house and shut the heavy door. There was no lock, but a piece of timber was placed so that it could be lowered across the door, barring it. The priests had used it to keep beasts and reptiles out. Jimmie lowered it and as he did, Carewe shot and killed a jaguar man who had head and shoulders through the window.

"My hat," he said. "That was close, what, what?"

"Darn right. Watch that window a minute. I'll see if there is any other way they can get in."

There wasn't. The jaguar men tried the window several times and found that to show a head meant that the head would be blown off, so quit trying.

"Not so bad," Jimmie said. "We can stick here until the south-west corner of the hot place is a skating rink. In the morning, the rest of—"

A CRASH against the door interrupted him. "Talking about morning," Carewe said, "do you think the door will last that long, old dear? That sounds like a jolly old battering-ram to me."

"It does to me, too," Jimmie answered. "I'll take that 'stick here' thing back." He went to the door. "About three more wallops like that one and—" The crash came again, and this time the door split from top to bottom, but the cross timber held.

"We can try the window, Jimmie," Carewe said calmly.

"They'll be ganged up thinking we'll do that. Only thing I can think of is to get on each side of the door and, when she goes, try to get out. It's dark and we may be able to."

"I say, that shook the giddy old fort, that last one. Maybe we can pry a block loose and—"

"Throw your flash up along the roof on that side," Jimmie said. "My brain must be made of mush. There's one that looks loose. Try it, Jonathan, Get up on the lever."

"It's loose," Carewe announced a moment later. "If you can get up here, Jimmie, we can push it out."

"The Red Gods must be looking out for us," Jimmie said as he climbed up beside Carewe. "It's on the far side. Say when, Carewe."

"Now!" Carewe said, as he pushed. The stone gave and fell, leaving an opening large enough for a lean man to crawl through.

Jimmie Cordie went first, and as Carewe followed, another crash came at the door, followed by yells as the jaguar men came in over the tree trunk they had used as a battering-ram.

Carewe lit on his feet beside Jimmie. "My word, that's two close ones inside of five minutes," he said. "What now, Jimmie?"

"The tall tree," Jimmie answered. "There's one down toward the dam. We've got to use our lights and take a chance that we can make it."

They made the tree, but without much to spare. The jaguar men had not heard the stone fall, being engrossed in the battering-ram operation, and in finding the two white men in the stone house. But once outside, after seeing the hole in the wall, one of them caught the flash of Jimmie's light just about the time the tree was reached. The jaguar man yelled and started for it, the rest with him. The lowest branch was some twenty feet up, and the trunk about eighteen or twenty inches in circumference. Later, Jimmie Cordie, in telling Red Dolan about what had happened, said, "I hadn't cooned up a tree since the Lord knows when, but I went up that one in nothing flat, and Carewe was five feet ahead of me."

The first limbs were not large ones, and Jimmie and Carewe kept going up, limb after limb, until the trunk forked.

Carewe stopped at the fork. "How is this, Jimmie?"

"All right, I guess. I've never been treed before, Jonathan. Is there room enough to watch both sides?"

"Plenty. I say, I left about half the skin of my arms and legs on that flamin' trunk."

"You shouldn't have been in such a hurry," Jimmie answered gravely. "Go down and get it. I'll keep house."

Carewe laughed. "I'll wait until morning. It ought to be getting lighter soon, Jimmie."

"I hope it does. This playing tag in the dark isn't what it's cracked up to be. I lost a little skin myself in that— Heads up! They're coming up. Let 'em get as far as that next limb. I didn't think they'd have the sand to try for us up here."

The jaguar men did have the sand, and, irrespective of the way that man after man tumbled from the tree, shot out of it by the two deadly Colts, others kept coming.

CHAPTER VII

THE END OF THE TEMPLE

IT WAS BREAKING dawn when Carewe said, "I've five cartridges left, Jimmie."

"Use your rifle," Jimmie answered. "I've got a few more than that."

"The buckle of my .30-30 belt broke on the way up, and the belt dropped."

"Yeah? Take mine. By gosh, these gents are sure sticking for the big show. Here come some more of them. I know now how the coon feels when the hunters arrive."

"I don't think I'll ever go fox hunting again," Carewe said as he buckled on Jimmie's belt after unslinging his own .30-30.

"From the looks of the reinforcements, I don't think you will, either, Jonathan," Jimmie answered, with a grin, "unless they have fox hunting in— You may, at that."

Both of them heard a shot, and, right after it, three more. Then continued firing, coming closer.

"That," Jimmie said, "is one of the most welcome sounds that Mr. Cordie's son Jimmie has ever heard."

The jaguar men heard the shots also, and the circle that was under the tree broke and formed a line to meet what was coming. Jimmie and Carewe saw the Boston Bean, the Fighting Yid, Grigsby and Red Dolan break through the brush and into the fairly clear space between the stone house and the tree. They advanced in a line with about three yards between each man, slowly and calmly, their rifles issuing death to all living things in the way.

The jaguar men charged, or rather started a charge, then broke and ran. They did not know how many more of the white men there might be, but they did know that those they had seen had weapons that the three-pronged knives could not stand up against.

Jimmie and Carewe sat in the tree and watched the advance, and it was not until Red Dolan yelled, "Jimmie! Jimmie, ye scut av the world, where are you?" that they revealed themselves.

"Quit making that noise, you big red-headed ape," Jimmie said reprovingly as he poked his head out between branches. "How can a gentleman get his sleep if bell hops with fog-horn voices run around paging him all over the hotel?"

"So, ye half pint av nothin', is that where ye are? Come on down."

"Oi," yelled the Yid gleefully, "at last I have seen Mistaire Cordie up a tree. Vait till I tell it to Mrs. Admiral."

Once on the ground, Jimmie asked, "Did you bring the treasure with you, gents?"

"Treasure?" Red Dolan answered. "Would we be thinking av treasure standing there on the bottom step waiting for the water to go down and hearing the shots av ye? Double shame on ye, Jimmie Cordie. Over we ran to get ye and the banty here widout a thought av anythin' else."

"My word," Carewe said. "We appreciate it, don't we, Jimmie?"

"We sure do," Jimmie answered. "That you value us more than the wealth of Montezuma touches the heart of old man Cordie. And now that we are all here, let's go back and get the treasure."

The Boston Bean laughed. "Any hunches about traps, Jeems?"

"Divil a hunch, Codfish. We'll take what we can pack and call it a day."

BUT THEY didn't. When they got to the rim of the clearing they saw, advancing across the depression from the far side, a regiment of Guatemalan infantry. One of the jaguar men who had survived the first attack on the knoll had fled across country and ran headlong into the advance patrol of the regiment. Taken before the officers, he had told of the white men and, after a little pressure, scientifically applied, also told why the white men were being attacked.

The colonel of the regiment swore a great oath about protecting the temple and ordered the regiment forward at the double. Incidentally, he and the rest of the officers became the advance guard. If there was anything like Aztec treasure around, they were going to reach it first—probably to keep it out of the hands of the wicked.

Red Dolan looked at the advancing troops and then at the temple. "Come on, Jimmie. We can beat the scuts to the temple. What are ye waiting for?"

"Several things, Mr. Dolan. Do you think that the six of us can stand off a regiment with one hand and collect treasure with the other and walk away with it?"

"Especially ven ve got it about one round of cartridges," put in the Yid. "Go get it a sword, Irisher, und den ve charge dem und run dem off."

"What the hell!" Red retorted. "Are we to stand here and watch them tin soldiers walk in and get our treasure, Jimmie?"

"You can sit down if you wish. Personally, I haven't lost anything over there that I remember. They may be tin soldiers, Red, but they've got lead bullets. We wouldn't get a hundred feet in the open."

"Do you mean to say that ye are going to let them—"

"How can we stop them, you big ape? Put a jaw tackle on for a minute. Let's get back a little ways. If they see us, they'll send a company around the rim and all we'll get is a running fight back to home sweet home. A fight won't get us anything. That hill back of the water gate on the right is a good place to hole up. We can see the temple from there."

"Yes, see them walk in and then walk out wid our—"

"We'll take it away from them by a surprise attack after they start home with it, Red," Jimmie said with a grin as they started. "You can fall on the regiment from the rear with a sword. The Yid can make a direct frontal attack and the Bean and—"

"Jimmie, are ye going to let them walk away wid it? Answer me yes or no, ye shrimp av the world!"

"No. Not if I can help it. All kidding aside, Mr. Dolan, six guns won't stop them from doing it. If we can frame something strong enough to make them think only of getting home and start out carrying as little as possible *en route*, maybe we—"

THE YID, who had dropped back to take a look at the troops to see how they were strung out, having in mind the working of the levers to either drive them back or to corral them in the temple, let out a yell. "Oi, look! Some von worked it dem! Look! Here comes it de vater und de snakes und everything! Oi, vorse dan before. A vall tventy feet high und den some. Dare goes it de Guatemala army back to de rim!"

By this time Jimmie and the others had reached the rim. The Yid had not exaggerated about the wall of water, tree trunks and all the rest of the seething madhouse of reptiles and beasts.

And the onrushing wall did look to be over twenty feet high, as the Yid had said.

"Mary Mother," Red said. "They are going to get caught! No, by all the saints, they'll make it. Look at them throwing away their guns."

"So would you, Old Kid Dolan, if that thing were rushing down on you," the Boston Bean answered. "That's twice as heavy as it came before, Jimmie. The priests must have a reserve swamp full of those gentle little house pets."

"By gosh," Jimmie Cordie said, "They made it just in time. Now I know we'd better hole up, pronto. They'll comb the country from the rim out with a fine comb to find out the how-come. They see us! There goes a company on the double around the rim to the right—and another to the left! Here's where we get into a hole and pull the hole in after us. They'll find the levers and—"

"Let's get into the hole," Grigsby interrupted, "and then figure what they'll do—also what we'll do, which is much more important."

"Vait!" said the Yid. "Are my eyes gone bad mit me or—vatch dot vater climb up de steps. Vat de hell? Is de temple sinking or is de vater rising?"

Jimmie Cordie watched for a moment, then answered. "Both, Mr. Cohen. It looks as if the priests had an ace up the sleeve. But what in the name of the angel chorus could they have engineered that would—"

Carewe laughed. "I say, old dear, it doesn't make much difference to us, does it, what, what? My word, look at her go down as if she were being lowered on a platform."

"There were more priests," Jimmie said slowly, as if explaining to himself, "and more hydraulic stuff that could send in a larger body of water and then, if the finals came, wash away the foundations of the temple with a powerful underground stream or pull them down in some way. There must be a series of levers hidden away and—"

"Quite right, Professor Cordie," the Bean interrupted gravely, "and now will you explain to the class just what is to be done about one thousand odd damn good and mad Guatemalans who think that we are responsible? Please note that the companies have again started around the rim, having been urged to do so by the gents who ran up to them."

"What the divil is all this talk about?" demanded Red. "She's going lower all the time. Do something, Jimmie, ye scut, or there goes all the treasure to hell!"

"Stick around with a shovel, Red," Jimmie answered with a grin. "You can dig it out without much trouble. If I knew what to do, I'd do 'er, old kid. Right now, all I can—"

There was an ear-splitting crash as the temple disintegrated and collapsed, throwing a geyser of water that almost reached the awed onlookers.

"There she went!" Jimmie gasped. "That will be all, gents. If the Aztecs feel that way about it, as far as I am concerned, they may keep their treasure."

"That's nice of you, Jeems," said the Boston Bean. "Does the fact that there are quite a few chocolate-colored gentlemen starting out to scrag us concern you any?"

"Not a darn bit," answered Jimmie cheerfully. "They threw most of their guns away. By gosh, I'd like to know how it was done."

"You suggested that Red stick around with a shovel," Grigsby said with a smile. "You might also stick around and investigate the engineering ability of the Aztecs, Jeems."

"I'm not that curious, George. Well, we saw it and we felt it and we owned it for a few minutes. Don't ever tell me that you have never been rich, Mr. Dolan. It's water under the bridge, gents. We will now—"

"You mean water over the treasure, me good man," Red corrected with a sigh of resignation.

"That's right, Red. As I was saying, we will now start for the river, playing pussy-in-the-corner *en route* with the Guatemalan army. Bean, you and the Yid take the point. Red and I will take the rear guard. *Allons, enfants perdus!*"

AS JIMMIE Cordie gave that order, the old priest whose companion had been bitten by the snake half fell, half climbed down from the uppermost branches of a tree far up on a hillside that overlooked the temple.

He fell to the ground from the last eight feet and blood came from his mouth. "Now, dogs," he shrieked, raising his weathered old hands high above his head, "now hunt for the sacred treasure of Montezuma! Now reach out your hands and see if you can touch it. I have fulfilled the order given by the mighty emperor! I, the last of the temple priests, have sent the treasure to safety. I—" He staggered to the tree which was hollow for about six feet up.

He reached in and covered two little levers with dried leaves. Levers not more than six inches high and an inch thick. Not that they needed covering, because, once pulled, they released forces that could never be re-harnessed. But the old priest covered them lovingly and patted the leaves as if they were the heads of children. "Stay there warm and safe," he said. "No one can ever find you, little ones."

Then he stood up and began his imprecations again. His mind went back to the days when the Aztecs ruled with glory and pomp of empire. Days that he had been told about all his life until it was as if he had lived them himself. He raved of engineers who built great temples and canals and cities on lakes, and water works controlled by one little lever.

And he told of how there were other gates, greater than the ones that had been opened, that held back swamps to which the one first released was as a mud puddle. That when one of the little levers was pulled, all gates opened and when the other was pulled, an underground river would wash away the earth on which the temple was built, and also the massive supports that held the foundation firmly, causing it to sink.

His ravings were not all about the temple and the protection the engineers had devised for it. He raved of ceremonies and human sacrifices and of many things. But always he came back to the taunting of the jackals who thought they could outwit the engineers and priests of Montezuma.

"For four hundred years we have been ready for you," he shouted in fanatical triumph. "Ready if the jaguar men failed! You think that you can drain the great swamps and then dig, dogs? See if you can find it. I, the—"

Blood came in a stream from his mouth and the old priest pitched forward, dead before his body reached the ground.

THERE WAS no pursuit by the soldiers. The colonel knew that the white men seen on the rim had nothing to do with the deluge and the disappearance of the temple. He was a native and knew that it was the work of priests. The white men could go where they pleased for the moment. He might hunt for them later, to stand them against a wall facing rifles, but now he had other business of more importance.

What the colonel did was to send the regiment out through the jungle with orders to bring in any priests they could find. The regiment found four—four dead ones. Even had the priests been alive, and had all the Aztec priests who had ever served the temple been there with them, they could not have raised that sunken edifice. It was gone forever, and with it had gone the treasure of Montezuma. The underground river had taken care of that—once for all.

"AND BACK we go," Red said bitterly as the six companions started, "widout even wan little gold plate."

"Look at the fun you've had," Jimmie answered, cheerfully.

The orders given the launch crew had been to patrol up and down the river, getting once a day to the place where the expedition had landed.

The trip back along the stone road to the knoll and from the knoll to the river was made much faster than the advance had been. This time they knew where they were going and had a path to go on. When they reached the river, the launch was in sight, coming up.

Jimmie saw it and laughed. "Well, we found the pot of gold at the end of the rainbow, George. Maybe it's just as well we didn't bring it home."

"I bring mit a sample, anyway," the Fighting Yid announced.

"Ye what?" demanded Red.

"I bring mit a sample of de pot of gold," the Yid explained, patiently.

"Oh, you did," Jimmie said. "What kind of a sample, Mr. Cohen?"

"Vell, vile de Codfisher und me vos up on de platform I decides to go it down und take anodder look. Things vos quiet und so I did. I found it a little skin bag und—" The Yid reached under his left armpit and brought out a skin bag. Not so little, either. He took off his hat and emptied the contents of the bag into the hat.

Jimmie Cordie and the rest stared at the priceless jewels that almost filled the hat. There was silence for a moment, then the Yid said, "Ve split dem six vays—after picking-out de best for Mrs. Admiral so she von't be mad dot ve didn't invite her to de party."

"Why, ye dirty tomb-robber!" Red said, then added hastily: "Don't drop the hat, Abie darlin'."

ABOUT THE AUTHOR

ANOTHER WRITER WHO makes his bow to readers is W. Wirt—a man whose life has been packed with adventures. We asked Mr. Wirt to stand up and introduce himself so that we can all get some idea of what sort of hombre can spin a salty yarn such as this. Mr. Wirt has the floor:

Born—Boston, Massachusetts, 1876.

People on both sides hard-boiled Maine and Massachusetts Presbyterians of strictly English descent. All but one—but that one was a direct descendant of one of Sir Francis Drake's captains. The King of Spain had a standing offer of one thousand golden crowns to the hombre that would present him with "That pirate devil's head." Every once in a while one of the elect breaks out. The rest of the family at once put it down to the old pirate.

My late pa was one of them, all right. I think he had more than his share of the blood. He was a special agent and one of the very few Americans who served in the Secret Service of foreign countries. He went here and there, all over the world, in the oddest places, from northern China to the South Sea Islands, from there to Alaska and way points. Sometimes for Uncle Sam in the Post Office Department; other times for other people.

My education and experience? They are part and part. If there ever was a scrambled one I had it. When I wasn't much bigger than knee-high to a grasshopper my pa began taking me along with him, whenever he could do so safely. I remem-

ber military, private, public and
every other kind of school in a
dim way. He'd leave me in one
somewhere, go and attend to his
knitting, then come back and get
me, and away we'd go again. But
the constant education I received
from him regarding the conduct
of "an officer and a gentleman"
under any and all circumstance
still remains vivid in my mind.
One month we'd be in England,
evening clothes after six as regular as clockwork, down at one of

W. Wirt

the big estates for the week-ends, then, in a month or a darn
sight less, we'd be in some "flop house" as poor broken-down
bums—I acting the part of the devoted son who wouldn't leave
his poor old ex-con father, and so forth.

After I reached eighteen I worked with him for a good many
years, and when he was called to join his venerable ancestors
I carried on alone. No matter where I was, in the Orient or
anywhere else, I missed him—with his cool laugh in the face
of death and his never failing, slow, amused drawl. His favor-
ite weapon was a sawed-off shotgun carrying buckshot. This,
of course, was for use in the places where the little yellow and
black brothers congregate mostly. I miss him yet, and always
will—and that's that.

I have been behind a badge for Uncle Sam some little time
and at present am still special agenting, but on my own, seldom
going out of the States and not hunting for any trouble at all,
having more than my share already. I've had my gun in the ribs
and ears of a few jaspers and used to say "Put 'em up!" so darn
often that my longhaired partner—now bobbed haired—every
once in a while wakes me up with a demand to know if I have
any good reason for poking my fi nger in her side and hollering
at her in the middle of the night.

Then there have been many times when the reverse English was in force and I did the reaching for the blue sky, promptly and in haste. All in all, I lived and rambled when things were wide open, no blue laws or anything, just help yourself to the mustard if you wanted any. And I am darn glad I did. Man, howdy, you could go over the mountain, in "them" days and see things—and do 'em likewise, if you wanted to.

I and Schley whipped the Spanish fleet together, I as a volunteer and Schley as a regular. There were a few others present, but we did most of it. In the late argument I did some "hush, hush" stuff.

My present standing? Well, been married seventeen years; have two children, boy and girl. Have an old place in Maryland near Washington, a police dog, three or twenty-six kittens and cats, an old "colored lady" named Medora to make the corn bread, plenty good old corn lick—I mean corn licorice—to drink and am "out of commission."

A lot of my old buddies drift through, hang their hats up behind the door and drink my said good old yellow-with-age corn licorice, eat some fried chicken and curse me in all the living and dead languages because I won't let go all holds and go wild-catting over the hills once more. They don't get a rise out of me at all. I'm like the colored man who, when asked if he wanted to make a quarter, replied: "No, suh, I done got me a quarter." All I want is peace and quiet.